A GOOD DAY FOR
SEPPUKU

A GOOD DAY FOR SEPPUKU

SHORT STORIES

Kate Braverman

City Lights Books | San Francisco

"What the Lilies Know" (published as "The Woman Who Sold Commu-nion" in *McSweeney's*, 2005 and *Best of McSweeney's*, 2006.)

"Skinny Broads with Wigs" (published as "Mrs. Jordan's Summer Vaca-tion," "Editors Choice" Carver Award, *Carve Magazine*, Volume 5, 2005)

"Feeding in a Famine" (published by Connotation Press online, June 2015)

"Cocktail Hour" (published in *Mississippi Review*, Volume 33 #1 & 2, win-ner of the Mississippi Review Prize)

"Women of the Ports" (published as "The Neutral Zone" in *San Francisco Noir*, Akashic Books, 2005)

Library of Congress Cataloging-in-Publication Data
Names: Braverman, Kate, author.
Title: A good day for seppuku : stories / Kate Braverman.
Description: San Francisco : City Lights Publishers, 2018.
Identifiers: LCCN 2017043863 (print) | LCCN 2017046533 (ebook) | ISBN
   9780872867222 (ebook) | ISBN 9780872867215 (softcover)
Subjects: | BISAC: FICTION / Short Stories (single author). | FICTION /
   Literary. | FICTION / Contemporary Women. | FICTION / Family Life.
Classification: LCC PS3552.R3555 (ebook) | LCC PS3552.R3555 A6 2018 (print) |
   DDC 813/.54--dc23
LC record available at https://lccn.loc.gov/2017043863

City Lights Books are published at the City Lights Bookstore
261 Columbus Avenue, San Francisco, CA 94133
www.citylights.com

CONTENTS

O'HARE

I love O'Hare Airport, with its unpredictable weather and constant gate and terminal changes. This is where I board my plane to Los Angeles. O'Hare is a zone with variables that can't be controlled. Cell phone service ceases and nobody can tell me no.

I wander corridors that end in cul-de-sacs where I sit alone in alcoves. Loudspeakers announce implausible destinations like Madrid, Prague and Tokyo. I pretend I'm someone else. I have a red or black passport, a different genetic code and a suitcase full with lace mantillas and hand-embroidered shawls. I'm subject to random acts of nature — lightning storms, tornadoes and lethal black ice. But that's at a distance so vast it's incomprehensible and irrelevant.

It's the summer of my 13th year and I'm supposed to make my decision. I must choose which parents I'll live with for high school and what foreign language I'll learn. I'm officially a teenager. I have a biological passport and carry tampons, lip-gloss and credit cards in my purse. My age has 2 syllables. And I count everything.

When I live with my mother and Marty in Beverly Hills, my bedroom is entirely Gucci pink — the walls and carpets, the cabinets with my TV and CD player, even the interior of my clothing and shoe closets. My mother took her vintage spring purse to a paint store and supervised the replication of a color only I possess.

My bedroom opens onto a tiled balcony where I can see the tennis court and swimming pool that's lit even at night. Halogen globes make shadows in the water seem alive and insistent, as if urgently communicating in a language I will someday decipher.

It's a June of Hibiscus and Magenta Bougainvillea. Night blooming Jasmine from Madagascar turns my skin fragrant. Marty says money alters planetary orbits and renders footnotes unnecessary. He indicates the terraced hillside garden surrounding the swimming pool.

"*Race ipsa loquitur*," he says expansively, agreeing with himself.

"And you only need a sweater at night," my mother adds.

My mother drives me to school in the mornings, even though it's only 4 blocks away. She wears a tennis dress and matching sweatband around her forehead. Walking is déclassé, she explains. It's for latchkey children. Or orphans. Or children of maids and gardeners illegally obtaining a Beverly Hills school experience.

"Walking is for peripherals," she clarifies.

On Wednesdays we have our hair and nails done at Diva Salon on Rodeo Drive. In a curtained room dense with Philodendrons and musk incense, we're given identical terrycloth robes lined with peach silk. A miniature Purple Orchid like a severed crab claw is tucked in the pocket. A willowy woman bows as she extends the robes like an offering.

We select identical colors for our manicures and pedicures. We are lacquered with apricot or strawberry. Then we meet Marty for dinner at the Club or Mr. Chow's, where we have our own table permanently reserved for us. On holidays, we attend services at Sinai Temple on Wilshire Boulevard with all the movie stars and industry executives.

The executives wear suits and have their own yarmulkes. The directors are bearded; their hair is long and uncombed and their borrowed yarmulkes perch uncertainly on their matted curls and keep falling off. They wear sunglasses and talk throughout the service. They make rectangles with their index fingers and thumbs. It's a geometry meant to show camera angles and close-ups.

On long weekends, we drive to Palm Springs or the beach house in Malibu. In between, Marty is invited to concerts at the Greek Theater and the Sports Arena. We don't need tickets like peripherals. Marty's name is on *The List*. We sit in the first or second row and go backstage with our special passes. We eat petit fours and palm-sized pizzas from Spago's with the bands. I shake hands with Mick Jagger, who wears a purple bonnet, and David Bowie, who wears lipstick. Steven Tyler shows me how to play a tambourine and lets me keep it.

Marty knows everyone because he's a record producer with 22 Grammy nominations and 9 Grammy Awards. When he greets a performer, his smile is suddenly abnormally wide, his teeth are enormous and inordinately white, and his hand reaches out as if by a mechanical extending device. It elongates dangerously and I think of the trunks of elephants and ivory tusks, swamps, cemeteries and poaching.

I watch the news with my mother. A river is swelling beyond its sand-bagged banks and houses look amputated at ground level. They drift past like a square armada with chimneys and dogs on leashes barking, and porches of Wisteria still attached.

"It doesn't figure," my mother says, filing her fingernails.

"The flood?" I ask.

"Floods. Rivers. They don't figure. Corn doesn't figure. Trailer parks with the obese in bathrobes don't figure." My mother pats my shoulder and smiles. "You'll learn."

A soaking wet woman who has never been to Diva Salon holds a sodden cat and a chair frame. Storms took her house, her daughter's prom corsage, her son's purple heart, and her marriage certificate. She points behind her floral printed bathrobe and indicates wood slats and glass panes scattered in mud. She's obviously a peripheral.

One afternoon I hear my mother say, "It's untenable." She's talking to my father on the telephone. "Why?" My mother holds the receiver in front of her eyes and stares at it like it's an object of alien technology. "You're joking."

My father does not tell jokes. He's laconic and rations his syllables. I imagine stray birds lodge in his lungs. If he laughed without warning, flocks of finches, the pink and yellow of chalk would fly out. Then I'd gather iridescent feathers and line a winter coat for him.

It's the word *untenable* that catches my attention. I would have passed barefoot through the living room, with its floor of hand-painted Italian tiles and Persian rugs with authenticated stamped certificates Marty keeps locked in his office safe. I might have crouched behind rows of Cymbidiums in 42 cloisonné pots. But the harsh certainty of the word, *untenable*, stops me.

Untenable sounds ominous and ugly, like all the *un* words — *unlikely, unhealthy, unemployed, unfortunate* and *unhappy*. *Un* words *are* like pointed stakes in a field with **No Trespassing** signs.

"She'll be in high school this fall. We're talking educational sequences with profound continuity implications." My mother is drinking brandy from a bottle she conceals in a cloisonné planter. My mother is in AA and she's not allowed to drink.

"Listen, old pal," my mother raises her voice. Her mouth is tight with frustration as if it has wires in it. Her eyes are cluttered like a pond overgrown with reeds and fallen red and yellow maple leaves like stained glass panels from a cathedral.

"It takes two weeks to wash the hillbilly off her. What about her interior? How's that going to wash off?" My mother finishes her brandy.

At dinner my mother watches my mouth. Her eyes are magnifiers. From the shape of my lips, she'll get an early warning. Selecting a foreign language has implications about character that last a lifetime like an appendicitis scar. Spanish is the language of the underclass. It's for bus boys and their girlfriends who won't get abortions because they believe God is watching. They're peripherals who don't figure. French, on the other hand, is the language of museums, fashion and money, style, diplomacy and ballet.

"There really is no choice," my mother decides for me.

I leave for Camp Hillel every June no matter where I live. But this time I recognize it's a definitive moment. It's a punctuation I didn't anticipate and don't want. I thought I could avoid this entirely, sleep through it or disappear in O'Hare. I'm like Alpine denied clearance to land, condemned to repeat monotonous circles. If it explodes in a cornfield or trailer park, it won't figure.

Marty's taking my suitcases, sleeping bag and camping gear out to the car. My mother is envisioning me in an apartment overlooking the Seine. My split ends and curls are gone, and my braces have been cut off with metal shears. I wear a beret and contact lenses. In spring afternoons, I am inspired and sit in the Tuileries reading Sartre and Simon de Beauvoir.

My mother and Marty drive me to Camp Hillel. Apparently this is an occasion necessitating the Rolls Royce. The weight of museums, revolution, democracy, ballet and existentialism ride in the back seat. As we enter Camp Hillel, counselors hold signs with **ARROWS** pointing to the dust and gravel pit designated as the camp parking lot. They salute as we pass. When our parents are gone the parking lot will return to its usual name. Sex Gully.

Marty slowly maneuvers the Rolls between Mercedes Benz sedans, Jaguars, Bentleys and SUVs parked at criminally dangerous angles. He steers with calculated deliberation like he's navigating a ship into a shallow inlet.

The parking lot is notorious. Fender benders and collisions are constant. Even small scratches require imported paint and take months to repair. There have been so many accidents, Dr. White includes a legally binding document promising not to sue in the Camp Hillel application package. You must absolve Camp Hillel in advance before entering the property.

Dislodged campers drag bedrolls and backpacks across gravel. Cameras slip off wrists and canteens fall from their shoulders. Fathers lean out windows exchanging business cards.

My mother hands me my purse which I'd dropped. "Monet," she whispers while I search for my assigned cot. "Degas and Camus." She continues naming famous French artists until a counselor asks her to leave.

I unpack my white Sabbath shorts and blouses. Chelsea Horowitz is taking German because her father is a Freudian psychoanalyst. I find a drawer for my jeans and rock band T-shirts. Jennifer Rothstein is pre-enrolled in Chinese because it's the most important language of the 21st century. Her parents are both cardiologists. Anything less than Chinese is a deliberate refusal to recognize reality. It's obtuse, like refusing treatment for a preventative valve or artery procedure.

I put my toothbrush and tampons in a basket in the bathroom. There are 3 toilets and 2 of them are broken. Tiffany Gottlieb already has an Italian tutor. Her parents own a designer in

Milan and a villa at Lake Como. They want her to appreciate opera, order from a menu with style, and not embarrass them.

Bunk 7 is named Golda Meir. It has torn screens on the windows and 2 showers marked **Out of Order**. The floor is cement. Somehow, I'd forgotten this. I place my pool thongs, tennis shoes and white Sabbath sandals under my cot. I inspect my mattress. Coils, orange with rust, unravel in multiples like fingers forced to repeat piano scales. They might be laminated worms and I suspect infection.

I cover my cot with an over-sized lavender sheet that belonged to my grandmother. Lilac trees bloom in 44 horizontal rows. It's been washed thousands of times and the cotton is softer than silk. It feels like skin. But it fails to stop the metal spokes that scratch my sunburn and mosquito bites.

Becky Fine is pre-enrolled in Russian due to her family heritage and the novels of Tolstoy. She has an appreciation for the Cyrillic alphabet that curls like waves in the Black Sea. Everyone's fallback is Latin.

Brooke Bernstein is committed to a Greek and Japanese double language program. She's sharing her cigarette with the rest of language-declared Bunk 7. I don't join them.

"What are you taking?" Chelsea Horowitz demands. "Canadian?"

I stare at her, flabbergasted. Chelsea Horowitz has dyed her hair platinum blond and it looks like a metal helmet glued to her skull. Stray pieces like starched straw jut out like errant stalks from defective seeds.

Chelsea Horowitz has a stress-induced amnesia. She's apparently forgotten last summer in Bunk 6, Esther, when she had mourning black dreadlocks and we were best friends. When she dropped her sleeping bag in the creek on our overnight, I gave her my extra blanket. We stayed up until dawn, shivering, and watching the stars make their singular circular transit.

After dinner we walked past the stables and into the Eucalyptus grove reeking of cough drops and confided secrets. Sometimes we held hands. Chelsea Horowitz swore me to eternal silence and told me the ethics committee had suspended her father. It was a harsh punishment for an unfortunate but essentially trivial episode with a bipolar Russian ballerina. Her mother had totally overreacted, and filed for divorce and bought an apartment in Haifa. She gave me her birthday opal ring. We wanted to become blood sisters, officially, but the cafeteria only gave us one plastic knife that broke immediately.

As soon as I wake up I go to the Health Center. Nurse Kaufman is a holocaust survivor. You could sever a major artery and she wouldn't give you a tourniquet. I loiter near the scale and jars of tongue depressors. Then I show her my abraded shoulder blades.

"This is a kibbutz, not the Four Seasons," Nurse Kaufman says. She gives me a band-aid, reluctantly. She's compromising against her better judgment and wants me to know I owe her.

In Bunk 8, *Delilah*, the Goldberg twins are in an experimental central European immersion program. They began in Hungary with blue-domed public hot baths and Klezmer recordings. They spent a night in a village of gypsies and interviewed them with video cameras. Each summer, they'll visit a different concentration camp and add another language.

I return to the Health Office. Nurse Kaufman glances at my puncture wounds. When she determines it's not stigmata, she loses interest. Golda Meir has dysfunctional screens and a division of mosquitoes has bitten me. I count 31 separate violations of my flesh. A spider walked across my back in 9 distinct bites. Nurse Kaufman dispenses 2 aspirin and a paper cup of tap water. She watches me swallow. She permits eye contact for the first time and writes a note on my chart.

Bunk 7 is sharing vacation photographs. Tiffany Gottlieb

wears a gold thong bikini, holds a beer, and waves from a boat on Lake Como. Chelsea Horowitz yells, "Yo, Canada," as I pass.

Chelsea Horowitz has been encouraged to say whatever comes into her mind because it could contain analytically significant material. Still, sometime someone's going to knock her front teeth out. I edge onto my cot. Soiled coils snap apart and jab my knee.

It's lights out, including flashlights and matches. I leave Golda Meir barefoot. I'm breathing rapidly in uneven bursts. I need to stand outside in the dark and quietly count the occasional meteor streaking silver and exploding like a 747.

The sky surprises me. It's a sheeted haze of monochrome gray like layers of smoke. In fact, it is smoke. The junior and senior counselors from UCLA and Stanford are lying on their backs in Sex Gully, chain smoking, passing joints, and pretending they're in the Israeli army.

I'm late for breakfast. My eyes feel like barbed wire is implanted in 2 horizontal lines like train tracks or stitches. My mouth tastes metallic as if my braces are leaking. It's lead poisoning. The Atlanta Center for Disease Control should be informed. They'll want samples and a quarantine.

Nurse Kaufman lights a cigarette. The Health Center is the size of a walk-in closet. A real medical emergency is for Medevac. Red Cross choppers fly over camp 2 or 3 times a day, staying in practice in case Dr. White presses the buzzer he wears next to his Rolex. Hypochondriacal disorders are for our own psychiatrists.

The Health Center is the size of a closet because you're supposed to walk in and walk out. Stray nests of ashtrays constructed from medical supplies sit on the counter between throat swabs and disposable thermometers. An empty jar has 4 cigarette butts mashed inside. It's symbolically concealed behind rolls of gauze and gallon bottles of iodine. Nurse Kaufman believes iodine is the universal solvent. If it doesn't hurt, it isn't working. You must feel the bacteria stinging as they die.

"Samples? Quarantine?" Nurse Kaufmann repeats. She expels smoke with purpose, forceful and direct like a bullet. Then she asks me if I want to talk to the Camp Director, Dr. White. I'll think about it, I lie.

Dr. White is head of pediatrics at Cedars Sinai Hospital where most of Camp Hillel were born. He's also head of child psychiatry. He's seen us in diapers and given us Rorschach tests. He's written our recommendations and testified at our parents' divorces. He definitely knows too much. He gleams, radiant with intimacies we'll deny under oath. All Camp Hillel avoids him. Everyone knows, if you're sent to Dr. White, you aren't participating effectively. Then your parents will be telephoned for a special conference.

Dr. White's office was equipped by the Mossad for global computer conferencing. He can talk to the Prime Minister in Tel Aviv and he can summon commandos. He can find your parents in Bali or Capri. He can force your mother to fill the screen with her hair wet from the ocean and her make-up washed into a blue smear. She squints through sun in another hemisphere, disadvantaged by the absence of contact lenses, sunglasses and lipstick. She stares blindly into the camera, confused and disoriented.

Dr. White can freeze the frame where a field of brown hair juts out above her lip like a just chopped crop and ground level stalks rise straight up. It's the guillotined field no one is ever supposed to see.

Dr. White can find your father and zoom in with one button. Your father seems isolated on a beach without a briefcase, stethoscope or towel. He is overly white and the size of an abandoned child. He's miniaturized and his tiny black eyes dart up and down the beach and then out to sea. He's desperate like a small mammal about to be captured. He looks like an albino lemming.

Global conference calls must be avoided. Gangrene and a fever of 105 are better than a televised confrontation your parents will never forget or forgive.

Dr. White can issue an edict that sends you home. In the hierarchy of not participating effectively, this is number 1. Everyone watches your jetlagged parents load your suitcases, backpacks, unfinished crafts projects, bedroll and wicker baskets of tampons and hair conditioner into their car. The trunk slams. You're put in the back seat and your parents tell you to shut up. They don't remind you to put on your safety belt. They don't care if you're decapitated on the way home. No one waves goodbye. Your bunkmates offer vulgar hand gestures and a chorus of enthusiastic boos.

I've been to Nurse Kaufman's 3 times. A 4th visit generates an automatic interview with Dr. White. I'm on unofficial probation. I find my rock band T-shirts and count them. 14. I arrange them alphabetically, beginning with Aerosmith and ending with Zappa.

Jasmine Weiss already knows Portuguese. Her parents bought a piece of the rainforest in Brazil larger than New Jersey. They own whole villages, including dwellings, artifacts, crops, livestock and people. They're on the Green Peace wanted list. They own 2 hotels on the beach in Rio de Janeiro, but if they return to Brazil, they'll be arrested. Jasmine's uncle parachuted in, professionally disguised by Stephen Spielberg's personal make-up team, but he failed to get below radar detection. Now he's in jail and nobody can visit.

I'm on a prison track, too. Even though I left my personality in an alcove at O'Hare, and assumed the identity of a stranger with an embroidered shawl from Malta and ivory hair combs from Mozambique, my camouflage is unraveling.

My mother and Marty will be forced to go to Family Therapy with me. My mother will have to cancel her tennis lessons, Diva Salon appointments and even the gardener. Then she'll have to change her colonoscopy and mammogram appointments. If rogue cells develop during the delay, if an atypical aggressive tumor appears like a volcanic island out of nowhere, metastasizes and invades her lymph nodes, it will be my fault.

Marty will have to abandon his mixing boards in the midst of a crucial, fertile chorus. He's generously shared his philosophy of song writing with me. Hook lines are like capturing wind in a sail. It's a triangulation that happens only once. It's like getting liquid and putting it all on the line. Then God throws you a 7. Marty's got his first 7 but Dr. White has ordered him to leave the casino.

His new band from Australia, the Wellingtons, who are actually from Sidney and attending a community college in Santa Barbara, won't get a Grammy nod. They won't even get an invitation to a party where the Grammy's are shown on a big screen in a restaurant in Malibu. They'll probably lose their green cards and get deported.

Orange coils spring open in my mattress at knee level and ricochet down to my ankle. Bull's eye. For some reason I think about Surtsey, an island off of Iceland in 1967. I consider how much of the Earth is still unknown. I limp and wrap a damp towel around my forehead. A forest fire burns between my eyes but it doesn't show in the mirror. I don't even think about Nurse Kaufman. It's a conflagration iodine won't put out. 23 Eucalyptus trees surround Golda Meir. They probably planted 24 saplings, one for each hour, but one died. And it wasn't replaced. I count the Eucalyptus again at dusk, searching for subtraction. I rub their purported, but unsubstantiated, medicinal leaves on my forehead. I stumble across a hollowed out scrub oak trunk. I trip on a branch. It's a bark carcass and I crawl inside with my flashlight and canteen, and try to telepathically transport myself to O'Hare.

I don't bother looking at the sky. Even Mars is gone, hidden by sheets of forbidden cigarette smoke like lead clouds at tree level. I close my eyes and let the glued horizon fall over me.

After martial arts and gymnastics, we have nature hiking with the botanist. The botanist is usually a graduate student from Santa Cruz or Davis, who reiterates, with each brittle leaf, desiccated seedpod, and severed insect leg or wing, that she isn't a certified expert. A wall of silence immediately encases her. We're a kibbutz and we don't indulge neurosis. We asked about bugs, not her existential crisis. We walk ahead, fanning out from our mandatory single line, and leave her behind, alone. She made herself a peripheral.

I am mute in the Main Hall at lunch. Horseback riding and swimming are next. My horseback privileges are suspended due to my undiagnosed limp and I've stopped swimming. Chlorine inflames my mosquito and spider bites. My thighs are yellow with scabs like colossal cellulite deposits that should be drained and I have no declared foreign language.

Chelsea Horowitz and the Goldberg twins occupy 3 of the 3 chaise lounges. They've been there for hours, painting their toenails fungus green. Chelsea Horowitz removes her gold-framed Prada sunglasses to stare at me.

"Can you say 'contagious' in Canadian?" she asks, voice loud and abrasive. The twins laugh on cue.

I avoid the swimming pool and spend afternoons in the crafts room. It's in the Rec Center basement and there are no windows. The ambience is discouraging. A sullen senior counselor on punishment detail rations art supplies. It's a bunker for the shunned and disfigured and campers with weight issues.

I sit near Lauren Silverberg. She has cerebral palsy and a portable flesh-colored oxygen tank protrudes from her spine like an extra appendage. Obviously she's a mutant. Lauren Silverberg shouldn't even be in Camp Hillel, but her father donated Citrus Hill. It used to be a mound with 2 hunched lemon trees. It was a conceptual homage to the Israeli citrus industry. Then Dr. Silverberg made it rise in tiers of trucked-in citrus trees and threatened a civil rights lawsuit.

Lauren Silverberg has trapped dozens of lizards in a plastic bag. They're still alive. She removes one at random and skins it with an art blade. Then she glues the band-aid sized scales onto a rock.

I decide to sit alone. I make papier-mâché masks of girls who removed their faces and hid them in airports. I've made 9 so far.

I sit with my bunkmates in the Main Hall. The chicken is passing my table as Dr. White appears. He's the cameo no one wants. Silverware stops moving and everyone sits up straighter. We remember our posture, our manners, and the value of small paper napkins.

Dr. White informs us that it's a thinking cap lunch. He pantomimes a triangular hat with a chin string that ties. Today, after lunch, we'll have Spiritual Discussion.

Spiritual Discussion is an unplanned activity, a back-up in case of rain or a heat wave with malpractice implications. Spiritual Discussion is the only time we see the rabbi, who is also still a student. The practice rabbis are stupefied by the weight of their responsibilities. The magnitude of post-historical interpretation and synthesis stuns and numbs them. They avoid Sex Gully. They swim but do not tan.

Dr. White assembles us into a co-ed group with four bunks. I'm in Golda Meir with a mattress filled with landmines and 11 linguistically pre-approved 13-year-olds who no longer share cigarettes or photographs with me. Chelsea Horowitz accused me of taking Canadian for my foreign language and I didn't refute her. I'm exposed, vulnerable, and deficient. I've made myself a peripheral.

Scotty is in Bunk 8, Shimon Peres. He comes to Camp Hillel every year, too, but he's been an undifferentiated part of the mosaic — the thin green medicated air above the stables, the partial shade of Eucalyptus leaking their chalky medicinal smell, and the chlorine lingering like a toxic eye pollutant.

We march single file to the foot of the terraced grove of lemon and orange trees that Dr. Silverstein's vision made manifest. The oranges and lemons look stapled onto scaly branches. We are told to sit there. We sit.

Our topic is the philosophy of the 10 Commandments and how they might be reinterpreted based on our unprecedented historical circumstances, which are global, technological and post-modern. We were given a typed copy of the 10 Commandments at Orientation, but I keep confusing them with the 12 steps of AA.

My mother and Madeleine are both in AA, but only part of the time. I wonder if the 10 Commandments are subject to relapsing. If you fail in a Commandment, if you've been intimate with farm animals or purchased false idols, if you've sacrificed your children to the wrong gods, if you've mortgaged your Beverly Hills house and jet time share to throw it all on the line for a 7 and crap out, can you go to rehab and return to meetings again? Can you go back to Sinai Temple?

I read the 10 Commandments during Study Time. I curl on my side on my cot and twisted iron springs dig into my thighs. Thou shalt not kill. Thou shalt not steal. Thou shalt have no graven images. Thou shalt promptly make amends. Do not covet your neighbor. Thou shalt admit you are powerless over alcohol and narcotics. Thou shalt honor thy mother and father, even if they're divorced, you're their only child, and they're trying to claw you apart.

Every summer my mother and Marty take me to a circus on the Santa Monica Pier. It's an annual family ritual. I'm afraid the Ferris wheel will leave me stranded at the top while Marty rocks the seat back and forth with his elongated arms. My mother and Marty hold hands as they walk. They eat French fries, despite the calories and saturated fat. I stagger behind them.

My parents laugh as a woman in feathers and gold stilettos is sawed in half. Don't they see she has the feet of a child, toes the size of grown-up teeth? Then the spinning cups promising the loss of limbs, and the miniature cars like metal coffins. Finally, a drum roll while a girl in pink sequins sinks into a spotlight. She smiles, wide and invitational. A man with pouches of blades takes her cape and tosses it aside. Then he straps her ankles and wrists. The wheel slowly spins. She's the object of knives and hatchets, and flaming darts like miniature spears. Everyone applauds when she survives.

"Remove the contrived pain from your face," my mother whispers.

Marty leans in, hearty. "It's show biz." His teeth are like glaciers. "Strings and mirrors, honey."

"Not like your home village," my mother points out. "You've got a real pillory."

"When is witch dunking season?" Marty asks.

"May through October," my mother tells him. "There's a hiatus for bow and arrow deer butchery."

"If they don't drown, they get barbequed." Marty shrugs.

Drowned and barbequed women must be peripherals to begin with. They're born that way. The 10 Commandments don't specifically mention circuses, but they're a subtext. I can't separate the 10 Commandments from the 12 rules of AA. Thou shalt carry the message to all suffering drunks and drug addicts. Thou shalt not do things to animals, particularly sheep, or sniff cocaine, one day at a time.

Then I'm back at O'Hare again, where, depending on conditions, regional aircraft fly me to Pittsburgh, Buffalo or Erie. I'm pretending I'm on route to Hong Kong or London. But my flight is delayed, departures are changing gates and TV monitors offer sequences of shifting instructions. Somewhere tornados blow roofs off houses and flood highways in small cities in regions of no consequence.

My father and Madeleine are waiting in the Pittsburgh airport. We'll have hours of two-lane roads with stretches of gravel and no light back to our farmhouse. I smell earth and shoots of what will be Tulips, Freesias and Iris rising to the surface like the red tips of infant fingers. Then we're on the dirt driveway to our house inside an apple orchard. Acres of wild grasses, shoulder high Mustard and Thistle grow between the barns and pond. Darkness is dimensional and primitive and I fall asleep immediately.

From my bedroom window, in my room of wood where nothing is painted, I study the Maple forest. It stretches for hundreds of miles in all directions like a secret undiscovered inland sea. Wind pushes through leaves like currents. There are fluctuating hieroglyphics in how Maple limbs swing and twist, purposeful and suggestive. This is also a language I will eventually comprehend.

Madeleine takes me on a morning tour of the farm. An apple tree has fallen in a snowstorm and lies on the ground as if sleeping. She shows me patches of strawberries she planted the season I missed, and where Dad repaired the gate and water pump. Then we bake pies in the old kitchen that has its own fireplace. We drive to Blue Heaven and pick buckets of blueberries. We can tomatoes, and peal and boil apples one wicker basket at a time. Madeline pours white and brown sugar, vanilla and cinnamon into the simmering pot. It's barely autumn and we're already preparing our winter larder. My father is in the main barn with his marijuana plants and magic mushrooms, his drying screens, plastic bags and scales. Then my yellow bus arrives on cue and I'm back in Alleghany Hills Middle School.

I don't wear my clothes from Beverly Hills. I leave them in my Gucci pink closet. I don't describe my bedroom with French doors opening onto a private terrace. I don't mention eating Italian cakes with Paul Simon or Madonna giving me a bouquet of yellow Orchids from her dressing room. They felt like lamps pulsing in my hands and I understood illumination then and how it's possible to see in the dark. I don't mention this either. It's just another detail that accrues to someone with a red passport and a parasol with hand painted Peonies and cranes on it.

I ride the school bus down Maple Ridge Road, but I'm really still in O'Hare, alone, watching passengers board airplanes bound for India and New Zealand. If I leave enough of myself in O'Hare, I'll continue traveling, watching islands rise and gathering phenomena without names or explanations. I won't become a teenager after all. I'll put my life on pause and remain a preadolescent for centuries.

We wait for Spiritual Discussion with our best posture and T-shirts tucked into our shorts. There's an intense heat wave, and Nurse Kaufman wanders gravel and pine needle trails with a canteen of Shabbat grape juice. The senior counselors are equipped with army issue binoculars. They're on fainting-watch.

When the Santa Anas blow and it's 103 degrees, malpractice

and reckless endangerment law suits take precedence. What if a camper passed out and received a head trauma with IQ implications? Or a fracture with dental involvement? What about a visible facial impairment resistant to corrective plastic surgery?

We form a circle beside a plaque indicating Citrus Hill with an arrow. Our practice rabbi, Just-call-me-Jeff, asks for opening comments. His forehead and cheeks are stained reddish, as if he's dotted with birthmarks or branded. It's iodine from the Health Center.

I begin counting pebbles and clumps of unnaturally rusty pine needles that remind me of old nails in a barn after a rainy season. Or the bellies of green snakes my dad finds under rocks in our creek. But these pine needles seem to be crawling.

Jeff leans into a Eucalyptus trunk. He has 3 band-aids on his wrist and iodine stains on his hand. I'm sure it's the residue of a suicide attempt. No one makes eye contact. No one responds. Then Scotty Stoloff, who is lounging on the cement hard pine needle throttled grass as if he's really comfortable says, "I have a problem with the commandments thing."

"A problem?" Jeff repeats.

"Yeah. If you look up the word 'commandment' as I have," Scotty produces a sheet of notebook paper from his pocket, "you'll notice words attached to 'commandment' include to tyrannize, oppress, dominant, inhibit and restrain. That's unconstitutional."

Scotty Stoloff's black hair is streaked with green and copper dye. His eyes are green, too. I stop counting pebbles and consider South Pacific lagoons, angel and clown fish, groupers, and lemon sharks. And swarms of miniature blue and yellow fish I snorkeled through in Bora Bora, parting schools of darting filaments with my fingers.

I feel like I'm back in O'Hare where seasons do not exist and all rules are suspended. I'm back in a region where codified laws, black ice and tornadoes don't exit. I press the pause button on my life and everything stops.

"Also the thou shalt not steal part. The dude in *Les Miserables*? 20 years in jail for stealing bread?" Scotty offers from his deceptive lounging position. His body is tense and alert.

"I see," Jeff says. He rubs his eyeglasses on his shirt, presumably to clarify his perspective. "Interesting point, Scott."

Our next round of Spiritual Discussion will be improvisational, Rabbi-just-call-me-Jeff says. He'll ask a specific question and we'll answer, one by one, going around the circle. Everyone will be called upon and, yes, a response is mandatory.

I'm sitting in the accidental middle with my ribs and shoulders bruised, and my thighs sacs of yellowing scabs. Scotty is in his one-elbow faux meditation position on the far left. If Rabbi Jeff proceeds clockwise, Scotty will have the last word.

"Imagine you're going to another planet," Jeff begins. "And you can only take three things with you. What would these three things be?"

Tiffany Gottlieb, who is slated to appreciate Italian opera and not get lost in Milan, says she'll take her family, her cat and her Walkman. Tiffany hates her older brother, Max. He has brain cancer. His head is shaved and black magic marker arrows indicate radiation sites. He is the city being bombed. And Tiffany Gottlieb wouldn't take him, with his bandages, catheter, IV tubes, monitoring devices and emergency oxygen tanks anywhere. He's terminal, a condition even worse than peripheral.

Brooke Bernstein's right hand fingernails are garnet; her left are iridescent blue. I assume this refers to her double language choices of Greek and Japanese. Her unmatched hands spread out like a fan on the thighs of her denim shorts. She's taking both her families since her parents are divorced, her dog Justice, and her diabetes medications.

Brooke Bernstein doesn't have diabetes and she doesn't

have a dog. She loathes her new stepfather. He's in the Russian mafia and slaps her mother on the face and pushes her against walls. Brooke keeps missing soccer practice and may be dropped from the team.

"The desperation of old women," Brooke revealed, summarizing her family catastrophe during a flashlight share and bond session. Obviously, it's her mother's fault.

Bruce Tuckerman, in Moshe Dayan, says he'll take the family Benz, in case there are roads on the other planet. He notes the importance of transportation historically, particularly the Erie Canal linking New York and Chicago, making Buffalo the 3rd largest city in the country. Barges are underrated, Bruce reminds us, reciting highlights from his history-of-taming America final report. We've all written this report, of course, and share his affection for barges. Then Bruce says he'll take a suitcase of seeds to start agriculture, and the family videos, so they can remember how things should be. Agriculture and personal history can fit in the trunk.

Everyone is taking their families, pets and Torah. Chelsea Horowitz is packing the classic pre-war Oxford dictionary, and the collected works of Freud in the original German. She has a duty to preserve their ambiguities and contradictions. She's also taking a sub-zero down sleeping bag and flashlight. That's at least 5 items, rather than 3, but no one notices. Then it's my turn.

"I'll take O'Hare Airport," I hear myself say. Each of its four separate syllables sounds strange and hangs in the hot-chalk lemony air. I offer only 1 item instead of 3. I can justify my 1 by the monumental amount of cement and engineering involved. By pounds alone, O'Hare should count for 3. Then I realize no one is listening. The Goldberg twins are asleep. Nurse Kaufman passes with a basket of damp hand towels. She takes pulses and gives out band-aids. Then we come to Scotty.

Scotty Stoloff's had nearly an hour to prepare his impro-visational response. I hold my breath and my mouth fills with yellow air that's thick and vaguely citrus sweet. I can't see his green eyes because he wears aviator sunglasses. He has a gold hoop earring in his left earlobe and his nose is pierced with a gold stud shaped like a miniature bullet.

In the flickering sunlight between Eucalyptus trees, his hair is streaked with bronze and red feathers. On a vision quest, he would find his guide as a hawk or golden eagle.

"I'd take a kilo of cocaine, a Tec-9 with a sling of clips, and a Cray super computer." Scotty informs us, removing his sunglasses. He glances at the circle of half-asleep liars with gen-erous indifference. There's no calculation in his green eyes or strain at the edges, no contempt or hostility.

Scotty inhabits an alternative region. We're remote and marginal to him. It's a kibbutz, not a four-star hotel. Nobody gets life support here.

I'm a 13-year-old without a declared foreign language and 37 infected mosquito bites who lost her face in O'Hare. It oc-curs to me that Scotty Stoloff may not come back to Camp Hillel next summer.

The dinner bell rings and Spiritual Discussion is over. Rabbi just-call-me-Jeff and Dr. White have to rethink the for-mat. During dinner, there's a rumor bunks Golda Meir and Shimon Peres are not participating effectively.

Bodies have on/off switches and mine is jammed awake. Scotty isn't in any of my activities. In fact, he sits in the lotus position in the empty Rec Center basketball court practicing calligraphy in his journal. Sometimes he plays drums and shoots hoops.

I leave my papier-mâché mask of a girl who removed her face before an Aloha flight to Honolulu. Her name is Lily and she hid her face in a potted Fichus tree next to an exhibit featuring states and their most significant minerals.

Scotty is in the lotus position writing in his journal. I sit on the warm wood near him. "Your answer was so cool," I say.

"I liked yours too," Scotty Stoloff replies. "Though O'Hare wouldn't make my short list."

It's a floor of wooden boards like puzzle pieces. I begin counting lines in the grain and the nubs of nail heads. 74 nails and 12 separate lines of grain in each board.

"I prefer Asian airports. Chaos impresses me." Scotty Stoloff closes his calligraphy book.

"What about an Aloha Airlines flight to Honolulu?" I ask.

"Hawaii is just another American state," he explains. "It's the next flight I like. Bangkok maybe. Or Hong Kong."

"In Hong Kong the umbrellas have red Peonies and birds painted on them," I tell him.

Scotty considers this. "Parrots?"

"No," I say. "Cranes."

Scotty nods. He opens his calligraphy book and writes **Hong Kong=Cranes.** Then I ask him what his foreign language is. I sit cross-legged. My yellow thighs' sacs and infected scabs make me feel like a reptile.

"Spanish," Scotty replies, determined. He lowers his voice. "It's the language of drug deals and arms smuggling," he reveals, whispering. "Want to move contraband, learn Spanish."

When he asks what I'm taking, I say, "Canadian."

In the burst of our laughter, I feel yellow as Orchids from Madonna's dressing room.

Then we're in the brutal glare of the dusty parking lot, waiting for our parents. We have our suitcases, backpacks, crafts projects, sleeping bags and pillowcases of dirty clothes in scattered piles. My crafts projects require an extra 2 cardboard boxes. I've made 16 papier-mâché masks of faces, and glued sequins and feathers on them. I've drawn black lines with arrows on their foreheads, indicating where the radiation should go. I suddenly realize my masks have no mouths.

Cameras, binoculars and Walkmen fall randomly on the gravel. Batteries and tubes of lip-gloss lay abandoned on bleached stones. I see my mother's red Jaguar approaching and run to find Scotty.

"Are you coming back?" I look down at my sandals and count gray pebbles in the gravel. 46. I can count the brown ones next.

He shakes his head no. "I'll be in Bolivia by next summer," Scotty reveals. In the sun his gold earring looks like it would burn my fingers if I touched it.

Unexpectedly, he produces a sheet of notebook with his address in a script like calligraphy. He extends it to me and I take it. Then Scotty snaps my picture and says, "Hey, stay in touch."

I can't see his green eyes through his sunglasses. There is just his black Sex Pistols T-shirt and how he enters a dark SUV and vanishes.

My mother and Marty begin their interrogation. They talk and I fill in the blanks. It's a multiple choice test. Camp Hillel exists to enhance me. Precisely how have I been transformed? My mother demands the first and last names of my bunkmates, in case she knows their parents. And the activities I selected? What new physical and artistic skills have I mastered?

Marty asks if I can make a horse jump over a fence. My mother wonders if I learned to play the flute. Was I invited to a villa in Lake Como? Am I going to the Brazilian rainforest? Did I try hard enough with the Goldberg twins? Will I be going to Cannes on their yacht? Most importantly, did I distinguish myself in a manner resulting in a certificate or plaque they can put in a frame?

My mother moves directly into the decision aspect. Am I going to stay with them? Of course, I'm going to choose Beverly Hills High over Alleghany Hills High, which doesn't even have a computer lab, or audio-visual or theater arts electives. Girls are required to take Home Economics and demonstrate proficiency with meatloaf preparation, which is a blatant example of retrograde gender oppression. Not to mention the fact that they don't even offer French, German or Latin. Chinese is not even on the horizon, not in my lifetime. They don't offer Spanish either, anymore, because Mrs. Burdick is pregnant and taking a year off. I don't mention this.

"English is a foreign language there," Marty says, driving. "Grammar is considered exotic."

"Like teeth. Know what a compliment is there? Nice tooth," my mother says. She doesn't smile.

I look at my sun blistered feet but there are no pebbles or pine needles to count. I begin adding up the number of lines in the leather floor mats. Then I start to count the small beige stitches.

"Look, darling," my mother begins, voice soft. She turns around from the front seat to face me. She unlocks her seatbelt and leans closer. "Isn't it time to get serious about your life?"

Her hair is dyed blonder than usual. She wears her blue contact lenses with Aegean blue eye shadow and Adriatic liner. Her lipstick is called Millennium. I have the same one in my backpack. It's red with a sheen that sparkles when lamp or match light touches it. It's a special imported blend that resists water and retains its minute glowing silvery flecks like recessed lanterns.

"I know your father told you things. And you probably told him we've become Republicans. That would inflame him. I understand the young automatically betray. And your father no doubt told you we 'sold out.' My mother laughs now. Her head swings back on her neck. "We didn't sell out. We bought in."

"My father didn't say that. About selling out," I tell her.

"What do they call it, then?" my mother presses.

"They say you found the right life for you," I reply.

"Sweetheart, this is the right life for everybody," Marty says. "Moses would throw his tablets down to come to this party."

I write Scotty that night. I tell him I'm going to O'Hare soon, and I have to make my decision. I explain the history of my parents' band, how I was born, and then my father, who played guitar and wrote songs, fell in love with Madeleine, the other singer and songwriter. And my mother, who played keyboards, fell in love with Marty, the bass player. The band lived as a commune and my father and Madeleine are the last ones left.

Marty became a producer and lawyer in Beverly Hills. I tell Scotty my father grows pot and Psilocybin Mushrooms under high intensity lights from Sweden in our barn in the Alleghany Mountains. Everyone in town thinks he runs an organic gardening business, but he actually sells drugs. I live in two places, but only feel at home in O'Hare.

I am suspended between mutually exclusive possibilities. I navigate encampments from tree level. I'm the girl on the high trapeze. My wires are disguised and I have my own gravity, rules and variables. I'm expected to cross regions with no bridges, diagrams or candles, no drum rolls or spotlights. And somehow I do in seizures of vertigo and fevers no one notices.

If an event can be explained, its mysterious origins and

destiny wash away. It's diminished and insignificant. I store details in unmarked Mason jars I hide — my parents' divorce, my Gucci pink closet just for shoes, my father's magic mushrooms in beds of dirt like babies in suspended animation, Marty's gold framed album covers and mechanical accordion arm.

If I don't connect the dots, circumstances remain weedy and intangible. They have no longitude or latitude. They move electrically through time, which is like a river with ports and Lilac branches strung with votives and orangey paper lanterns. You can't find this on a map and it has no landing strip.

Scotty immediately answers my 9-page letter with a special delivery envelope. At the end of his calligraphy letter he's added a **PS** in plain block letters. **YOU'RE NOBODY'S CHILD.** We write each other almost every day.

I've come to the final week when my decision is due. My choice will shape my destiny. The farm is a squalid cul-de-sac, a village of peripherals. I am to go back to my father and Madeleine and pack my necessary mementos and then return for school in Beverly Hills in September.

Of course I can visit my father and Madeleine whenever I want. I can spend my vacations and summers there, if I prefer northern Pennsylvania to French Polynesia or Italy. It's just the matter of school, of being settled, on track and participating effectively.

At night, the swimming pool is implausibly turquoise, as if painted and starched. It looks glutinous, like you could get stuck in it. I walk in and out of rooms, turning lights off and on, off and on. I count the crystal vases in the living room, 11. In the kitchen 18 copper pots hang from their antique copper rack. There are 29 rows and 19 columns of hand painted Italian tiles in the entrance hall below 5 skylights and 14 Fichus trees.

I watch my mother and Marty play tennis. I'm suddenly

afraid of the pool. I count my mother's prescribed 50 laps. She actually does 34. The gardener subtracts 3 scorched Pink Camellias and adds 5 Hibiscus bushes in their place, 3 yellow and 2 red. He loads his truck with 6 different sized shovels and 3 green hoses coiled like ropes or creek snakes. I memorize his license plate.

Marty is in his office with the 22 framed record covers of the bands he's produced hung on the creamy white wall behind his back. His 6 platinum record plaques hang across from his desk. He wears white tennis shorts and stares at his just-delivered FAX machine. He looks stunned.

I try to remember the 10 Commandments. "Do you bear false witness?" I ask.

Marty is surprised. "I'm an attorney. My license obviates such distinctions. I've never had a contract seriously challenged."

That night, my mother is stretched out in a chaise lounge by the pool. She's drinking cognac disguised as root beer. I sit next to her. We wear identical tropical print bathing suits and I realize our legs match precisely. We have thin ankles and our tanned flesh adheres seamlessly to the bone like some newly invented millennial clay was poured over them. My mosquito and spider bites have gone into remission.

"Do you steal?" I begin with my mother.

"I would never steal." My mother doesn't hesitate.

"What about the Millennium lipsticks you took?" I ask.

At our last Diva Salon appointment, when her stylist wasn't watching, my mother took 3 lipsticks from the shelf and slid them into her purse. Later she gave me one.

"That's not stealing." My mother smiles. "That's called slippage. I'm a regular customer. They expect established clientele to take samples."

"But is it wrong?" I want to know.

"Stealing? Of course it's wrong." My mother bites her lower lip and a dent forms in the red gloss.

Marty drives to the Malibu house for what may be my last weekend of the summer. He's tan and wears a Dodger baseball cap. The convertible is down so I yell through wind.

"Do you steal?" It's the only Commandment I remember.

"My pen is heavier than Pete Townsend swinging a guitar. It has more force than an enraged diva with her mic at max." Marty's eyes are on the Pacific Coast Highway. My mother is already in Malibu with Maria preparing the house.

"I don't draw up contracts, honey. I devise war plans." Marty shows his ivory teeth. "I really build prison camps."

"But you did steal." My voice is raised, competing with the salty wind. There are 5 of what my mother terms real restaurants and 8 traffic lights between Santa Monica and our house on stilts in sand. The night beach glistens with mica like tiny shattered stars.

"You mean the commune days? Sweetie, those are times no one remembers, including me." Marty is driving his birthday Porsche. He passes a house, swerves, and pulls over to the shoulder of the road. He stares at a house and his mouth is half-open.

"Geffen's having another party," he says. His voice is a mixture of anger and stunned admiration. Perhaps that's called coveting. That's against the law.

"You grew drugs with my dad. You traded drugs for guns and sold them to the Weathermen. You and Dad robbed an armory," I point out.

"That's hearsay and inadmissible," Marty replies. "We

needed Marshall amps. Madeleine had Stevie Nicks' dress designer on retainer. Retainer, no less. It's ancient history. The rules were different then."

Marty's words are spaced with precision like a mathematical equation proving the existence of gravity and why you can't go faster than light, not even in a Porsche. Marty can say anything, with his stretched wide lips and teeth like infant tusks. He can take a lie detector test and pass it.

"What about the dude in Les Miserables? 20 years in prison for stealing bread when he was starving," I remark.

"He's got a malpractice action against his attorney. No question," Marty decides.

At the beach house, I walk along the lip of the ocean counting stray pebbles and pieces of damaged clamshells. Later, I'll count beads of mica like miniature fractured mirrors beneath my feet. This is how you learn to walk on glass and not get cut. After dinner, I'll carry a calculator and count sand particles.

"Tell us your most memorable Camp Hillel experience," my mother begins. Maria has prepared her special salad with avocadoes, crab and pecans. Marty cooks steaks on a grill on the terrace just above the slow slapping waves.

"Spiritual Discussion. Scotty Stoloff said he'd take a kilo of cocaine and a 9-millimeter gun to outer space." I'm wearing my Millennium lipstick. My mouth is encrusted with camouflaged metal discs. If the wrong person kissed me, my lips would make them bleed.

"That's disgusting." My mother puts down her fork in slow motion. She looks like she's just accidentally discovered gravity.

"I'm calling the Camp Director now." Marty stands up. "That's absolutely unacceptable."

"I'm shocked," my mother decides. She stares at her fork. She has what appears to be a glass of orange juice near her plate. I know she put vodka in it.

"Don't call the Director." My voice is too loud. I glare at Marty and add, "I mean it."

I want to leave the table, but I don't. I finish dinner. Then I go to my room, close and lock my door, and begin packing. I wrap all 16 masks separately and take an extra suitcase.

My father and Madeleine wave to me in the corridor of the Erie Airport. We run to embrace each other. When we walk, I'm in the middle. My father holds one of my hands and Madeleine holds the other.

My dad's gray van is like the skin of winter. It's made of rain, clouds and wind. It's a hot summer night. Even though the moon is nearly full, the stars are astonishing, strewn like confetti, and more abundant than mica in sand. The stars aren't broken pieces, but separate entities, each in its appointed place, spinning and burning. Dad plays a U2 tape. It's *Joshua Tree* and Madeleine sings the chorus.

"In Spiritual Discussion, I met a guy named Scotty," I begin.

"Did you fall in love?" Madeleine inquires.

"I think so. Practice Rabbi Jeff asked what we'd take to another planet. Everyone lied. They all said they'd take their parents and dogs. But Scotty said he'd take a kilo of cocaine and a Tec-9 with extra ammunition."

Madeleine laughs. "Sounds like someone we know."

"Not me." My father isn't amused.

"You at 13 maybe," Madeleine amends.

My father turns up the volume and Madeleine knows all the words. They don't ask me what my plans are. Or talk about the most important thing in the world, participating effectively. They don't want distinguished certificates suitable for framing. They don't want me to go to the rainforest the size of New Jersey. Or Lake Como, not even if the Goldberg twins take me on their yacht.

I leave my suitcases at the front door and sit on my bed in the wooden room and look out at the Maples. Even in the dark, they're relentlessly and unapologetically green, as if no circumstance can alter their condition. Later, they'll be burgundy and magenta, claret and bronze.

I mail Scotty an O'Hare Airport postcard. I sit on the porch, eaves entwined with Wisteria and abandoned finch nests. I watch the mail truck come and go. 8 pick-ups pass on the dirt road. I walk to the creek. I stand at the well. Then I follow the perimeter of the property and return to the house.

Madeleine is in her music room. It was the attic the band used as its official rehearsal space. My father turned it into a real music room for her, one slow refinement at a time. He glued acoustical tiles onto the walls and put skylights in the ceiling. When Madeleine plays piano and writes songs, she can look out the thermal paned glass windows and watch the forest run through its seasonal progressions.

Maples have scales and melodies. Wind sounds differently in red and yellow leaves than it does in green. It's more like horns and brass. When leaves turn burgundy and magenta, the forest is fragile and tinny, like it's filled with clusters of miniature cymbals. Winter is drums and castanets and all forms of percussion.

Madeleine is playing guitar, sitting on the floor, her back leaning against the wall. She's lit incense and cranberry scented candles, but I know she's been smoking pot. I determine this by how her body is inordinately airy and receptive to sway, even though there's no wind in the room. She could float away but won't. Her hair is long and falls across her face, streaked with a gray that resembles currents of silver. Her hair is a smoky mirror. I can watch her head and know what she's thinking.

"Do you steal?" I ask.

"Everybody steals," Madeleine says. "We all dip from the same trough, dear."

"So you steal?" I press.

"It's unconscious. Sounds and images live inside. They mutate. When you write a song, you don't even realize the palette you're really using." Madeleine puts her Martin acoustic guitar across the pillow near her leg. She gestures for me to sit beside her. I stand where I am.

"I mean things," I say.

"Things?" Madeleine repeats.

"Like clothes or lipsticks or boxes of candy." I stare at her. "Or guns."

Madeleine says, "No."

"Why not? Because it's wrong?" I am tall above her. I'm a sapling, intrinsic to this forest. I have my own dialect of shadow and metamorphosis.

"No," Madeleine replies. "Things you can buy don't interest me." She picks up her guitar.

"Why do you keep writing songs?" I demand. "Mother says it's ridiculous. There are no 40-year-old unknown singers. Zero." I make my fingers form an **o**. I hold this **o** in the air between us. I move my **o** up and down and jump from one foot to the other. "You're never going to sell anything!" I scream. My voice bounces off the tiled walls.

"I'm not trying to sell anything," Madeleine says.

"So why do you do it?" I need to know.

"It brings me pleasure." Madeleine strums a chord progression. A minor, G and F. Then she plays C, F and G. She plays it over and over, at least a dozen times. "Those are 3 chords you could build a world on. I'd take them to another planet."

I walk outside through acres of shoulder-high wild flowers and into the big barn. My father wears his white lab coat and washes Psilocybin Mushrooms in the sink. They're veined with purple, as if they're organs, pulsing and alive, waiting to be transplanted. The marijuana plants are eight feet tall. Soon my dad will cut them down and hang them up-side-down to dry from ropes strung between the rafters. As they cure, resins accumulate in the buds. He'll sort the buds by size and quality and vacuum-seal them. The leaves are compacted into bricks, weighed and packaged in plastic and canvas.

"Mom and Marty are Republicans now," I reveal.

"So what?" My father runs water over the mushrooms and places them on the drying mesh. His hands are steady and nothing spills.

"Don't you hate Republicans?" I'm confused.

"I don't hate anyone in particular. I'm an anarchist." My father spreads mushrooms across the mesh in even rows, none of them touching.

"Why didn't you go back to school when the band broke up? Like Marty?" I decide this is a good question, even though it isn't directly connected to the 10 Commandments.

"I was happy as I was," my father says.

"But you could have made lots of money. You could have been important," I point out.

"I'm important as anyone," my father says.

My father dries his hands with a towel. He crosses the dirt floor to where I stand. He wraps his arms around me and holds me pressed against his chest. I hear his heart beating, each individual increment of pump and flow, and I do not count them.

"Do you steal?" I finally ask.

He releases me from our embrace and stands an arm's length away, examining my face. It reminds me of when he looks in a mirror, shaving. Then he says, "No."

"Why? Because it's wrong?" I'm not wearing my red lipstick with the dangerous disguised stars embedded in them. My mouth is stark and small. It's a winter mouth now.

"There's nothing I want," my father says.

It's the cusp between summer and autumn. It occurs to me that transitions can be crossed by trapeze. The grass beneath my bare feet is a soft half-asleep green like pond water. Deer are sighing and pawing between Maples. It's the end of blueberry season. Apples redden in baskets. I hear squirrels and fox, finches and owls, crickets and frogs. There are more sounds than I can count, but I just want to listen by the pond until all the stars come out.

WHAT THE LILIES KNOW

Amy Gold hears the rumor and instantaneously recognizes it's true. She's being denied tenure. Then Alfred Baxter Coleman ambushes her in the corridor. Alfred Baxter Coleman, the ABC of the History Department, stage whispers the terminal news to her. He executes his standard mock Indian mime, emitting a sort of emphysemic whoop, and his arthritic fingers anemically slap his thin lips, sporadically, with no discernible rhythm. Whoop whoop. He ho. He ho.

What he actually says is, "No way, Sweetie. Told you."

He's intimated this for months. Amy ignored him.

She stumbles into her office and reaches onto her desk to steady herself. She picks up the first object she chances to touch. It's her phone book. She holds it in her palm like a magic stone, an amulet, a medicine bag. The pages are fragile as petals or antiquities. It's an artifact with disasters between the lines.

On this particular morning, she dials her mother. Then she waits for her mother to answer. Raven Gold is an integral component in her arsenal of weapons of personal destruction.

Raven is the core, her plutonium centerpiece. Amy needs an action to definitively express her rage and grief, something like a hand grenade or bullet. Raven can pull the trigger.

Cellular service, with static intermittent voids and uncertainties involving wind currents and angles, has finally come to Espanola. Theoretically, they can now communicate directly. But Amy Gold cannot talk to her mother. They speak as if with flags the way people do at sea when conditions are mutable, possibilities limited and primitive. They choreograph pieces of cloth. The planet is compressed into a basket of fabrics. They wave at each other with rags.

Raven removes language and logic. Cause and effect are illusions. Raven has an unscripted life. No scrawls in the margins, and no footnotes.

Her mother has a cell phone now, but Amy is still rendered childlike and vulnerable. She presses the phone hard against her ear until the metal hurts. This is foreshadowing. Amy counts the rings. Twenty-five.

"They didn't give me the job," Amy begins, her thoughts spinning chaotic and circular.

"You're surprised?" Raven laughs. "You're not a team player. You always wanted a rank and serial number. The right uniform. Play first string for the military industrial complex."

Out the fifth floor window ersatz palm trees are stunted by sun, and the air is oily and smeared. Outside is a slice of Los Angeles in early summer. Hills are a brutal stale green with brittle shrubs like dry stubble.

"Do you know how long it's been?" Raven asks, softer now. "Since you called?"

"To the hour," Amy answers. She tells her mother precisely how many years, months and days passed since their last conversation.

"I'm impressed," Raven admits.

"You're always impressed by the wrong things," Amy says. "Men who add fast without scratch paper. Chess players and piano players, no matter how mediocre. Women with trust funds who sew their own clothes and bake breads."

"I'm a simple country gal. You were always too smart for me," Raven offers.

"I want to see you now." Her words are sudden and tumble into the hot-stripped morning like dice hitting a wall and she wonders if she means them.

"Then get in your car. You'll be here tomorrow," Raven says with surprising urgency. "Just check that AA crap at the border."

"I'll leave half my IQ, too," Amy offers. "As a sign of good will." After a pause in which Raven fails to construct a reply, Amy asks, "How will I find you?"

"Ask in the plaza. Anyone can tell you where."

Her mother hangs up. No more details. Just anyone. In the plaza. It's like a treasure hunt. Or eating peyote and letting it happen. That's what they did for years. Let it happen. They camped on mesas and the rims of canyons. Raven had a boyfriend with a jeep and a sawed off 12-gauge under the seat. His 9-millimeter was in his backpack, and he had a .32 semi-automatic in his pocket. A man, one man or another, who played drums or bass in a band, just returned from Australia or Japan. They stayed in the juniper forests for weeks. Finally, insect bites, sunburns and infected cuts made them return. Sometimes Raven just wanted a hot bath.

"I demand perfume," Raven laughs, half-dressed on a plateau, her bare shoulders sculpted as if by centuries of wind and a gifted potter's hands. "I must have musk and a new hat with an extravagant feather."

They find towns with a hotel sporting an old west motif. Durango or Aspen, Las Cruces, Silver City or Santa Fe. Her childhood is a sequence of lead glass windows and crimson floral carpets, mahogany paneling and authentic antique saloon doors. The card tables and upstairs brothel are gone but somehow manage to assert themselves, not quite visible and completely intact. Chandeliers emit a tame filtered light like pueblo churches. Late afternoon is cool, and the amber of honey and whiskey. It's the color of an afternoon shoot-out.

It's the era of the commune and just before boarding school. Raven's boyfriends have what they call business in town. They take unplanned flights to Los Angeles and Miami. Raven drives them to and from airports. Small planes land on salt flats in the desert where there are no roads, and Raven has flares, flashlights, and a basket of still warm tamales and rum in a jug. Amy is wrapped in a down blanket in the backseat. Why do they lean into one another whispering? She knows they're dealing drugs.

Amy doesn't confront her mother. They already speak in code, in a network of implications and arrested partial sounds like passwords. Between them, flannel and denim and gingham scraps wait to become a quilt that won't be stitched. Plans for a house built of adobe on the mesa above Espanola that her mother somehow owns stay a rolled-up document, a parchment hollow inside a rubber band. It's a navigational chart for a sea they won't sail. Their ideas drift off, despoiled, weightless; they abort themselves.

Amy is leaving. She's been accepted to a boarding school in San Diego. The provost pronounced her test scores impressive. He's encouraging. It's possible a college scholarship may eventually be granted. In hotel rooms with lead glass windows and red velvet curtains, she studies brochures for colleges in Vermont and Massachusetts.

In between, she just lets it happen. They return from the mesas, their vision quest Raven calls it, with their filthy clothing, ammunition and stray pieces of peyote stuffed randomly into plastic bags. It's the best hotel in town and the bellman carries their trash bags with the gravity afforded real luggage. Raven is instantaneously elevated to Madam.

It's usually a suite. Her mother's boyfriend of the moment enters cautiously, his hand touching the gun in his pocket. He eases into rooms, opening closet doors and shower curtains. He glances at the street below, scanning for indications of an ambush by DEA agents, Zeta flunk-outs trying to make a name for themselves, or freelancers.

After weeks in canyons of juniper, sage, and pinion, cafes and boutiques are a fascination. It's another form of foraging. She spends afternoons in tourist gift shops. She's lost so much weight on their plateau vision quests, eating only dried fruit, crackers and an occasional rainbow trout, she fits into size 2s on sale racks in Pocatello, Alamosa and Winslow, where the women have either run away or gone to fat the way domesticated animals do.

In an Indian casino near the border she buys a hot pink mini skirt for 2 dollars. It feels like abraded Teflon. Eventually Raven has to cut it off her with scissors. Amy buys a silver blouse the texture of steel wool. She stumbles in neon pink spike heels and pretends she's Brazilian.

She rides a dawn bus to work from the favala. She's a clerk with ambitions. Her name was Gloria but she's changed it to Marguerite. Her married boss takes her to hotels on Sundays after mass. Through the slatted terrace blinds, birds and cathedral bells in cobblestone plazas drift in, and the festive fluttering bells from old trolley cars with electric spokes that sizzle. A choir of indigenous orphans from the mountains offers an incoherent rendition of "New York, New York" and "Take Me Out To the Ball Game." It's mutilated by distance, intention and what resists translation. Nuns draped them in novice habits and glued gauzy angel wings to their shoulders. They're barefoot and hungry.

Further, men in cloaks of magenta and electric blue feathers from jungle birds play flutes. In the plaza spreading beyond the cathedral, swarms of pigeons and yellow butterflies almost touch the faces of old women selling dried corn strung like beads and Chiclets arranged like miniature pyramids. Beyond, there's something rhythmic and insistent that might be an ocean.

We are all clerks with ambitions, Amy decides then, stretching her insect bitten legs out on a brocade bedspread in a restored hotel suite in Colorado or New Mexico. She is fourteen or fifteen years old. Raven and her boyfriend are out doing business. They leave three hundred dollar bills on the brocade and instruct her to get an ice cream soda and go shopping.

Beyond town is thunder, glaciers on mountain peaks, then desert and finally San Diego Pacific Academy. Amy Gold imagines boarding school will be similar to the commune. But the sleeping and eating arrangements will be superior. San Diego Pacific Academy has desks and electricity and a library. Bells ring and they have specific and reliable meanings.

Now it's noon in Los Angeles. She packs her office. It's the end of the semester and she won't be back in the fall. Alfred Baxter Coleman, chair of the promotion and tenure committee, has successfully convinced his colleagues they don't need her. She's only half-Indian, after all. Christ, she was born in Laguna Beach. They've hired a Palestine to replace her. It's a more profound historical statement and irrefutably global.

Amy wraps a pottery vase in the school newspaper. Ink encrusts her fingers and she feels soiled to the bone. She doesn't want to put her books in cardboard boxes again. It's an obsolete rite of empty repetition. It's the opposite of propitiation. It's failure in a cardboard box the size of an infant's coffin. Even her fingers resist.

The square book caskets. She's been carrying dead texts from state to state, up and down flights of apartment steps bordering alleys and parking lots, Bougainvillea and Oleander strangling on cyclone fences. Amy realizes she doesn't want the books anymore, period.

What she wants is a wound that bleeds and requires sutures and anesthesia. What she wants is a cigarette. Amy gathers her cosmetics and tape cassettes from her desk drawer. She takes the gym bag with her tennis racket, bathing suit, jeans, diamondback rattlesnake boots, flashlight and mace. She wraps her raincoat across her shoulders and thinks, *I'm down the road. I'm out of here.*

She wants someone to call, "Professor Gold?" Then she can reply, "Not anymore." Her response will be fierce and laconic. It will deconstruct itself as you watch. Then it will explode in your face.

Amy Gold shoves U2's *Joshua Tree* into the cassette player. She replaces it with a *ZZ Top* cassette. Yes, it's an afternoon for the original nasty boys from Texas. They provide a further dimension to the concept of a garage band. After all, you don't have to just rehearse there. You can throw a mattress on the floor, invite your friends, drink a case of bourbon, shoot coke and orchestrate a gang rape. Maybe she should get down even further. Maybe it's an afternoon for chainsaws and a massacre.

She turns onto the freeway, and considers her final encounter with Professor Alfred Baxter Coleman. In instant replay, her knees wobble and she almost falls down. But she doesn't. She manages to stay on her feet and give Alfred the finger. If she wasn't having a seizure of vertigo, she would mace him.

Los Angeles is at her back, a solid sheet of grease that's not entirely unpleasant. That's why she's been able to inhabit this city. Ugliness is a kind of balm. Beauty makes her uncomfortable. She instinctively averts her eyes from a flawless face the way some recoil from a car crash.

Amy Gold relentlessly attempts to annihilate all certified versions of perfection. The conventionally sanctioned snow-dusted mountains above wild flowers in alpine meadows that look designed to be photographed and sold as posters. She's repelled by images resembling calendar covers. They're faux artifacts of what you didn't actually experience. And she loathes towns with contrived lyrical names that could be the titles of country western songs. They're an accompaniment for the plastic scorpions tourists buy in stores with moccasins made in China and ceremonial headdresses of dyed turkey feathers.

That's why she left Raven the southwest interior of the country. Amy took the coasts and gave her mother everything else. That is their real division of assets. She took abstraction, hierarchy, and systematic knowledge and left Raven the inexpressible, the preliterate, the region of magic chants and herbs. It was a sort of divorce. Her mother could have Colorado, Arizona and New Mexico, and she would get her doctorate.

Raven accepts landscape as her due. She expects and collects it. Raven, staring at a sun setting in a contagion of magenta and irradiated purple. It's begging to be absolved. Raven nods in acknowledgement, shaking her waist-length black hair as clouds pass in a flotilla above them. She pauses, as if expecting the skies to actually part.

Raven, wind-blown and barefoot is prepared for the sky to form a tender lavender mouth and confess everything. It's the third or fourth day of a peyote fast, and her mother is a pueblo priestess, accustomed to tales of routine felonies and unavoidable lies. Transgressions aren't absolute. They're a matter of interpretation. Raven takes her form of communion beneath an aggressively streaked sunset the texture of metal. Amy knows the sky is a conventional polite lie. It's politically correct misdirection. There's something else behind clouds, a subterfuge of malice.

Her childhood is incoherent, images that stall stylized and suspect. They might be postcards. That's curious, she realizes, they didn't take photographs. Even when her mother married the magazine photographer, there were no cameras, no visual artifacts.

"You can't paste this between album pages," Raven says, standing in a meadow, her bare arms stretched out like twin milk snakes. Her paisley skirt is ripped to her thigh and wind-swirled. This what, precisely, Amy wants to know.

"Experience can't be reduced to a 4 by 6 inch still," her mother says. "People stick their loves in cellophane prisons. They incarcerate images. Then they put these cemeteries on coffee tables. They're mockeries."

Raven is topless on a mesa festooned with pinion and juniper, tilting her face to the sky, memorizing a spectrum of purple that runs from lilac and velvet iris to crushed antique maroon. It's an alphabet bordered by cobalt and a magenta that's gone a step too far, and committed itself to red. Amy wonders what can be distilled from such a sequence. You can't arrange it like paint on a palette, or orchestrate it to sound like flutes or ferry bells. You can't order it into stanzas or paragraphs. In short, it's entirely useless.

Her mother exists in a series of indiscriminate moments, each already pre-framed and merely waiting for lighting cues. Raven poses with a canyon lake as a backdrop. Amy half expects afternoon to dissolve into a car commercial. This is what she resists. No to the plateaus of northern New Mexico. No to the vivid orange intrigue of sunsets you could stencil on T-shirts. No to men who spend summers in sleeping bags, backpacks filled with Wild Turkey and kilos of cocaine. No to Raven in August, scented with dope and pinion, sleeping oblivious under lightning and an outrage of stars.

"I've been tattooed," Raven laughs in the morning, making coffee over a fire of purple sage. "Look." she angles her face toward the new boyfriend. Her face is tanned peach, without a single line or freckle. Amy possesses a secret accumulation of invisible injuries. They're the most exquisite. If there's an entity Raven calls Buddha, it is these clandestine self-inflicted lacerations that attract him.

"You can live myth or be buried by it. It's your choice," Raven says. It's her cocaine voice, vague and distant and leaking light. "I've been more intimate with this canyon than all 5 husbands combined," she confides. "It's revealed more. And it's been more generous."

Amy is on the periphery, simultaneously chilled and parched. She is not a team player. The sky is relentlessly alien. Plateaus are layered like a chorus of red mouths that have nothing to say to her.

Before nightfall and the desert, Amy Gold stops for gas. In a convenience store, fixed in the glare of anonymous waxy light, she decides, on inexplicable impulse, to change her life. She deliberately buys a pack of cigarettes, though she hasn't smoked in eight years.

"Vodka," she says, pointing to a fifth. The two-edged syllables are inordinately pale and mysterious, like something you can't procure on this planet. *I've been too long without the traditions*, she thinks. *Eight years. I'm estranged from my true self. I'm broken off at the root, amputated. I must graft myself back.*

She wonders if she can still score amphetamines in a truck stop. They're probably just kitchen bennies. White crosses, manufactured in basement labs, and sold as the trucker's other fuel. Last time she copped roadside speed, she got a two-day stomach-ache and the sensation that a 747 was landing on her head.

Danger excites her. Once she glided between trucks somewhere near Albuquerque, walking between the enormous cabs oily with bold unapologetic streaks of red and yellow like war paint. There are enemies and rogue bands everywhere. She notes the enormity of the wheels. The truck stop is a metal graveyard not unlike elephant and mastodon burial grounds.

We know ourselves through architecture and indecipherable charred hieroglyphics. To see the monumental trucks at rest is like watching men when they don't know they're being observed. Men in their natural state. Their posture softens, they slap each other on the back, show one another their rings and tattoos, and laugh often and easily.

She is with Big Jeb. He's impatient. There's a new girl in the aluminum trailer behind the restaurant. 15 and a natural blond from Alabama.

"It's show time," he says. He nudges the small of her back. It's the way a cat rubs against your leg.

"Got any whites?" she asks in her fake southern accent, leaning into a fierce crimson cab, her lips stretched into a smile that hurts her teeth. And, of course, the driver does.

"You mad?" Big Jeb asks later.

Amy translates his question. He means angry. She says no.

"Well, don't tell your mother," he says. His voice is light. It's not a threat. He's asking for a favor.

Amy smokes a cigarette, sips vodka and smiles. She takes another drink. There is no other way to cross the Mojave, she assures herself. At 3 a.m. she turns off the highway, finds a fire road, places her gym bag under her head as a pillow and falls asleep gripping the mace in her right hand.

She wakes stiff and feverish and drives to Santa Fe, singing with ZZ Top and drinking vodka from an orange juice bottle. Did she learn that from Wade or Gus? Who coached her on the southern accent and how to carry, conceal and shoot a weapon?

"I did all I could," he tells Raven. She is leaving for San Diego Pacific Academy. He sounds disappointed. Her mother nods sympathetically.

Amy is startled to realize that Raven's boyfriend was serious. Was it Big Jeb or Big Sam, Hawk Man or maybe Wade? Who positioned beer bottles on sand banks with tender precision and showed her how to put bullets in them? Who captured snakes for her to shoot, and bent to demonstrate how to remove the rattles and make them into earrings? Who explained spoor on trails and how to determine what coyotes, raccoons and rabbits had been eating?

Amy didn't encounter men with multi-syllabic names until boarding school. She was stunned when strangers voluntarily offered their last names. It hadn't occurred to her that people reveal this information. When asked, she automatically provided an alias. Marguerite.

⁊҃

Amy Gold checks into a new hotel near the plaza in Santa Fe. She's disoriented. Everything is some manifestation of adobe, cement and mud. Buildings are a tainted orange and degraded pink. Houses are set behind walls like African compounds. The walls are designed to keep the inhabitants in. They're ubiquitous, as if mandated. Here dirt and all its forms are not only obligatory, they're deified.

She's erased clay in all its permutations from her repertoire. In the millennium, we survive by aliases, photo shop and selective amnesia. It's a new spiritual expression. It's the first global mantra. We reclaim ourselves so that we can discard and bury them. Our AOL and Yahoo versions were insipid squalid forays into the wilderness within. We know better now.

In her senior year at San Diego Pacific Academy, her

elective choices were pottery studio or wood world. She chose the later. The boys built a two-story house with a graceful staircase and balconies. She made small boxes and glued sequins and chipped tiles on them. Her latches fall off. She says they're jewelry boxes. She defends herself. She's a clerk with ambitions and no, they don't have to close. They're conceptual. The wood master wants to flunk her. But she already has a scholarship to Stanford.

The swimming pool is deserted. Everyone must be buying necklaces of plastic dyed to mimic turquoise and fringed jackets made in Thailand. Or else they're stumbling up Canyon Road in their new boots that don't fit. Canyon Road, with it's 2,000 galleries, features what you've already seen. You know what's on the walls and pedestals before you walk in. Tourists find the familiar reassuring.

It's landscapes of Rio Grand gorges rendered in O'Keefe reds that look like lacerations. Then the heads of Indians in bronze. And bronze horses. And bronze Indians on bronze horses. It's the third or fourth derivative generation. Still lifes of vagina sunflowers. And landscapes reiterating their original psychedelic palette. Now they're actually spraying them with glitter.

Amy stands at the edge of the swimming pool. The water reminds her of Hawaii. The blues are so vivid and unadulterated, the elements seem participant.

As a child, she lived in Maui for three years. Her mother was married to Jerry Garcia's photographer. Ed. Big Ed. The ocean beyond their lanai possessed a clarity only certain sunlight, strained and purified by currents and anointed cloud configurations, can impart.

The swimming pool is the turquoise of traditional Indian jewelry. There's an enticement to this blue, with its suggestion of revelation and sacrament, of opening an enormous chamber into the world as it once was, into thunder and stone and sacrifices designed to engender an incandescent intelligence. It's the turquoise of time travel, camouflaged salt flats at dusk, and prayer.

This terrain renders ideas and artifacts inconsequential. That's why everyone was moving here, the ones who hadn't migrated to Hawaii or Mexico. But she has no interest in this obvious and generic surrender. Such a seduction would admit the squalor of her ambitions and what they imply, namely the incontrovertible value of acquiring systemic knowledge. Amy swims three hundred laps. It does not clear her head.

She sits on the bandstand in the plaza. Late afternoon is the adobe of dust and apricots. The sky is a swarm of storm clouds and two rainbows appear in precise twin arches. As they break into Cubist fragments, Amy realizes they're the DNA of the sky. Then she looks across the plaza, directly at her mother.

"Amethyst," her mother calls, already moving towards her, awkward and determined. They embrace and Raven smells unexpectedly sweet, like vanilla ice cream and spring grass.

Raven's hair is entirely white and tied into a ponytail with a piece of rawhide.

Raven in dusty black jeans. Her Saturday night end of the trail outfit. And she's profoundly tanned. It's not a skin coloration one can receive through ordinary daily living. It's clearly a statement, no doubt the result of pronouncing the diminishing ozone layer an establishment rumor that has nothing to do with her.

"Too many tourists," Raven says, talking out the side of her mouth. "Let's go."

Amy follows her mother's jeep along the highway toward Taos, and then off and onto a road so sudden and narrow it seems hallucinatory. They wind up a dirt road of sharp curves and loose gravel. Her mother parks alongside a tiny yellow trailer.

"It's temporary," Raven says, indicating the trail structure with a dismissive flutter of her left hand. "Like life."

"Right," Amy answers. They are proto-humans, banging on stones. Language has barely been invented. They communicate by drums and smoke singles. She follows her mother, climbs three stairs into the trailer, and pauses, all at once listless and exhausted.

"Old hippies don't die. They just quit drinking, take their milk thistle and liver enzyme counts." Raven offers an unconvincing smile.

"Liver enzymes?" Amy wonders.

"Hep C," Raven says.

"You have hepatitis C?" Amy is startled.

"We all do," her mother replies, flat and off-hand. "I hope to live long enough to get Medicare."

"Medicare?" Amy repeats.

"Medicare is just a word, like democracy and justice. It barely exists," Raven says.

Her mother sits cross-legged on the floor at a low table, a child's table, rolling a joint. When she offers it to her, Amy takes it. She left AA at the border. And half her IQ. Wasn't that the deal?

The trailer is so minimal it seems unoccupied. There's a tape deck that runs on batteries, a plate in what must be the kitchen and a bowl of bananas, strawberries and two onions. What's become of the Navajo rugs, the carved oak furniture, the Mescalero Apache tribal wall hangings, Hopi baskets and masks? And where is the Santa Clara pottery?

She remembers the era they called the Harmonic Divergence. The commune dwindled. It dried up overnight like creeks in summer. First AIDS. Then the crisis no one anticipated. Their foundation was the exploration of human consciousness. Insidiously and inexorably, their beliefs were culturally degraded, marginalized and then outlawed.

They were a band of conceptual renegades, biochemical pioneers in an aesthetic frontier that was abruptly fenced. Suddenly, satellites provided surveillance. They were shorn of legitimacy. There's no glamour in being a designated leper. Criminals have no justification. But there were treatments for their aberrant inclinations. Antidepressants. Rehab. AA. Support groups and disability payments. Everyone took the cure.

"I'm too old for this," one of the Big Bobs or Big Jebs said. "I'm not taking a dump in mud in winter. Not at 45."

There was attrition. Drugs were now controlled by men with computers in Nassau and Houston. Big Wade and Big Jake had arthritis and diabetes and the wrong skillset for the emerging global market place. They dispersed, took their medications for depression, and meditated in shacks on canyon rims, proclaiming themselves Zen masters. They had tape decks and bags of Prozac, Paxil, Zoloft and Metformin. And shelves of SSRis and Tricyclics. Nothing worked, but it was free. Some found apartments in town with electricity and watched CNN on 16 inch black and white televisions.

The Espanola property accrued to Raven. She was the last one left, keeping the faith in derelict rooms lit by kerosene lamps, incense and candles. Rooms collapsed around her. The roof fell down in chunks and walls disintegrated into powder. That's why she purchased the trailer. And what was that green square outside? Was Raven growing marijuana?

"Corn." Raven is amused. "Subsistence economy. Tomatoes. Squash. I put seeds in the ground. I eat the plants. A simple life. Much too boring for a professor like you. But you always thought me dull."

Not dull, Amy wants to correct, just affected, predictable,

and formulaic. The trailer reminds her of a boat, ingenuously compact, deceptively pulling in or out of the miniature closets and cabinets. They had a boat in Maui, she remembers later, when winds rise and batter the metal sides in a sudden squall with lightning.

They are laying side by side on twin cots like berths, rocking. The trailer sways and Amy thinks, *We are floating through metaphors and into symbolic oceans, clutching our charred text as life preservers. We make a telephone call. Or stand in the glaring light of a liquor store on the edge of the Mohave and the course of our life is changed.*

Once during the thunderstorm, Amy sits bolt upright and for an inconclusive moment, thinks she sees Raven standing naked at the tiny window, weeping. Her mother by moonlight, whitened, whittled.

"I'm a moon crone," Raven says, directly to the night.

Her mother has sensed her movement, her intake of breath. "I'm 52 and haven't had a period in years. I'm on hormones and I'm still burning up." Raven turns toward her and speaks into the darkness. "You don't have to fear me anymore. I'm not a competitor. You removed my 9 heads. Hydra is gone. You beheaded me. See me as I am."

"Are you lonely?" Amy wonders, uncertain. She's an ethnographer and Raven is her subject.

"Lonely?" her mother repeats. "I have two friends. New Mexico and Bob Dylan. He wrote the soundtrack for my life. When he dies, I'll be a widow."

Amy wakes at noon. Raven has assembled sleeping bags, a tent, stacks of camping equipment and a variety of canvas bags under the awning in front of the tiny yellow trailer.

"Let's rock and roll." Raven is enthusiastic. "Mesa Verde. I feel a spiritual experience coming."

This woman has absolutely no sense of irony, Amy thinks.

She inhabits an era of oral tradition, intuition and omens. The constellations aren't named. One worships flint and thunder, bargains with stars and drums in solitude.

They drive north, Raven taking the curves too fast. Amy assembles a random list of what she hates about the Southwest. How everyone is making jewelry and searching for shrines. Santa Fe is an outdoor theme mall. Silver is a wound that gleams. It's a cancer. It lays itself out in strands of necklaces and belts, a glare of dead worms, obscene. The entire Navajo nation is home in a stupor, smoking chiva and crack and watching TV while numbly pounding out conches and squash blossoms. It's sickening.

Amy remembers a town on the way to Las Cruces. Shacks where she sees lava mountains out a broken window. Her real father is coming down from the reservation to see her. He's out of prison. Amy hasn't met him. Big Ed or Big Jeb are buying pot. Or maybe selling it. The adults are eating peyote.

Her mother and a woman she doesn't recognize sit on the floor in the lotus position, stringing necklaces and laughing. The TV is on maximum volume, picture and sound wavering, ghosted and distorted. She became dizzy, and perhaps she fainted. She is carried to a car. It's a special day. She is certain. Yes, it's her thirteenth birthday and her father doesn't come down from the reservation to see her after all. Later, the woman reaches through the car window, dangling necklaces. She offers her beads, silver and turquoise. Amy shakes her head no.

"Mesa Verde is a revelation," Raven reveals. "The Buddha must have built it."

"Didn't extraterrestrials do the construction?" Amy asks. "Aliens from Roswell with green blood and implants in their necks."

Raven smokes a joint. Amy Gold turns away, angry. She rejects the concept that enlightenment can be geographically pinpointed, that one can chart a route, follow a map, drive there, and purchase a ticket. Spirituality has been reduced to another commodity. Can't Raven comprehend that? Probably not.

Amy experiences a disappointment so overwhelming it erases the possibility of speech. She drinks from her vodka bottle surreptitiously, leaning against the car window while afternoon falls in green and blue pieces against her face. The time space continuum is fluid and it's flowing across her skin. It's breaking across her flesh in a series of glass splinters.

They spend the afternoon in Indian ruins, peering through holes and slots implying windows. They climb reconstructed steps and wood ladders into the cliff dwellings. The repetition of identical ceremonial rooms is relentless. She feels sullen and futile.

"You're still a bitter child," Raven says, voice soft. It's not an accusation. "You have a one word vocabulary. All you say is no."

"You're the queen of yes. What did it get you?"

Silence. Amy is wondering what the Anasazi did, how they lived. They smoked pot, no doubt, and strung beads, got drunk, hunted and gathered herbs. In between, they engaged in acts of domestic violence and child abuse. Now a slap, then a torn hymen. Human nature hasn't changed. In 641, a pope decreed that a man could have only a single wife. But there's no evolutionary adaptation to support that opinion.

Amy wants to discuss this with her mother. But Raven doesn't have the attention span. They crawl through a tunnel, dust settling across her forehead like another coating of adobe or clay, a decorative filigree. They stand on the rim of the canyon, their shoulders brushing. It begins to rain; thunder echoes off rock and the ground shakes. It's like being in a shooting range.

Raven is out of breath. "It's the ancient ones talking," she manages.

"Christ," Amy says. "You'll end up a tour guide."

"Big Red's a guide in Bandolier. He's got a uniform and a pension," Raven tells her with a rare edge. Is she jealous?

Amy touches the emergency pint of vodka inside the rain poncho her mother handed her. When she isn't watching, Amy finishes the bottle.

"You don't have to drink like this," Raven said. "Pot is easier on the liver. And it's more enlightening."

In a deserted campground, they walk in mud up to their calves. Raven is wearing a stylish leather coat. It simply materialized. It's like that with her mother, the costume changes, the inexplicable appearance of accessories, the silver belt pulled from a bag, the mantilla that's both a veil and shawl. Amy is shivering.

"West and south," Raven decides. "The first decent hotel where it's hot."

Gallup is a few disappointing blocks of pawnshops and liquor stores that seem to be lingering posthumously. A community center with windows broken, and a tennis court with the pavement ripped. The net has been hacked up with knives. She imagines playing on the court, bits of glass making her footing slippery. She could fall, sprain an ankle, get cut. But that scenario is too simple. The wound she's searching for, what she's stalking, is more profound and permanent.

"The whole infrastructure is going," Amy notes, glancing at the gutted swimming pool, the brown lawn laced with glass. "It's not just the cities."

"My infrastructure is going. But government pills and AA aren't my answer." Raven stops the car. There is a pause.

"Listen, I had boyfriends," her mother begins, almost whispering. "When you were 10, I was the same age you are now. But nobody laid a finger on you, Amethyst. You are my jewel. Everybody treated you right. I made sure."

Late afternoon is a chasm of shimmering crimson that seems vaguely Egyptian. Raven gets out of the car and hands her the keys. "Your turn," she says. "Surprise me."

Amy drives west across desert. She stops in a liquor store, buys four pints of vodka and hides them. She drinks and drives until Raven wakes up, moaning. They're almost across Arizona.

"What's this?" Raven asks, mildly interested. She rubs her eyes, can't find her eyeglasses and opens her map. She examines it, concentrating. The map is upside down.

"Laughlin. It's a déclassé Vegas on the Arizona-California-nia-Nevada border. Feeds off the retirement dollar. It's nickel and dime all the way. They let them park their trailers free. Hope they'll toss a quarter in a slot machine on the way to the john. It's the collapse of western civilization. The final capitalist terminal. You can watch the empire fall here. Come on. We'll love it." Amy is incredibly festive.

She pauses in the oasis of lobby surrounded by casinos. They're cavernous. They're the magic caves where Ali Baba and the 40 thieves hid their gold goblets and chests of coins and rubies.

It's oddly familiar, the assault of neon on walls, the leaden clinking machines and spinning wheels. Then the islands of green felt of card and dice tables. She understands this electric palette. The neon ceiling is like a cathedral. The neon-draped walls are layered in birthday cake pink and yellow icing. Come on. Spend a buck. It's a holiday.

Here are men in cowboy hats and boots with spurs who recently won a minor event at a second tier rodeo. They have the prize money in their socks. And men who just buried their wives and have ten thousand insurance dollars in their sports jacket pockets. This is what they got for their 30 years, five of it spent going to and from chemo. The money is in a roll with a rubber band around it like another type of ring. This time, they'll marry fortune.

Here are women who just sold their mothers' wedding rings for four hundred dollars, their divorced husband's bass boat and tool set. Nearly three grand in total. They wear flower print cotton dresses, and acres of pink and what might be bathrobes. They sit on stools, considering each quarter with deliberation, calculating their possibilities and counting their change. They extract one dime at a time, rationing themselves, and waiting for the right second, the anointed juncture, to spring forward and pull the lever.

Everyone moves in exaggerated slow motion through the neon drifting from the ceiling and sliding off the slot machines, making the air thicken like cornstarch. All carry coins in plastic cups the size of ice cream sodas, faces devoid of expression. Their limbs are stiff, arthritic. They look jetlagged and confused. They look like they need wheelchairs and want to go home.

Women on social security in mini skirts and fishnet stockings thread their way between the mock islands, carrying trays of free drinks. Only the dealers are swift, flipping out cards like whirling dervishes. Here come the royals. You've barely added up your hand and they're already reaching across felt and raking the chips back in.

Bells are the punctuation, the music of the casino. Bells signaling a payoff and the impending cascade of nickels and dimes. Bells announcing the start of a new keno game. These bells don't ring with the authority and purpose of churches. Or the promise of thrill like ferry and carnival bells. They don't mark the hour. They're designed to keep you from the walking coma you suspect you're in. They're like alarm clocks. Then the blast like a siren that doesn't require translation. Jackpot.

This is the new American score, Amy thinks. It's not a house, forty acres with a pond and mule and some stray grass to barbeque on anymore. Medicare is just a word, like democracy and justice. This is the global world of the dwarf dollar and the failure of gods and tradition and language itself. There's been a mass reduction. Even fantasy is truncated, amputated, stuck in a box in the basement. In this new century, we just want one good weekend.

They have a suite on the 17th floor with a view of the Dead Mountains, a swath of the Mojave, and the whip-thin blue chalk line of the Colorado River. Millions of women and men are also standing at windows, at this precise instant, realizing their lives are nothing they thought they would be. Sun is a slap across their mouths.

Amy Gold feels a rising excitement as they ride the elevator back to the lobby. She listens to bells from slot machines and the constant tumbling nickels flowing into steel shells suggesting mouths. Of course, this is what you hear at the end of the world. It isn't a whimper after all. It has nothing to do with anything human. It's the sound of symbols in motion. It's the sound of tin.

Raven is changing a ten-dollar bill for a foot-high plastic cup of quarters. She's changed her clothes, too. It must be Act 2. She's wearing a maroon caftan encrusted with tiny beads that sparkle and gold high heels. She has a canary yellow sash around her waist, bangles on both wrists and oversized sunglasses with gold frames. Two old men stare at her.

Amy hasn't had the right accessories for any of the towns or situations of her life. In the lobby of the River's End in Laughlin, Amy regrets the silver she didn't buy in Aspen. And the squash blossom in Taos. She should have taken the birthday beads she was offered by a laughing woman on peyote. Or even a turquoise bracelet from a pawnshop in Flagstaff where she saw thousands in rows in display cases. The Navajo nation was divesting itself of its semi-precious stones for beer and crack and it was horrifying. She didn't want any of it, not even for free.

Neon drifts like party streams and bolts of crepe paper. Or spun glass in the crimson of the plumes of jungle birds thought to be extinct. They didn't disappear. They're here, at the River's End, in their giant electric aviary.

She should have acquired a silk shawl somewhere, brass hoop earrings, a skirt in a floral print or a chiffon dress, fall leaf colored and embroidered with flowers, iris and pansies and violets, perhaps. And a straw hat with a flagrant yellow silk flower. She could have made herself into a garden. But she was a professor of no. Maybe she was born this way.

The tinny bells don't come from cathedrals or ships. They're machine proclamations of impending money. And it occurs to her that no accessories could possibly be right for this occasion.

"Let's check out the river," Raven suggests. She's put on mauve lipstick and a citrus perfume.

Outside the casino, air cracks against her face. It must be 110, Amy thinks. 115. Heat rolls across her flesh, laminating it. This is how time takes photographs.

It's how you get into the eternal line-up. It has nothing to do with Homeland Security or INTERPOL.

They walk into liquid heat. Huge insects perch on the ground. Clusters of scorpions. And nests of roaches and maggots.

"Crickets and grasshoppers," Raven explains. Her skirt is a compendium of all possible shades of purple. Her skirt is wind across dusk mesas. Raven brings her climate with her. She wears sunset around her hips and asks, "Are you OK?"

OK? Is that a state with borders? Or an emotional concept? Can you drive there, get a suite, break a 20 for buckets of dimes? Should she reply with a flag or a drum? And what is in the arc of light on the side of the parking lot? It's a confederation of hallucinatory swooping forms, too thin to be birds.

They're creatures from myth. They've broken through the fabric, tearing through time with their teeth.

"Bats," Raven says. "Can't you hear them?"

Everything is humming. It's a corrupted partial darkness, too over-heated and streaked with arrows of red neon to be real night. It's grazing above the surprisingly cold river. Amy touches it with her hand. The riverbank is studded with abandoned construction sites, iron grids with no walls, roofs or windows. It's a ghost town.

They stand on a sort of loading dock. The terrain is increasingly difficult to decode. What is that coming toward them? A sea vessel? Yes, a mock riverboat calling itself a water taxi.

Raven reaches out her tanned arms, and helps her climb down the stairs. "You're going to vomit," her mother whispers. "You're drinking too much. You could never maintain."

The boat motion is nauseating. The water taxi crosses one thin strand of river, disgorges silent passengers who seem already defeated, and takes new ones to the other bank. The water taxi rides back and forth, back and forth, ferrying gamblers from Arizona across the river to Nevada where it is legal. Everyone is somber.

Amy Gold closes her eyes and counts the rivers she's been on or in with her mother. The Snake, Arkansas, Rio Grande, Mississippi, Columbia, Missouri and Wailua, and now this ghastly Colorado in July where she doesn't have the right accessories, not a scarf, bracelet or shawl. And what do they call this? The Styx?

"You're not smoking," Amy realizes.

"Even bank robbers quit," Raven replies. "Even guys in the can quit."

It's the last ride of the night. The driver repeats this twice. He's accustomed to passengers with Alzheimer's and hearing aids, canes and walkers. And she's been in the boat for hours, her head in her mother's lap. She's finished her emergency pint of vodka. She manages to stand, and pauses on the dock.

There's an anomalous movement in the river. Some rustling denting the water the way tuna do in shallow bays. Then the water looks like submerged dogs are running just beneath the surface. Two boys are doing something with white flowers. They toss bouquets into the muddy river and the flowers are instantly, savagely ripped apart.

Amy is startled by an agitation beneath the surface. Enormous fish circle around the wood planks. They must be four feet long. There are severed palms in the water. People have removed their hands and these grotesque fish are eating them. The hideous dark gray fish. It's a ritual. They must supplicate themselves.

"My God," Amy says, wondering if she should jump in. She's an excellent swimmer. She learned CPR. She takes a breath.

"Just carp." Raven is tired. "Hundreds of large carp."

"But what are they eating?" Amy has a pulsing ache that begins in her jaw and runs through the individual nerves of her face. Fine wires are being pulled through her eyes. Perhaps they're going to use her for bait.

"Bread," her mother says. "Look. Pieces of bread."

Yes, of course. Slices of white bread. It is not the amputated hands of virgins. It's not the orchids the Buddha promised. It's bread from plastic bags. And we are released. We are reprieved. Enlightenment does not announce itself on the map. It is random, always.

"Where are you going?" Raven demands. "You're sick. Let me help you."

She is frightened.

"I'll come back," Amy says.

"You haven't been back in since San Diego," Raven says.

"You left too soon, Amethyst. Fifteen was too early, baby. And you're not going anywhere now."

Amy Gold is moving through the lobby; she's running, and she's way ahead of her mother. She's been way ahead from the beginning. That's why her attention wanders. It's always been too easy, she remembers, finding a path between islands of machines with glittering gutted heads. She possesses the secret of this age. It's about the geometry of cheap metal. And she knows where the parking lot is and she has the car keys.

Amy Gold stops, paralyzed. She understands this moment with astounding clarity. No. She's not going to pack her office at the university. She's not going to carry books through corridors, one cardboard box, one square casket at a time. We decide the components of our necessities. We design our own ceremonies of loyalty and propitiation. And history fails to explain the significance of accessories. The silk sash around your waist can be a fishing line. Or a noose to hang a man with. Why isn't this even a footnote?

Raven is reaching through the garish neon, her palms open, waiting to receive something. Pages from the original Bagavaid Gita? The UFO invasion plan? An Anasazi document inscribed in glyphs on bark in a lime ink unknown for a thousand years?

"Give me the keys. Give me the booze and cigarettes," Raven commands. "I'm taking you home."

Her mother is a sly predator bird who avoided capture. She's infertile, arthritic, and she's lost her claws. Her liver is diseased and her nest is lit by kerosene and candles. She'll be safe there. She will receive the correct instructions and this time she will listen. When they drive through the Four Corners, through the region of the Harmonic Convergence, this time she will hear.

Her mother is driving, white and stiff in the darkness, a

woman with lines like dried tributaries gouged into her face. She gave birth to a daughter she named for the distillation of all strata of purple. Raven wraps a shawl gold as a concubine's solstice festival vestment around her shoulders. This woman will give her tenure. Amy leans against her mother; her eyes close and she is completely certain.

The architectural drawings can be salvaged and revised. They can build with hay bales now; it's cheaper. They can do it themselves. After the adobe walls and kiva beams, they'll tile the floors. Later they'll plant chilies. Then half an acre of lilies, Calla Lilies. They can have a roadside stand in April at Easter. They'll be known throughout the northern plateaus as the women of the lilies. Some will call them the women who sell communion.

They'll be known only by rumor. It will be said that the solitary raven of the mesa received a miracle. There was a brutal severing and a long season of mourning. Then, inexplicably, since this is the nature of all things, the unexpected occurred. Hierarchies are irrelevant because they do not examine central and recurring events. There's the unknowable trajectory of inspirations that prove to be barricaded cul-de-sacs. Or a king has an aneurism, issues a final edict, and families collapse, and villages vanish.

As there is lightning and cataclysm, droughts and wildfires, so too exists the revelatory accident. Are we not reconfigured as we cross rooms, strike matches, and catch moonlight on our skin?

On a mesa above Espanola, where the Rio Grande is a muddy creek you can't even see from the highway, it is said that one day a lost daughter bearing the name of a sacred stone was somehow returned.

SKINNY BROADS WITH WIGS

For precisely twenty-five years, Barbara Stein has required her advanced placement English class at Allegheny Hills High School to produce a three-page creative essay describing their summer vacation.

Introduce yourselves to me, Mrs. Stein has asked a quarter century of 10th graders. *Begin with the last three months.*

In return, she's presented with listless landscapes like postcards selected at random in convenience stores or found accidentally in a stranger's drawer. Cities meet their harbors, waves unavoidably fill the centers with anonymous paint-can blues, but it's all secondhand and detached from the speaker. They're merely views without fragrance or the possibility of vertigo.

Her students omit the ambiguously provocative areas of their Julys and Augusts. They replace them with predictable travelogues. She is presented with formulaic montages of interchangeable beaches meeting cliffs with the remnants of fortresses and rubble of cathedrals and lighthouses.

The images are the certified version of location and event,

but they're a censored translation, generic, erased of danger and revelation.

This is so impersonal; it might have been transmitted from another planet. In red ink she writes, *Nice image, but what are the sounds of summer? The specific smells of your July?*

Mrs. Stein believes catastrophe has a distinct texture and climate. Summer disasters are deceptively intense and enacted under stark white light. It's garish and has nothing to do with illumination. It's the flash of a camera freezing your face with a comprehension of circumstances you don't suspect you know. That's why you reject the photograph. It isn't because the angle is unflattering, but rather the image contains gestures and dialogue occurring just behind your shoulder. It's in the hallway or on the pier, a subtle text you pretend doesn't exist.

Tell me about the quality of light, Barbara Stein instructs, *and you'll find out who you are.*

Some students begin to listen. They consider the periphery of their lakeside villages — the implications and the words they don't actually hear but subconsciously intuit. On certain summer nights the prolongment of divorce is unmistakable — it's an edgy scrape across an unwashed plate, an unexpected slap on a face, a slammed car door, a phone call in a voice too rapid and soft in a back room with the lamps shut off. The correlation between betrayal and darkness is obvious. One must listen beyond thunder and crickets, past wind blowing the motel banner advertising free dinners for children in six colors.

If you've trained yourself, you can hear disease and derangement growing. Cancer is sudden and yellow and smells like rotting tropical fruit and algae in neglected aquariums. Sickness favors surfaces like plaster hallways, mesh screen doors, and plastic kitchen counters in rented bungalows. Sometimes it appears after lightning storms as if electrically incited. Divorce has its unique architecture and undertow. You must search for this while you're fishing. It's not in the bucket of bait or on the nylon lines. Instead it's in the wakes boats carve on water like a legible script.

This is a good setting, Mrs. Stein inscribes on the margin of a student paper. *But I think there is more you want to say. Don't be afraid. The page is your best friend.*

Mrs. Stein is intimate with the core of summer. It's the khaki of tents and sleeping bags and army uniforms. It's the khaki of camouflage.

Her students entertain the notion that she has unspecified powers, perhaps of a telepathic nature. Yet Mrs. Stein is known as a teacher you can trust. You can tell her about your mother's new boyfriend and how you're having trouble sleeping. Mrs. Stein doesn't demand specific information or what was actually suggested in the barn or pick-up, and the events that followed. She understands what you're not saying. You can reveal yourself to her in a way you can't to the guidance counselor who will report your confidences to the principal.

Barbara Stein is an expert keeper of secrets. It's curious no one suspects her of also possessing them. That's what keeping a low profile, rarely confiding in another human being, and buying your clothing from the LL Bean catalogue does. It renders the most salient aspects of your personality invisible. In an age of labels and categories, one can effortlessly disappear.

Barbara Stein is, in fact, festooned with clandestine hieroglyphics. If her subterfuges were made dimensional, shaped perhaps into ornaments, she could be Allegheny Hill's annual Christmas tree. She would sparkle with the radiance of her concealment, her omissions, and what's growing in her periphery and margins. There's the matter of where her daughter is, and how she hasn't spent the last twenty years of winter nights alone. If Barbara Stein told the truth, she'd blind you.

Her students respect Mrs. Stein's courage. When the schoolboard banned *The Catcher in the Rye* and *The Diary of Anne Frank*, she continued teaching these books. She drove all the way to Pittsburgh to buy paperback copies. She purchased them with her own money. When the board threatened to fire her, she replied, "Fire is a weapon against truth. After all, they fired Joan of Arc."

Students in graduate school return to pay their respects. Mrs. Stein doesn't encourage this. She doesn't save their postcards with literary allusions or their trinkets from England and Greece. She doesn't read their publications and has only an abstract and minimal interest in their achievements in the field of the written word.

Mrs. Stein doesn't think there is much field left for the written word. It was once a frontier, a primitive meadowland like the acres of shoulder high Mustard, Purple Thistle, and Golden Rod beyond her apple orchard and gardening plots. It's become a squalid cul-de-sac, a footpath littered with garbage you can't find on a map. The quality of books has changed in her lifetime. They're constructed from a different sort of paper and poorly bound, as if intended to be discarded. They're like cereal boxes rather than sacred artifacts. She's seen exhibitions where text was used as a graphic element — letters were selected for their shape, rows of words were pasted into columns forming geometric patterns. These representations didn't offend her.

In truth, few of her students want to read, not even the brightest and the most verbal. They've been inundated by more images in their fourteen years than entire libraries contain. Sentences and paragraphs are tedious, irrelevant like fortress walls. They don't believe books provide revelation. Words are a version of stone.

Her students spend afternoons in computer chat rooms, employing aliases, and inventing constantly evolving identities. They exchange texts they mistake for accurate approximations of their values and psychology. They don't recognize they're engaged in acts of fiction.

Once she mourned the passing of the poets. She recognized that, when they became obsolete, something of what was intrinsically human would be extinct. So it was for the bards with lyres and the carvers of canoes who navigated Pacific islands by the sound and scent of currents. The Gutenberg Printing Press lasted five hundred years, certainly longer than airplanes or cinema will. The technological revolution is an abrupt compression, a swing toward an incremental and collective synthesis. Who is to say half a millennia of books are not enough? She keeps these thoughts to herself.

On Maple Ridge Road, her neighbors perceive her as neutered and eccentric. She's beyond fertile and therefore harmless. She's a middle-aged woman, predictable in navy and cranberry, who does her own gardening and house repairs. In late summer she sells eggs and blueberries from her yard. She looks like she'd defend Emily Dickinson's honor with her own life if it came to it. Barbara Stein is viewed as a distillation of English literature and the teaching profession itself.

If there's a sense of tragedy in her eyes, it's an ancient wound — or the result of childhood abandonment. There are rumors of an unfortunate early marriage and a problem with a daughter. But it's nothing anyone can verify. Invisible women do not invite serious investigation.

Mrs. Stein is aware of the multiplicity of rumors surrounding her. Some are perennials, flaring like banks of May Daffodils, Tulips and Lavender Crocuses. They have a short season. Then the anomaly of annuals that stun but don't return. In point of fact, she has more than a passing interest in the powers of intuition. Mrs. Stein suspects she might be an adept. When she's luminous with clarity, she can, in fact, see. She penetrates the ordinary to an enormous brilliant core like an inland sea. It's a region of pure marrow, detailed and unspoiled. She could trace it with her fingertips.

The inland sea is a body she can open. She's learned its subtle anatomy and how to subdue and characterize it. Ridges of bone are maple leaf green, the surrounding tissues are chartreuse, and the fluids are a jade she can split with her lips.

Mrs. Stein has a natural affinity for landscape and its seductive promise. All women in gardens sense there is a further purpose. Women on their knees in dirt are engaged in conspiracies of disguised eroticism. The shears, gloves and baskets are blatant props. Any woman gardening is prepared for acts of love.

"Menopause is turning me into a witch," she told Elizabeth.

That was the last time they spoke. Elizabeth is her only child, the daughter she is going to Los Angeles to find. That's what Barbara Stein does, secretly, during the two weeks of her summer when she has the budget to leave Maple Ridge and search for her daughter. She's been doing this for twelve years.

"You were always unusual," Elizabeth said, her voice raked raw and hollowed out. That was three months ago when she still had Elizabeth's latest phone number. Barbara Stein inscribed it in her leather directory, in a section filled with discarded Elizabeth phone numbers and addresses. These are kept under D for daughter.

Sometimes she just layers blank papers with the ten phone numbers the way her infatuated students reproduce the name of the object of their desire. They're engaged in acts of magic — a kinetic incantation, the pencil and paper are flints and there's an angle that can produce fire. Her students wonder if this is the meaning of geometry and why mathematics is required. It's an attempt to stem delirium.

For decades, notebook pages of —

Brian

Brian

Brian

Brian

Justin

Justin

Justin

Justin

— fall from folders onto her classroom floors. The repetition of the printed patterns, the crude calligraphy spilling beyond the margins, the curves and etchings suggest the deliberation of engineering and construction. Who is to say these are not novels about love?

She last spoke to Elizabeth three months ago. Barbara Stein was surprised when her daughter answered the phone. She told Elizabeth that her life was a simple arithmetic of addition and subtraction. She had lost her hormones, her interest in men and sex. She had insomnia, needs eyeglasses and a prescription for sleeping pills. Her hair fell out in clumps. The veins in her legs rose like so many summer flowers, lilies and peonies pushed from below.

These manifestations were not the ordinary residues of age, Barbara Stein intimated, not mere spider veins embossing her thighs and calves. Her legs were like dusk avenues where ritual processions passed and stalls on riverbanks offered Carnations and Chrysanthemums for altars and cremations.

"I'm being tattooed while I sleep," she told her daughter.

"You always wanted a tattoo," Elizabeth said, voice husky from cigarettes, whiskey, sequences of strangers mouths, and some unspeakable vast fatigue.

"We were going to get them together. Remember?" Mrs. Stein remind her.

Elizabeth was increasingly breathless, as if calling from a public phone on a rush hour boulevard above a subway. There's too much noise and static on the line. But it's better than a beeper.

"You sound exhausted," Barbara Stein realized. "You're not taking your medicines."

"You're clairvoyant," Elizabeth managed. "It's too hard. They disrespect me at the clinic. Nurses won't touch me. They give me the same forms to fill out. They won't let me use their pencil. And you always wanted a tattoo, Mommy."

During college, her roommates returned from weekends in Boston or New York with moons carved on their shoulders and bracelets of flowers engraved around their ankles. Barbara Stein craved this ink and envied them. She couldn't have a tattoo, of course — her parents denounced it as unacceptably vulgar.

Her father was a rabbi. Her parents were, in their way, sophisticated for their historical moment. It wasn't about the Torah, her father was quick to point out. It was about commerce. God was the family trade and a tattoo would be bad for business. It was that simple.

But her parents are dead and she's being etched from beneath as she sleeps. Why not choose the actual design? When she gets to Los Angeles and finds Elizabeth, she will get a tattoo. Perhaps they'll do this together — select a symbol, an emblem, a celestial configuration.

On her final morning, Barbara Stein thinks about tattoos, constellations and the history of carving images into flesh. All cultures practice this and interpret the positioning of moon and stars as recognizable objects. It's a perpetual night of cause and effect.

Barbara Stein slides her suitcase into her gray Volvo. She assembles stacks of AAA maps and state pamphlets listing motels and local attractions. She realizes, with sudden urgency and discomfort, she wants a summer vacation distilled to three pages.

Eric, the teenage son of her closest neighbor, arrives. She gives him the last of her instructions. He'll feed her cat Grace for the next two weeks and pet her for ten minutes every day. He'll pick what's ripe in the garden.

Eric follows her into the vegetable and herb plots, noting where she keeps the shears, gloves, trowels, shovels and baskets. She demonstrates how the beans must be cut, the tomatoes and strawberries picked and stored. He's a polite boy, shy, serious and attentive — a city boy, excited to be standing where vegetation rises enormous over his head. Jack in the Beanstalk. Yes, it is true. Behold. This is the birth of cities and epics. The grain you hold in your palm is the history of this planet.

"What about the vet?" Eric asks. "Do you go to Dr. Sutter's clinic?"

Barbara Stein tells him that she doesn't. It's an odd admission and she regrets it.

"What if she gets sick?" Eric asks. He stares at her grey tabby. He's concerned, "Okay, but if it's more than fifty dollars, just put Grace to sleep," Barbara Stein tells him.

The boy is stunned. Her new neighbor is a surgeon from Philadelphia. The doctor had bought Professor McCarty's house, and his wife virtually gutted it. Their family made what they term a quality of life move. That's what the doctor's wife, Amanda called it. Barbara Stein isn't sure what this means and she doesn't ask.

The McCarty house was a sequence of maple, ash, hemlock,

oak, and cherry. Walls were made from two hundred-year-old barns and doors salvaged from churches and government buildings, courthouses and town halls. The ceiling beams were once railroad ties. Now the interior of the house is a uniform light oak. Any surface that can be coated has been painted white. Glass and marble have been installed over the hemlock and cherry. The railroad ties are gone, replaced by a series of skylights.

"It's a bare beginning," Amanda said, urgency and threat in her tone.

On the few occasions they've met, Amanda spoke incessantly about her personal crisis. During mandatory student orientation, Amanda discussed the possibility of a second life, simplifying her life and changing her life — as if those concepts were interchangeable. Amanda did not mention her son. Eric sat in silence and looked out the window.

Mrs. Stein was tempted to tell Amanda that only the simple simplify their lives, and having a second life was more typically characteristic of psychotics. The only plausible verbal description was, in her opinion, changing your life. But behavior modification lacks immediate gratification and happens, if at all, one imperceptibly slow detail at a time. Then Mrs. Stein recognized she had little to say to Amanda.

The doctor and his wife send Eric to buy eggs, transmit information about the state of Maple Ridge Road, and inquire if she needs anything from town. They would prefer to ignore her entirely, but Barbara Stein has a certain status in Woods End. They volunteer their boy as intermediary.

"Mrs. Stein, I'm not sure I can handle putting Grace down," he says, uncertainly.

"People make too much ado about animals," Mrs. Stein says. "They should spend more time on babies and less on kittens."

"That's not what my mother says," Eric tells her.

"How old is your mother?" Barbara Stein asks.

"Forty-seven," Eric replies.

Mrs. Stein laughs. "You mean thirty-seven," she corrects.

"No, she's forty-seven. We just had her birthday. I lit the candles myself. Math is my best class," Eric assures her.

Barbara Stein doesn't think it's possible that she and Amanda are the same age. When she's with the doctor's wife, she feels matronly, arthritic, and peripheral. Amanda is lithe and eager within her entirely discretionary universe. She plays tennis, goes to yoga classes, and hosts a bridge game on Tuesday afternoons.

When Amanda decided she wanted a garden, she simply ordered one. A landscaper from Buffalo came with a soil expert and drawings, two men to dig and a crew to fence. Her ornamental plum trees were put into the earth larger than Mrs. Stein's are now, after fifteen years of growing, of wind and ice storms, of what happens when you take an idea and let the elements define its destiny.

When Barbara translates this process into human terms, she thinks of her daughter. Lena is her name now. Her West Coast working name. She's been Lena for more than a decade. Lena doesn't want to live unconsciously, but rather one incremental step up. She wishes to inhabit an enormous post-op, permanently on the cusp of surgery. Lena, under the squalid palms of Los Angeles, in her private version of a recovery room, waking from an operation, calling out for Demerol and morphine and getting it. Nurses are eager and competent. They bring syringes, adjust pillows and smile.

Lena, in an apartment by a bay studded with fragile vertical palms that seem superimposed, stitched unconvincingly into the landscape. Lena, in her invented perimeter where it's artificially cold and hushed, the bleached white of nurses' uniforms and anesthesia. Lena wants to be in that post-op zone forever, at the edge of coming to and then being put under again, to float in her own inland sea. For her daughter, every day feels like surgery. Sunlight cuts like a razor and must be avoided. Each morning she is knifed and stitched. Night is an abuse. Gravity and air sting and wound her. Voices startle her and she trembles. That's why she gives herself injections for pain.

Elizabeth is a heroin addict and a prostitute. The order is important. If heroin were dispensed freely, Elizabeth would not be selling her body. Elizabeth would not be HIV positive. Elizabeth has AIDS now. In the clinic, the nurses and technicians believe she's a criminal, a woman without rights or even the privileges of the terminal. It takes Lena three hours to ride the buses to the hospital. They arbitrarily cancel her appointments and deliberately misplace her chart. They pretend they don't remember her. Lena waits shivering in corridors through their entire shifts. They want her to die.

Barbara Stein thinks about order and disease as she drives, as highways change numbers and there's nothing for her to see anymore. It's a journey she takes every summer.

She remembers searching for Elizabeth in Idaho, in fields of barley and alfalfa. She tried to find her in Kansas City in regions of corn and soy beans. In between were rocks, gravel, abandoned farmland — derelict barns and boarded shut bars, the metal shells of gas stations going to rust. Then the interchangeable motels, anonymous restaurants, featureless towns and ersatz suburbs that might be San Diego or New Jersey.

She avoids cities with their boulevards that could be Baltimore or Dallas. American streets with shops' racks of cheap faux leather yellow and green jackets and rice bowls and back-scratchers from China no one wants or needs. Stores that have **Going Out of Business** signs on display windows the day they open.

Night is worse. Every shop is locked behind black iron grates. In between are bars lit by flashing red neon. It's the standard greeting of the great superpower. Buy some junk and get drunk.

Barbara Stein could only afford motels on the margins of cities and in strips along interstates. The designated areas for travelers on budgets. This was what America wanted for itself — a subterfuge of monolithic uniformity. This's the mirror in which America looks at her face and concludes that she is normal.

Elizabeth couldn't bear looking at her own face in its entirety. Elizabeth's skin was blossom subtle, not delicate but rather rare like certain fabrics— thick silks, pure light wool and cashmere. Elizabeth has a spring face and her dark brown hair smells like espresso and harbors. When Mrs. Stein held her daughter, she breathed in her skin.

Elizabeth at thirteen and fourteen, before she ran away, had the scent of a river — the Ganges or Nile, with all the intrigues intact. She was the reason for pilgrimages and shrines, why people read texts beside vases in museums, why they collect pebbles from beaches, tiles from temples, and why they take photographs.

Her daughter with her raw silk face couldn't bear sunlight and feared it. Mrs. Stein transformed the backyard. She dug and cemented holes in the backyard for canvas umbrellas. She cemented rakes and brooms in the ground and wrapped sheets and tarps to their tops. patches of shade fell geometrically as a sequence of squares. Her daughter, trembling and fevered, crawled between the canvas oases.

One early autumn afternoon when the maple forest was the yellow of votive for prayer and the red of heretics, she dragged a fifty-pound bag of cement toward her backyard. Sheriff Murphy drove down Maple Ridge Road toward campus. He saw her and stopped his patrol car.

Sheriff Jim Murphy carried the cement into her yard. He

took her shovel and dug. "How big a tent you plan to pitch?" he asked. His eyes were hazel and he squinted as he looked at her yard.

"As big as circumstance demands," Mrs. Stein replied.

"Can't keep her under a canopy indefinitely. It's unnatural," Sheriff Murphy decided.

The sheriff handed her his card. "Need something, call me," the sheriff said. "Anytime. I'll come. Count on it."

Mrs. Stein nodded. She no longer believed anyone could help her.

Elizabeth lives near the ocean. She'll probably die near the ocean, too. Since she came to the West Coast, first to Seattle, then Portland, San Francisco and now Los Angeles, she's rented an apartment in sight of the water. Barbara remembers this as she takes the last of the freeways to the final exit on the western edge of Los Angeles, at the bay called Santa Monica.

Elizabeth's telephone is disconnected. It takes Barbara Stein all morning to find the yellowed stucco apartment half a block from the beach. The manager has never heard of Elizabeth or Lena or a dark haired woman resembling the photographs Mrs. Stein supplies. "Could be a blond or redhead now," the man says. "They're all skinny broads with wigs."

Mrs. Stein stands in the entranceway, trying to envision what Elizabeth would have seen. The bay lacks the spectacle her daughter craves. Elizabeth requires seas like the Grenadines and Aegean, defined strata of purples and startled turquoise. Elizabeth wants a permanent Yucatan Caribbean, a patchwork of reefs beneath her skin forming a channel of depth and current only. There are no mirrors or monetary constrictions. You have fins and gills and glide through coral.

Can you say chartreuse, Elizabeth? Can you say cerulean?

Do you know what is halfway between Borneo and Sumatra? A tiny island called Palau Kebatu. I'll take you there someday. And the Bay of Bima to Komoda. Then Sumba, finally, and Bali. That's what she promised her daughter.

The beach is a congestion of tourists and the bay looks oily and degraded. It smells tangy like citrus that's gone bad from a wide-open sun that doesn't play by the rules. The sky is vague and restless as if remembering a nightmare. Starched white Oleander along the fenced parking lot reminds her of nurses' uniforms. Elizabeth might have made that association. She would have been drawn to the burgundy Bougainvillea spilling across the sides of the shabby apartment building where the paint has been abraded by wind and sand and formed what looks like scabs. Still, such an extravagance of claret vines would have caught her attention, even stumbling drugged in darkness.

There's a boardwalk below the slow slope of hill of two-story stucco apartments with identical balconies where Elizabeth and Lena no longer live. Barbara Stein must touch this ocean, anemic and drained of blue as it is. She thinks of her English class assignments about the meaning of movement in American literature. The American experience is about physical passages. The Lewis and Clark Expedition. Manifest Destiny and the wagon trains. The European immigrant migrations. Jack Kerouac and the Beatniks. In any event, Barbara Stein must keep walking.

Maybe we each have our own personal manifest destiny, she thinks. It sweeps us from the Allegheny Mountains of northern Pennsylvania to a strip of pavement studded with yogurt shops perched between acres of soiled sand.

Mrs. Stein finds a splintered bench engraved with knife-etched graffiti, gang names, the slang for sexual acts and assorted scatology. It's much too hot. The sun seems lacquered. It has the texture of paint. Skaters in their bikinis already inhabit a future century where all disease has been eradicated. Elizabeth can sell her body to the whole navy and then take a shower, two weeks in Cancun, rinse it off, heal in salt waters, and be done with it.

"Just don't bury me," Elizabeth had said. "Promise."

"I promise, yes," Mrs. Stein told her daughter.

They were talking on the telephone. Her daughter has been too long on this earth as it is. Her daughter, subsisting by acts of desperate translation. She negotiates the ordinary and redesigns it for her personal biochemistry of necessity.

"I'm an alien on this planet," Elizabeth said. "They'll burn me for free at the clinic. Let them."

Further south Barbara Stein sees a courtyard partially in sand. It's dense with excessively magenta flowers and tattered palms, their texture rank. There's no logic to this stunted progression, she thinks. Women stand at windows facing the ocean. They wear slips and imitation silk kimonos and have syringes of heroin in their fingers.

These women are like Lena. They have divested themselves of their birth certificates and the longitudes and latitudes of their origin. Their documents proved inadequate for survival. Maybe, like her daughter, they were once named Elizabeth. They rebirthed themselves and became Lena, married to a brown tar she burns with a match in a spoon, turned into a fluid like a muddy river she sticks in your vein. The price is your life and she knows it. That's why such women have faces that are epics. Their eyes are like the one lighthouse on the last peninsula at the end of the world.

Barbara Stein crosses the ragged beach. She suddenly remembers college when she once wanted to collect waters and preserve them in labeled bottles. She wanted certain rivers as merely symbolic ornaments — the Amazon, the Mississippi, the Danube and Seine. They were like one-night-stand rivers, brief encounters she name-dropped at a dinner party. She came to know other rivers with intimacy. The Snake in Idaho during three successive summers when she almost found Elizabeth. Then the Colorado which began as a creek in the Rocky Mountains when she thought Elizabeth was in Denver. She followed it west into the California desert.

It's a light blue afternoon. Sand offers disappointing tiny fragments of broken gray clam shells. Barbara Stein must acknowledge this region with her hands. Los Angeles is a port, after all. All ports contain certain traditional elements. Sailors and the women they buy, and cargoes of kidnapped girls and smuggled rubies? Refugees float in oceans, hidden in cartons, drinking rainwater and burning with fever.

It's an ordinary afternoon, boys on bicycles, women hanging T-shirts on ropes. The obligatory fishing boat comes to the dilapidated pier, water a listless bleached pastel. Barbara Stein knows the new wharves of contraband are inland. The stolen computer chips and software, the prototype vaccines for cancers, formulas for extending lifespan and magnifying intelligence. They're kept in offices in Dallas and Baltimore.

The ocean is cooler than she expected. She places a damp hand across her forehead as if it were a kind of bandage, as if she might faint. She stands by the water until sunset, waiting for Elizabeth to call *Mother, Mother*. She's prepared to turn from this bay, which tells her nothing, and embrace her daughter. She stands until the sky is livid and brutal with red and it looks alive and in pain. Somebody should put it out of its misery. Somebody should put a bullet in it.

It's sunset. Barbara Stein walks south past tattoo parlors, bistros and piercing shops. On the boardwalk, women younger than Elizabeth when she first ran away stick out their palms for dimes. Their eyes are sheeted portals. They have tornadoes in their faces. Still, they're some version of her 10th grade students with their round faces and wide-into-the-wind eyes. They could wear the clothing of Allegheny Hills High School. In a group photograph, they would look like cousins or classmates.

Barbara Stein isn't going to find her daughter and she isn't getting a tattoo. She is forty-seven years old. She's lived longer than Billie Holiday and Frida Kahlo, Judy Garland and Anne Sexton. Of course she wanted less, took a measured route, but still, there's a triumph in the simple enduring. Elizabeth will not live this long.

Barbara Stein considers all the women of Los Angeles and Boston, Rio de Janeiro, Bangkok and Shanghai. A legion of middle aged women strolling boulevards named for royalty, psychotics and saints. They could feed one another's broken and ravaged daughters. In Barcelona and Amsterdam, in all port cities where the ships come in and children lay on pavement, we must offer them bread and carry them home.

She knows that some children don't want just one box of crayons. Some reject certain colors entirely and scream when offered yellow or red. Some won't color within the lines. Some are like Lena and can't tolerate the air of this Earth. On boulevards named for queens and madmen, teenagers in Salvation Army jackets look up from the pavement, twitching and dazed, longing to be fed like malformed baby birds.

When Ulysses encountered the lotus-eaters, his crew threatened mutiny. They had to be dragged back to the ship, kicking savagely. Some girls can't simply dial 911 and come home.

At Venice Beach, Barbara Stein sits on a bench facing a billboard where a model in a bikini posed in front of lurid green palm trees. HONOLULU written in pink neon at her bare feet. I am forty-seven, she thinks, and I will never see my daughter again. It's time for the women to remove themselves from the posters where they are imprisoned. They must peel themselves off the images of implausibly flawless island resorts. They must separate themselves from the overly representational, the vulgar red orchids and garish yellow plumeria. They could climb down feet unsteady on asphalt and then begin walking. With each step, they would enter the enormity of their own unscripted lives.

But in the millennial global warehouse, which is not a village, our offspring curl fetal on sidewalks. We have learned not to notice them. They don't register. They're below our radar. We step around them as we once did foreigners with sores and scabs. They are lepers and consumptives. We must not speak to them.

Meanwhile, we are exchanging inappropriate confidences with counterfeit companions in an electronic vacancy. We are intimate with people in Madrid and Tokyo we've never met or ever will. The children at our feet are bad girls. They deserve to be sick and suffer. Rather than entering an astonishment we've become rigid and laminated. We do not even exchange your real names and serial numbers. We are all prisoners of war now and the Geneva Convention no longer applies. That's what her students are telling her.

Mrs. Stein walks past fortune-tellers on blankets at the sand's edge. They're reading cards and palms as they have for six thousand years. Body-pierced young women who could be in her Allegheny Hills classes, returning to the apartment where Elizabeth briefly lived. She stands near the squat stucco building her daughter no longer enters or exits, memorizing its unique characteristics — the four aggressively vertical palm trees, how the sun is white, gritty as if layered with microscopic glass chips, pieces of cactus, and splinters from strangers' teeth. Sun is a relentless deliberate assault, a series of flesh wounds. A fuchsia on a back balcony, stems like manic dangling and longing for the pavement. They want a mouth full of gravel. They want to be burned at a clinic for free.

Perhaps Elizabeth noticed the almost full moon and smelled the White Star Jasmine in the alley making the darkness scented and drunken. The Eucalyptus, vaguely medicinal, chalky and mysterious. Things bloom in dusk harbors where the trade winds have been and gone. Barbara Stein realizes, if it were the end of myth, there would be nothing to write about.

There are smuggled girls in shuttered alcoves behind tattoo parlors. Girls who ran away in journeys begun by prank and accident. The flesh is an acquired taste like opera and shellfish. Some girls need a tutor to show them the ropes. Teach them the tricks. Turn them out. Girls who couldn't conceive of the cliffs between Ravello and Amalfi. Big Sur and Malibu were equally distant. The highway to Hana, jungle-side Maui, was beyond their ability. Athens and Shanghai felt contrived in their mouths. They were afraid of capitals.

They were simple as stones and bells. They smelled like glass on October afternoons. They were less than a thumbprint. They didn't wear make-up, want to speak French or tour the Parthenon. Denim was fine. Spandex and bronze did not occur to them. They hadn't heard the whisper that says *lush are the ladies of the lamps, lit from within, heads dyed copper as coins.* That's why they needed a razor scar on the cheek, a fractured arm and black eye. You'd be surprised. That's all it takes.

They remember April when they were still cotton panty girls. They had collections of arrowheads and butterflies and a drawer for just bows. Then the powders and injections and days turned Technicolor. They carry their accidents with them. Their coats contain a sadness that doesn't require translation.

In this darkness, pirates and magicians, exiles and alchemists camouflage themselves as beggars. Names and identities are manufactured and exchanged for cash. Flesh is bartered for packets of brown fragments resembling tree bark. The air is charged. Lamplight is calibrated an elegant 14 carat, tinged with pear. Such a light can burn in deserted rooms for years, with no fear of suffocation or fire.

If we believe in sin and retribution, then antiquity must be continuous. The Minotaur is in the Allegheny Mountain farmhouse. He's your mother's new boyfriend. In pastures, bulls with bronze feet breathe fire. The Cyclops is your uncle. He's coming for supper. Yes. Again. Brush your hair and put on that pretty dress he got for you. It's not too short. You could thank him better. How's that going to hurt? Want to get a reputation for a cold heart? And you don't need GPS. You know where the labyrinth is. It's past the path to the tool shed and patch of corn behind the trailer.

Barbara Stein stops on the edge of the Mohave and buys postcards of Los Angeles. She drives east, crossing the desert and mountains. She must accomplish this journey on her three-hundred-dollar budget. Three days of sunlight like sheets bleached a pure white and leaching the air, absorbing events until they're rubbed away past intention.

She must patch her roof before the ambush of winter and tend to her garden — the canning and freezing and the ritual of blueberry jam. Then she'll manufacture a three-page essay encapsulating her summer vacation. She'll describe tropical vegetation, the colossus of wild magenta Bougainvillea blanketing the bamboo fenced edges, and the boardwalk with its skaters and fortune-tellers. She'll note the Pacific was paler and cooler than she expected. She'll say she might have seen a movie star wearing a baseball cap and sunglasses in a Jaguar, Mercedes Benz or Ferrari.

She has the postcards to provide the authority of detail — the bay below cliffs the color of flesh where wild purple succulents cling, and on the tame exhausted waters, fishing boats return in the late afternoon. Sometimes the fraudulent laminated illusions are enough. Conventional versions can also serve. Who is to say experience can't be distilled to a 4x6 photograph?

She won't write anymore margin notes in red ink. We live by aliases and don't even reveal our serial numbers. She won't mention the stucco apartment on the low sloping hill near Ocean Avenue and Marine Street where her heart broke. These are coordinates she'll be buried with.

Science has methods for reconstructing villages jungles swallowed. Aqueducts, bridges and temples are reformed from a chip of rubble. They can decode architecture in reverse, inventory the crops in warehouse wharves, and catalogue the birds in royal aviaries. Capitals known only by obscure footnotes and rumors are discovered beneath hundreds of feet of sand and routinely resurrected with the statues of warriors, holy scrolls in earthen jars, and concubines' solstice gowns intact. Portraits of princesses are painted from a fragment of skull bone. Surely then the restoration of one woman's life is possible. In this way, we will someday gather our daughters and bring them home.

FEEDING IN A FAMINE

Megan Miller returns to the farm in July or August when the river is low and the air yellow. There's been a six-year drought. She looks across the barley field to the twin silos and interprets them as reassuring. It's all a sequence of impressions to which we assign meaning. I could call them sores or anchors, she thinks, deliberately selecting the later.

Eleven Cottonwoods line the front fence. She counts them anyway. There's a new horse in the pasture. There's always a new horse in the pasture. She's been told his generic name several times but forgets. Blacky. Honey. Wheaty. Rusty. She can't remember them from season to season. There's a take-home message here. One must not fraternize with livestock. To give them names implies a psychology, a personality, an emotional involvement. The next thing you know, you're screwing sheep and everyone in church knows precisely the category of your sin. They smell it. It's a capacity they've developed, like scenting sudden wind changes and ominous indications in shifting cloud structures.

She calls this horse Lady Gaga. "Hey Lady," she yells

through dense sunlight, across channels where voices are effortlessly lost. It strains the mouth to carve syllables into the laminated glare. The Sargasso is with us, Megan thinks, in our suitcases, our briefcases. We unpack salty red kelp as we do our silk suits. And the horse comes running. Megan waves a carrot she prepared in a slow motion, stood at the sink pealing with a dull knife while watching the aluminum coated silos. Such containers are festering lesions or acts of revelation. The farm is ground zero. And the silos her first punctuation. They rose from the ground like metal teeth.

Her father passes, almost grazing her shoulder, and climbs into his pick-up truck. "You're going to spoil that horse," he warns. He shuts the truck door hard, but it's not a slam. That would be too decisive. Still, it's a clear dismissal.

Megan observes her father drive away. This is how she remembers him, precisely, in insomniac nights in Paris, Maui and Los Angeles. He leaves a deliberate funnel of dust and the irritating scratch of gravel scattered beneath him. It's an unmistakable threat. He's a man of tornadoes and flesh wounds, surrounded and camouflaged by untouchable elements, stones, wind, motion, and the ripped air that leaks through wire fences. You know his plaid jacket better than his face.

An area is defined not only by what it contains but also by what is missing. That's what Megan thought three days ago when they picked her up at the airport and drove home. She saw thunderheads and smelled damp barley. Fields like sea grass wind cut paths through. Perhaps this is the specific absence she is trying to fill or define, some weedy fluid movement loitering at her borders.

We carry intangible mistakes and garish miscalculations we never reveal. Megan recognizes they are simultaneously indulgent and brutally irretrievable. She glances at the barley. It's a piece of her that's been removed. It's an amputation.

Megan is assaulted by the absolute knowledge of place. She surrenders to it, the river swollen with sun and insects, heat blowing in, thunderheads circling like gray walls growing up from the ground. Clouds are a speckled bouquet in reverse; a mysterious expanding fabric a woman initiated in such practices would know how to pick. Here all materials are saved, arranged and stitched. It is always quilting season.

August is white and yellow moths, monarch butterflies, oriels and golden eagles. Dust turns the sunset red and exquisite. It redeems and elevates the flat fields of wheat and barley, alfalfa and potatoes. There's an insistent indication of gold between sheets of leaden gray and she thinks, suddenly, of medieval illuminated books.

That first afternoon, watching her father carry her suitcases into the house, Megan realized climate and personality are intimately linked. It is possible that geography is a form of fate. The valley is entirely ringed by clouds. They rise from the earth like a sort of crop. Potatoes are flowering with tiny white buds and if she ran the division of nomenclature, she would call the blossoms comafaces.

It's two o'clock and Megan inhales heat from the unpaved road where her father drove away. It feels brittle, could settle on skin the way dust does, pollens, particles from plants and stalks when they're cut and everyone's eyes run. Harvest tears. But there's more in this air, an underbelly tarnished with bits of wings from dying butterflies and yellowish feathers from sun-bleached hawks that often fall, a further layer of stained accumulation.

The posts on fences are ashy, the identical color of gravel in the driveway. Everything is chipped off, rubbed away. Even horses in the pasture with stalled summer across their backs are muted, dazed. The one blue spruce by the highway looks parched, neglected, scrubbed out. It's merely an inconsequential blue afterthought, easily erased. There's residue to this thought containing a darker implication, a midnight blue of bruises, perhaps. It's not a psychological resonance but three-dimensional; you might actually see it in a mirror.

"She's so dark," her mother repeated. "That's the darkest girl I've ever seen." Dylan was four that summer, black haired and olive skinned like her ex-husband. A girl with enormous dark brown eyes who laughed and tanned easily, wanted to touch and ride the horses, swim in the river, pick flowers, eat peas from the garden, feed the chickens. A four-year-old from the season of infinite yes.

"I've never seen a child that dark," her mother said again. "So dark and so small. Is that normal? You get her tested? She going to fade out? Is that her permanent complexion?"

Megan has not brought Dylan back. Now she wonders why she returns to her hometown, continues this pilgrimage in reverse, this journey where she expects to find nothing and does.

Restless, she drives the gray pick-up her father doesn't use anymore. She parks on River Street, one block north of Main, and walks toward Maple. If the town had a center, this would be it. If there were answers, they would be here under the accidental circle of tall pines. In such shadows, one can engage in acts of personal architecture and invent a strategy for reconstructing seminal events.

Megan squints into sunlight. Morning comes at her in fragments, as if she's an accident victim with extensive memory damage. She has a form of selective amnesia. That's why she returns to the actual site where place should reveal itself as definitive.

Megan spends much of her life picking out shards like a woman stumbling from a car crash. She is paralyzed in a long startled, moment of pulling splinters of glass from her skin. There's a sharp, gritty irritant she can't identify. That's why she returns each summer. It's an archeological excavation. Decades of dust, sun and relentless digging pass before the unearthing of one gold bowl, an orb of what might have been a concubine's earring. Or one singular coin with the face of a princess known only from rumor. You stand on a plateau, wind anointed, staring at the face of a god in your palm. There is danger in this heat; in the way thunderheads assemble above her shoulders when she isn't tracking them. You must constantly bear witness. Now a crack of thunder behind her, close like a warning shot. And could it have happened here, on Maple or Main or River Boulevard? The specific coordinates she is searching for?

Megan Miller returns home like a journalist sent to cover a catastrophe. It's an assignment. She's collecting evidence, prepared for body counts, mass graves and vistas of burned acres. What she finds instead is Joe Carlson's Fountain, Drug and Prescription. A woman could drink a milkshake at the counter while filling her pain killer supply, in one swoop like a hawk. Mrs. Carlson is seventy-nine. She can barely count. Megan can pass fraudulent scripts, give Mrs. Carlson telephone numbers of non-existent doctors in Los Angeles or New York, and confuse her with area codes and unusual spellings. Then Megan remembers she has already done this many times.

Outside is thunder like a plane straining at a blue edge too fragile to be a real border. It's a juncture created by intention and rumor, composed of insects and feathers clinging to the underside of yellow air. It has nothing to do with her. Neither do the desolate stranded silos, derelict barns and brittle roots of Cottonwoods along irrigation canals that seem trapped and trying to claw up from the dirt.

It's raining when she walks into the house. Her mother sits at the kitchen table, smoking a cigarette and playing solitaire. No lights are turned on. Rooms are cool hollows, suggesting bones and forests, images from a children's book. A yellow dishrag lies on the table beside seven piles of cards. But her mother isn't drying or dusting anything.

Megan realizes her mother engages in domestic chores only when her father is home. When her mother hears the pick-up truck in the long driveway, she empties the dishwasher, sponges surfaces, piles plates, moving her fingers and objects through space. When her father is home, her mother washes clothes, puts them in the drier, and busies herself with fabrics and how they are folded, stacked, ironed, stitched and carried. She wonders when her mother began preferring cotton, china and silverware to her husband. She suspects her mother is living secretly. Her father doesn't know his wife possesses a deck of cards. She keeps cards in a box in her apron pocket. Her mother is surreptitious, layered, and indecipherable She has her own climate now, her own seasons and storms, and rivers that relentlessly change and bend.

Perhaps this is what naturally accrues to rural women. They learn camouflage, notice subtleties, the way a trail winds, how a bent branch might contain information that will save your life. One becomes adept at finding niches you don't tell your children or neighbors about. What appears to be a lethargic primitive state is actually an evolutionary adaptation.

"I always used to know what you were thinking." Her mother stares at the nine of diamonds. Fields of barely and potatoes and willows slung along irrigation canals tremble between thunder. Lightning now, hot neon pink streaking directly at the ground. Her mother is not looking out the window. "I used to know," she says.

It's not a question or accusation. It's so neutral, without emotional direction, that the statement is less than a gesture with incidental sound. It's like placing plates in a cupboard.

Her mother is leaning over the table, studying a black king. Lightning is lavender and forked.

"What was I thinking?" Megan asks.

"That last year. You'd walk across the yard, pressing hard, leaving your boot prints in the snow. See these tracks, you'd say. Remember them good. They're the last marks of me you'll ever see."

"That was cruel," Megan realizes. "I'm sorry."

"No need." Her mother places a red seven below a black eight. "It was your way. You were heading out and telling us. Fair warning, fair enough. We didn't think you'd get that scholarship. Whole year early for college. Never had your senior prom. No graduation pictures. No corsage. But you were right. Those tracks faded and they never came back."

"I always come back." Megan is defensive. "I come home every year."

"Some girls have a phase." Her mother slides a red seven below a black eight. "You were different. No phase. You left and you were gone."

"Are you saying you missed me?" Megan senses she's being baited, but takes it anyway.

"I don't even remember you," her mother says. "What's there to miss?"

Megan walks into the bedroom she is sharing with her sister. The room her father built into the earth, paneled with pine, constructing one wall out of gray stone he carried in his truck from the quarry. He mortared all August, working in silence in the long late afternoons of sunlight, hammering and painting the extra room he didn't believe they needed. He hauled and nailed and knelt with his back turned away, his face and hands to the wall. Rage entangled in the ridges of his muscles like vines on certain trees, tendrils growing into and over the branches, strangling them.

Her younger sister, Martha, sits on the bed smoking. "You don't come back to see us. You come back for us to see you." Martha doesn't shift position. Her words are small rocks.

Martha has been discarded by a man a sane woman wouldn't have given her telephone number to, let alone married. Martha has been abandoned by this man and left with three children under the age of seven. Two boys and a girl, blond and bland like everyone else in the region. Their names are inspired by television programs, so contrived Megan cannot remember them, like the horses, Paint Spot or Brownie. These children wear the syllables of characters from ports and capitals where they will never go. Paris, Brittany, Austin, Kingston and Wellington, Chelsea. Three children with features Megan cannot remember. They are generic, sturdy, already solid and fleshy, a good harvest. She couldn't pick them out of a line-up.

Martha chain smokes, follows her around the downstairs bedroom where she now lives with her three uniform children, her plain wrap kids. Martha is tracking her, resting a hand on her rolling acre of cotton flowered print skirt hip, and says, "We're some sick ritual for you. Something you do before the verdict comes in instead of a prayer. You think we don't know?"

What does Megan actually know of the intelligence of these people, their ability to synthesize? Martha is convinced all attorneys are dirty, greedy and corrupt. She has a T-shirt with a rendering of a white shark. Beneath the caricature, block letters spell out *LAWYER*. Martha wore this shirt at the airport.

There is a further level of disdain she recognizes in her sister. Martha considers it absurd that a woman should work, or rather and more precisely, that a woman would deliberately choose this. Women only work from necessity, from external and unavoidable harsh circumstances, like death or abandonment. A good woman would be taken care of. Everyone knows that.

"You come by once a year, flaunting yourself. Get yourself a new name. Megan. Mildred wasn't good enough, right? You're a brunette. You're a redhead. You're getting an abortion. Then you're divorced. You're smoking pot. Then wed up a Jew boy. Now it's lifting weights. Yoga and sailing. You know what?" Martha stares directly at her face. "You use us. We're your private clinic. We're your private mirror. Don't you think we know?"

Outside is lightning pink and lavender like neon party streamers. Outside is rain on fields and horses, everything a sodden dark green. Outside is a driveway leading to an interstate, more fields, and a tributary winding to the Snake River. When she looks up, Martha and her children are gone.

Obviously, what she needs to see isn't in the house at all, but rather in the distance. In the morning, Megan drives into town and buys a pair of low power binoculars and a book titled *Birds of the Western States*. What she is searching for is beyond the frame. It requires the aid of a technological device. It must be behind the silos or on the edges of irrigation canals, past the barns and gully of cloud, a slice just beneath the horizon.

Megan drives back to the farm, one hand resting on the box containing the binoculars. She's forgotten what it is to drive a truck, to be intimate with a machine, the gears that feel abnormally warm in her palm, the spectrum of metal motor sounds you must listen to. She can't drive with the radio on, it's too distracting. There is nothing on the radio but religious sermons and country western songs, a squalid repetition of alcohol and poorly educated people without recognizable options whining about it in strict and predictable rhyme schemes.

Megan Miller spends the afternoon on the south field where the irrigation canal is. She studies the book of birds with its intimidating glossy pictures. She can't identify anything. They all look like big black birds or medium sized black birds.

There is more to classification than she anticipated. She spots magpies and hawks. The golden and bald eagles are easy, and the oriels and robins, pelicans and seagulls. Everything else eludes her. How does it fly? It flies well, she thinks, furious with the text. It flies with authority.

Later, she hears her brother Matthew say, "She's got binoculars." He is talking to her father, reporting in. "Looks like one of them tourists from California. Dressed up like she's on safari." There is laughter.

The city where she now lives is a region of collective contempt for her family, a contagion. For a moment, Megan feels she has been ambushed when she least expected it. But that's the point of an ambush, after all, she remembers.

Matthew is engaged in a singular process of subtraction and reduction. He is continually divesting himself of what he learned in school, even to the level of grammar. They used to read plays out loud together. She recalls a winter of Tennessee Williams in the basement. They memorized and recited their lines with conviction, acted them with cleverly assembled props. They had lighting cues. Martha designed and sewed costumes. Then it was another winter. They had aluminum paper crowns and swords. Matthew glued on a beard. Perhaps it was Chaucer. Her brother had a beautiful voice. Some actors can read the telephone book and bring tears to your eyes. Matthew could do that, naturally.

His hold on words is each season lessening. They have failed him. Or perhaps he is growing in reverse. All the attention to the ground is pulling him in. Soon he will communicate in a sequence of grunts and slaps. Then he'll be ready to marry someone like Martha.

In the late afternoon she drives the old pick-up to town.

She is going to call Karen Kaplan, her partner and best friend. Megan promised to telephone but she hasn't. There's no cellular service in the valley. And she cannot physically force herself to use the one telephone in the kitchen at the farm. She senses her mother in the air, in the wires, in disguise, tapping in, listening and recording, saving words for a future sabotage. Megan exists on the farm in a paralysis, as if she's had a stroke. She must separate herself by seven miles of interstate before she remembers how to use her credit cards.

"Why do you do this?" Karen Kaplan asks. She is talking about the farm, Idaho, and her summer ritual that has nothing to do with purification. "It's perverse. You could have had Shelly's condo in Kauai. Dylan's in camp. You could have gone anywhere. You do it to make yourself feel worse. Admit it."

Megan considers the possibility that her summer returns are an obvious propitiation. It is her ritual supplication, her unique blood letting to insure her own crops. Harvests of clients with injuries. Fields of clients who are victims of fraud, irrefutable negligence, breech of contract, misconduct that has a criminal code clearly attached to it like a price tag on a suit. And the bad faith that is someone else's fault. Megan glances at the river across the street from the phone booth, the river slow as if damaged slides through the center of town. It looks dull and beaten in early August. She is prepared to tell this to Karen, to reveal this as an absolute confession, but she doesn't.

"I'm collecting Jewish lawyer jokes. They're Neanderthals but they have rocks and clubs. And there are so many of them."

"As your attorney, I advise you to stay out of the mashed potatoes and gravy," her partner offers, voice too light. Megan detects her concern. "Limit your biscuit intake. Remember Los Angeles lent. It comes the spring of your 15th year and it lasts through your first grandchild. Keep your priorities, dear."

A small corridor of laughter. It feels sticky and contrived.

Her words and reasons are weak, exposed and inadequate. The inside of her mouth is dusty.

"I always used to know what you were thinking," her mother says. She holds a cotton cloth for washing or dusting. It's a prop.

Her father is watching television. Her mother looks directly at her and the words are an accusation. Her mother rinses dishes and smokes. She brushes a strand of gray hair from her eyes, barely glances out the window at the view she has memorized. At the end of the barley fields are two silos stranded above an irrigation ditch. Then the purple etch of Morris Road with the railway crossing and cemetery and the roof of the new high school. They were building it when she left for college. She remembers enormous piles of bricks.

"I used to be able to read your mind," her mother says. There is sorrow in this, but Megan cannot determine why or for whom. "You'd be looking out at the potatoes. But I knew you were seeing bridges and cities on the other side of the ocean."

"Yes," Megan says. "I was." Is this the door she must walk through? Is this the sudden portal you cross and find the other and more vivid world?

"But now. . ." Her mother pauses, lights another cigarette, straightens an invisible wrinkle in her apron, loses her train of thought. Her mother looks each year increasingly like Central Casting sent her for a farmwoman crowd shot. They all are. Her father and Matthew and Martha and her children named after detectives and districts.

Outside is a sunset that dust has turned into unexpected strands like lava. There are islands of purple embossed above a molten orange that might be Hawaiian. Summer opens like an oven. Megan waits for her mother to remember that she is speaking. "Now you've been those places," her mother points out, turns to examine an area of linoleum near the door. She extracts an envelope from her apron pocket. It's a stack of post-cards Megan sent in what appears to be chronological order. Her mother places them on the kitchen table. They are merely another set of cards. But there are more than fifty-two. Oahu. Paris. Venice. Bali. Amalfi. Tahiti. Shanghai. Prague. Rio. Bora Bora.

"Was it worth it?" her mother asks.

That's the question, of course, the matter of worth. You bring in your acres and what is the yield? There is the computation of planted field to pound, to ton. People are no different. Is that what her mother is attempting to measure? Did she plant at the right time? Were the seeds spoiled? Was the effort appropriate to the product? Or is there something else, more primitive than even the biblical? After all, Megan has sacrificed her blood, her kin, the village of her birth, her ancestors, the incontrovertible rituals and borders, the bones of the ancient ones. She violated them on a molecular level, brought the black haired daughter from the foreign tribe into the world. This is unforgivable.

When a witness is encouraged to engage an unnecessarily ambiguous question, particularly one with an implication of damnation, it is best to equivocate. Megan can negotiate this obvious treachery. "Worth it?" she repeats. "Well, that's difficult to say." In the morning, Martha screams at her. "You don't come at Christmas when we could use some decoration." Her sister is following her down the driveway, into the road. The three standard issue children she has spawned are in various stages of ambulation behind her. Megan walks toward the road that leads to a trail with a marsh. She has her binoculars around her neck and the book of birds under her right arm even though she rarely identifies anything with certainty and wants to abandon the entire project. Big and black, or is it perhaps merely charcoal gray? How large must it be to be considered big? What of other markings, colors around the neck, the bands on the legs and, of course, how it is flying? It's using its wings, she wants to scream. That's how it's flying.

Megan cannot master the book of birds. She cannot articulate flight patterns and body characteristics. It seems incredible that she grew up in this region and can barely name what is flying or growing, trees or bushes or birds. How did she manage to miss all this? Did she spend her adolescence sleepwalking? Was she already living in Los Angeles, surrounded by another vocabulary of vegetation and necessity, even then?

"No. You don't come at Christmas when we could use something festive," Martha informs her. She has left her three children in the gravel roadside and they sit down, reach out for small stones, and dig with them. Soon Martha will leave her children at a daycare facility in town while she returns to her job in the photo developing section of Smith's Supermarket. That's what she did before her disastrous marriage. She spent her days in an enormous blue cotton smock counting out pictures of men exhibiting their rainbow trout while smiling sunburned from boats and docks. And women at barbecues, holding up spatulas and infants, raising them to the camera like banners or trophies. Megan remembers photographs muted by too much sun, all the backyards, lawns and moorings blunted, beaten into conventional submission. Even the water looked barely alive, undernourished, anemic.

"Don't you dare look at me like that," Martha sneered at her in the supermarket once. "Don't stick your nose up. It's an honest living."

Now it's a high plains August, baked green with flashes of neon white lightning in the night storms. Megan remembers thunder after midnight, how the air was vacant after the strikes and the shake. She considered the possibility that the house might collapse. She felt not bruised but numb.

"No, sir," Martha screams. " You got better stuff to do for Christmas. Hawaii with your boyfriends of the Hebrew persuasion. Skiing in that town where Oprah does with all the movie stars. You come when the river is low and the air stinks. That's how you remember us. You come with the dust. You come to feed in a famine season."

She crosses the highway, a demarcation she suspects Martha will not venture and she doesn't; she turns back to her three gravel-sitting children. It's always a disappointing yield with not enough to go around, Megan thinks. Who are you kidding?

Suddenly, she remembers an August when she was ten. She went to Y camp in town for theater week. They put on a production of *Little Women* and she was Jo. Later, she won the summer county library award. The prize was dinner at the pizza parlor and a game at Bowlero in the mall next door. She had to read forty books to win, including *The Yearling* and the entire *Anne of Green Gables* series, nine in all. Megan thought her achievement was worth more than a slice of pizza and twenty minutes of bowling. That's why she stood in the parking lot crying. There is the matter of worth and value and the moment when we set our price per pound.

Martha stands on the edge of the highway. "You pretend you're coming to see us," she says, voice high and wavering. Behind her wind is blowing. "You come back for us to see you. Your new implants and hair-dos. Don't pretend." Martha laughs and it is harsh, brush and wire, gravel and wild fires. "But that's what you do. That's what keeps you in feed. Lying and pretending."

Martha is experiencing a contempt so vast it's completely beyond the known human range of expression. She is rocked with a silent laughter that makes her body violent. It is swollen and mute and terrible. Then she starts crying.

Megan walks toward the trail that leads to the marsh

where there are bird feeders on poles and numerous nests and she is certain she will not classify anything. We become the landscapes we inhabit, she thinks, the molecules in the air we allow to enter our lungs. There is nothing random about this. It's volitional. We consort with textures and fragrance, the shadows they cast and what they imply. We are infiltrated and redesigned. Of course there are spirits of rock and sky, reasons to worship eagles, hawks, the flight of geese and cycles of the moon, all moons, those named and charted and those still encased in their unmolested and hidden sleep. But this is only a partial explanation.

In the afternoon, Megan rides her bicycle out Lincoln Boulevard past the town limits to the ridge where she can see the Oregon Trail markers, the two pieces of mountain she considered indisputable as a child. They were what she would always navigate by.

It is mid August and patches of barley on the low hills are round as wells. Wind rolls through them like waves. Everything is some gradient of yellow, a golden swirl in unceasing motion. It is precisely the hay fields van Gogh painted, the dried grasses battered by their own hurricanes, perpetual, rising and falling as the Earth breathes. It occurs to her that, if she watches the barley field long enough, if she finds the one absolutely accurate angle, she will know what van Gogh was thinking.

It had nothing to do with absinthe or inhaling fumes from turpentine. Such an interpretation of van Gogh is trivial. The fields actually swirl as if painted and lacquered. They reveal the entire history and etiology of yellow and the wind is a hieroglyph a lucky woman might decipher.

For six consecutive days, just at sunset, one lone black elk passes a few yards in front of her parked bicycle, almost brushing the wheels. He crosses the highway, ambles into the scrub around the barley. It's the color of twilight then, a suspended washed out purple that elongates and has no edges. The moment of borderless held breath. Megan is waiting for an indication, perhaps magical, like a stumbled upon enclave of lavender scented with prairie rock no one has seen before. If she could discover and resolve this, it might be possible to determine where home actually is and go there.

The next morning, Megan witnesses a storm form around her. She rides her bicycle into a squall and finds herself in the absolute unblinking yellow center of it. The gold bull's eye. It's like a nest. She is in the barley field on the top of the ridge where she spends afternoons attempting to determine what van Gogh knew. The sky is black, she is surrounded by it, but she stands in a circle of sun. Then it comes at her, gray and black clouds distinct like bats flying at her face, moving like predators, shockingly fast. She watches them approach and thinks, *Then come, already. Come.* And the squall is wind and rain and then a sequence of sudden pink lightning she simultaneously smells and hears. The air is a wound you put sulfur in, she thinks. You can put it in me.

She lies down in wet barley. Her bicycle has fallen over. It is raining hard. There are so many women within me, she realizes. Women with histories of tin and feathers. Women with veins of infected yellow water. Women abandoned by their fathers and mangled by August, by voices that ricochet through screen doors, by sirens and cursing. There are dialects of stones and bullets. Then she puts her head against the ground and lets the rain enter her.

On the plane the next morning Megan takes a window seat. Her mother and sister are standing against the fence waving handkerchiefs. She wishes her mother would ask her now, as the plane races across asphalt, what she is thinking. Now, at the juncture between ground and air when all things are possible. She is thinking van Gogh knew we are less than islands. We are anomalous rock in a stretch of bad ocean, one boulder in a thousand miles of aggrieved waves. We stand as long as we can, dreaming of yellow, our feet bleeding in sand. Then we collapse.

Her mother and sister, the fence and landing strip are gone. The sky is an immaculate blue like the painted capes of certain saints on cathedral walls. Megan knows women are traditionally traded for a string of beads and a few cows, a horse, maybe. Where is the surprise in this? It is a perpetual cycle of poor harvests when you consider drowning the girl children.

Of course, rumors persist. There are ambiguous disappearances. A woman here or there invents techniques to elude detection and escape the compound. There are trails in mountains and methods to extract water from cactus. Some women scale the walls and reap years of fortunate seasons. They don't count livestock, measure grain or define themselves by harvests and droughts, floods and contagion. They refuse to save discarded fabrics like they were holy relics. Some women reject induction into the society of females who stitch quilts. They change their names and destinies, slip off their shoes at 27,000 feet, ask for a scotch on the rocks, close their eyes and wake up in another millennium.

COCKTAIL HOUR

Bernie Roth is not going to get his twenty-year service plaque in the lobby. The hospital he founded has been purchased by Westec Medical Division. Bernie Roth is merely the former figurehead of an ad hoc insurrection that has no meaning in the realm of litigation. The project coordinator makes it clear that his presence is unnecessary, in fact, it's intolerable.

He leaves the merger meeting three days early. Bernie Roth takes a midnight flight and his green-tinted contact lenses sting as he drives from the airport directly home. The house is perched on a cliff of purple succulents above the ocean that is, today, a dark blue like certain fabrics where you see the grain and stitches.

Chloe designed their house with an architect from Milan. It's a three-story Mediterranean villa with arches, balconies, a turret, orange tiles on the roof, and graceful windows of leaded glass that face interior courtyards enclosed by Bougainvillea draped walls. And it's not painted pink, Chloe has meticulously explained. It's a salmon terra cotta.

Chloe's car is in the driveway. It's a weekday and she

should be out. He notices her car with surprise and relief, realizing that if she hadn't been home, he would have called her and asked her to return immediately.

He finds Chloe in the bedroom, standing inside her closet, apparently arranging clothing. She is wearing a silk kimono imprinted with red Peonies, her blond hair is tied back in a ponytail and she seems startled to see him. She actually touches two fingers to her throat in a gesture of surprise when she looks up, and her mouth is momentarily wide. He starts to embrace her but, but for some reason, stops, and lays down on the bed instead.

"You're three days early," Chloe says. There's something accusatory in her tone.

"I was invited to leave," Bernie explains, prone. "I'm not getting my plaque."

"Why not?" Chloe asks. She glances at him, briefly, then continues moving clothing through the 120 square feet of her cedar closet.

Spring-cleaning is inappropriate, he decides. Insulting and dismissive. Bernie wants a scotch and he wants her to lay down with him, in that order, now.

"Their focus groups don't like plaques. It reminds the consumer of death. Their lobbies are strictly ferns with central gravel fountains. They're identical, like McDonald's." He closes his eyes.

Bernie waits for Chloe to offer consolation. A drink and a quick tennis game, perhaps. It's still early. They could have lunch, walk on the beach. Then he could tell her his joke. Westec Medical Division. WMD. See, there are weapons of mass destruction, after all. They're just not in Baghdad. They're in La Jolla.

Bernie Roth is aware of an agitating interference in the room. He must remove his contacts. His vision is blurred and scratchy, as if his eyes are being clawed. "What are you doing?" he asks.

"I'm packing, Bernie. I'm not getting my plaque, either. I intended to be gone before you got back." Chloe resumes her closet activities.

He sees now, the selected dresses and suits and skirts hanging in one area, an assembly of shoes and purses already on the bedroom floor below the French windows leading to the mahogany bedroom terrace. Her entire set of luggage is in the corner, garment bags, cosmetic cases and assorted carry-ons. The suitcases are nearly filled.

"Where are you going?" Bernie sits up. Is this an unscheduled Book Club related journey? A prize-winning poet must be fetched at an airport and properly entertained? Is there a problem with the children? Maybe he needs a scotch and a cup of coffee.

"I'm just going, Bernie. That's the point. Not where." Chloe pauses. "I'm leaving you. This. Us. La Jolla. I'm through."

"You're leaving me? As in a separation? A divorce?" Bernie stares at her. "Now?"

"Affirmative. Sorry about the scheduling. But it's always something. The siege of festivities. Christmas. Birthdays. Valentine's Day. Our anniversary. Departures tend to be awkward." Chloe looks directly at him. "Can you give me an hour or so to wrap it up here?"

"Wrap it up here? What is this? A movie set? You're divorcing me and you want me to leave our bedroom now?" Bernie repeats.

He examines the bedroom as if he's never quite seen it before. Their bed has four oak posts supporting a yellow brocade canopy. The walls are an ochre intended to suggest aged stucco. Ochre, not yellow. A stone kiva fireplace is dead center across from the bed. Navajo rugs lay over glazed orange Spanish tiles.

The ceiling is a sequence of Douglas fir beams somehow procured from a derelict church in New Mexico. Bernie assumes her decorator hires bandits. An elaborate copper and glass chandelier with a history involving Gold Rush opera theaters and saloons hangs suspended from the middle of the beams. Chloe insisted it was necessary, despite the earthquake hazard. It was essential for what did she call it? The hybrid Pueblo Revival style?

"I have a list and this is confusing. Yes. Why don't you make yourself a drink? I'll join you downstairs in a bit, OK?" It's not a question.

"Isn't this sudden? I've been preoccupied with the merger, but—" he begins.

"Actually, it's a coincidence. It doesn't really have to do with you," Chloe says, over her shoulder.

She extracts a pair of fire-engine red high-heel shoes. She holds them in her hands, as if determining their possible flammability. Or is she weighing them? Is she taking a special flight? Are there baggage limitations? Is she going on safari?

"We've been married twenty-four years. I must have some involvement." Bernie entertains the notion that this is a ghastly practical joke, or the consequence of an anomalous miscommunication. A faulty computer transmitting a garbled fax designed for someone else entirely, perhaps.

Chloe is within her fortress of closet, on her knees, nonchalantly evaluating pocketbooks and shoes with both hands. She does have a list, he notices that now, and a pen where she checks off and crosses out items. She's also listening to music. Bob Dylan live, he decides. It's her favorite, the Rolling Thunder tour. Or the other one she plays incessantly, Blood on the Tracks. They made a pact when Irving and Natalie went to college. She would not play Bob Dylan in his presence. In return, he would not subject her to John Coltrane or Monk. No Dizzy Gillespie or Charlie Parker, either. Chloe deems his music agitating. In fact, his entire jazz collection is, by agreement, kept in his study, as if they were vials of pathogens. Or slides of children with pre-op facial deformities.

Bernie stares at her back for an arrested moment, in which time simultaneously elongates and compresses. Then he pushes himself up from the embroidered damask pillows with their intimidating wavy rims of thick silk ribbons requiring handling so specialized he fears them, stands unsteadily, and walks downstairs to the kitchen. He pours scotch into a water glass.

Outside is a tiled courtyard with a marble statue of what he assumes is a woman rendered in an abstract manner embedded in the center of a round shallow pool with a fountain. Flowers that resemble lotuses but aren't drift slowly across the surface like small abandoned boats. He realizes the petals form a further layer of mosaic. So this is how his wife makes stone breathe. Then he reads the Sunday *New York Times* front page twice. The script is glutinous, indecipherable. He pours another scotch and dials Sam Goldberg's private emergency cell line.

"The WMD negotiations? You're still there?" Sam doesn't wait for a response.

"I'm at lunch with a client, Bernie. Can I get back to you?"

"Chloe says she's divorcing me," Bernie begins.

"I'm representing her, yes." Sam sounds equitable, even expansive.

"You're my best friend," Bernie reminds him.

"I love you both. She came to me first. I'll call you back." The phone goes still in his hand, which feels suddenly numb. He remembers that his hospital is now simply part of 250 small medical facilities owned by a corporation based in Baltimore. He is merely one of 12,500 doctors they choose to employ.

Bernie climbs the wooden stairs to their bedroom. Chloe is placing shoes in an enormous cardboard box. "Imelda Marcos had fewer shoes," he notes. He's wondered about her shoe accumulation, the pumps and stilettos and platforms, how odd for a woman who habitually wears sandals or is barefoot.

"Won't you need a porter or two?"

"My job is over. The chauffeuring. The scheduling. Tennis lessons and matches. Music classes. Not to mention the soccer practices and interminable play-offs. The surfboard transportation logistics. Piano recitals. Ballet productions. The play dates," Chloe pauses. She reaches for something in a drawer on the far side of the closet. She withdraws a package of cigarettes. She lights one and faces him.

"Listen. It begins in pre-school. These kids don't play. They have auditions. If they pass, if they get a call back, a sort of nanny-chaperoned courtship ensues. It's loathsome." She expels smoke. "Later, it's worse."

He hasn't seen her with a cigarette since Ion and Gnat first went to nursery school. The fumes are infiltrating the room, further irritating his contacts. Bob Dylan is whining off-key and out of time, contaminating the air, now on an auditory level. It should be labeled a posthumous rather than live performance, he decides. He shuts off the switch.

"I didn't know you still smoked," Bernie said. "Or that you hated the children's activities."

"Soccer did me in. Soccer, for Christ's sake. How does soccer figure? When did that make your short list? How many professional soccer stars has La Jolla produced? It's just crap." Chloe is vehement.

"We accepted division of labor as a viable vestigial tradition. But you could have refused," Bernie counters.

"You can't say no to soccer. It's the new measure of motherhood. It's the fucking gold standard. I sat in parking lots between chauffeuring, feeling like Shiva with her arms amputated." Chloe finishes her cigarette. She uses a yellow shoe with a red flower at the toe for an ashtray.

"Let's have a drink downstairs," Bernie suggests. His voice is reasonable. He is able to produce this effect by pretending he is someone else entirely, a concierge or a waiter. "I'm finishing the Laphroaig."

Chloe consults her watch. It's the Piaget he gave her when their son entered college. His wife shrugs, the kimono sleeves drifting briefly from her sides like twin cranes skimming an inlet, hunting.

"One drink," she assents.

They sit in the kitchen. He considers the Westec buy-out. For two decades, he entered the hospital each morning and paused in a gesture of respect near walls engraved with the names of doctors who had achieved their 20, 25 and 30 year status. Next year, he would have had his own 20-year service plaque installed. Chloe has already arranged the catering. He would be permanently mounted beside Milstein and Kim, McKenzie, Fuentes and Weintraub. They were there when Northern San Diego Children's Clinic was built, the landscaping just put in, the first Bougainvillea and Hibiscus bushes growing against still dusty cinder blocks. Chloe planted pink and white Camellias the next year. Then Wisteria and Roses.

Bernie realizes the kitchen floor is actually a composition of hand-painted tiles, purple and blue Irises and Violets. The stems and leaves are a raised green enamel suggesting channels and veins. So this is how she prepares their meals, barefoot, standing on a version of cool garden. He finds cheese and fruit in the refrigerator and bagels in the cabinet. A china platter with ornate silver handles he vividly recalls packing in plastic wrap and hauling in a special crate on a plane sits between them. Where were they returning from? Portugal? Prague? Chloe averts her eyes.

"I love California Lent. It comes the spring you're fifteen and lasts the rest of your life." She looks tired.

"Just gain a few pounds and let's stay married." Bernie spreads cream cheese on a bagel. It's stale. Chloe smokes another cigarette.

"I'm leaving a few pounds early. I'm one of the last original wives. Do you realize that?" Chloe asks. " I'm forty-six. Let's just skip menopause and the obligatory trophy wife syndrome. We did our jobs. Now the task is finished."

"We had a deal. We agreed to be post-modern," Bernie points out. "No empires with historically disastrous ends. No mistresses with unnecessary dangerous complications. No tax fraud. No start-ups or IPOs. Just us, with plausible defendable borders."

"We did that. You built the clinic. I did this." Chloe indicates the formal dining room with her fingers, and by extension, he surmises, the entire house and grounds, courtyards, swimming pool and tennis court, gazebos and rose gardens.

"You saw it as a job?" Bernie is amazed.

"It was a performance art piece. Remember when Book Club discovered one man shows? Spalding Gray. Laurie Anderson. We went with the Weintraubs on opening night, remember?"

Bernie Roth thinks for a moment. Then he says, "No."

"It was the hospital benefit that year. A bit arty for you. We went backstage.

"Elaine had Laurie Anderson's entire tour profile. We realized we were earning more than she was. We had our own multi-million dollar performance art pieces. We just had smaller venues and a limited audience. Elaine Weintraub, the original wife. Before the current version. The ex-TV late night weather girl? The anorexic redhead with the room temperature IQ? Jesus. Elaine Weintraub was my best friend. You don't even remember her." Chloe finishes her scotch.

"Our marriage was an art piece, a performance?" Bernie is incredulous.

"The four piece choreography. The lessons. Sports and tutors. Surfing and swim meets. The theme birthday party extravaganzas. Christ. Not to mention the gardeners I bailed out of jail. The maids with alcoholic boyfriends. Their secret abortions. The relentless complications. The emergency loans. It was 24/7 for 20 years. And I'm not getting a plaque either." Chloe stares at the table. Bernie pours more scotch.

Outside is sunlight that surprises him with its nuances, its fluid avenues of yellows that are not solid at all, but tentative and in curious transition. Streaks like gold threads waver across the surface of the fountain, a filigree embossing the koi. Bernie thinks of brass bells and abruptly senses a clash in the air. So this is the sound of a day being sliced in half.

"I walk through this house and it's like being trapped in a postcard." Chloe indicates the living room table, a square of in-laid mahogany completely covered with framed photographs. She picks them up, one by one. "Agra. Bali. Rome. Luxor. Maui. Everyone holding hands and smiling. It's a laminated version of reality."

"But this was our life," Bernie realizes. He stands near her. "You wanted Thanksgiving in a Beirut back alley? Easter in a Turkish tenement? That wasn't our experience. What's encased in glass is, in point of fact, the truth."

"Really?" Chloe sounds bitter and combative. She is still wearing the kimono with the extravagant sleeves that seem to suggest intention. She has put on pink lipstick and diamond earrings. She has brushed her hair. Perhaps she sprayed her wrists with perfume. Then her skin would be a distillation of all things floral and vanilla. "This isn't truth," Chloe said. "It's an advertisement for consumption."

For a moment, Bernie thinks she is alluding to tuberculosis. TB is rebounding globally. Half of Europe tests positive. Studies suggest nearly forty percent of New York City college students have indications of exposure. Malaria is also making a spectacular comeback. Polio is a possibility, too. Its crossover potential is seriously underrated. A major influenza epidemic is inevitable, actually statistically overdue. Of course, small pox could be the defining epidemic of the millennium. Then he realizes his wife is not talking about infections. He holds a silver framed photograph selected at random. "You don't appear to be suffering in Tahiti," Bernie observes.

"I didn't suffer. I just wasn't engaged. It was like filling stamps in a geography game. More accumulation. Just like the grotesque children's activities." Chloe seems to be considering another drink.

"Grotesque?" Bernie repeats.

"Piano. Cello. Guitar. Ballet. Gymnastics. Basketball. Karate. Theater arts. Choral group. Ceramics. Mime. What kid has that plethora of aptitudes?" Chloe demands.

He is apparently meant to say something. "I have no idea," he admits.

"They don't have affinities or longings. Every stray spasm of temporary enthusiasm gets an immediate new uniform. They lack affection and discipline. Activities are another form of consumption. Now a video. Now a violin. Now Chinese. Now a chainsaw." Chloe sighs.

Bernie considers the possibility that he may pass out. He barely slept at the negotiations, which were not mediations, but rather the inordinately slow unraveling of a fait accompli. His hotel room was curiously uncomfortable, the sheets and towels abrasively starched, the walls a deliberately muted blue reminiscent of an interminable depression. The sense of transience in carpet and upholstery stains disturbed him. There were lingering odors he couldn't identify. Perhaps it was perfume, insect repellant, spilled wine, suntan lotion and something intangible that leaked from a stranger writing a postcard. He had insomnia for the first time since he was an intern and nightmares about his father.

"What are you going to tell Ion and Gnat?" Bernie tries.

"I've taken care of that." Chloe almost smiles. There is strain around her mouth. It's as close to a sneer as she can permit herself. Her genetic code doesn't allow her to further distort her face.

"You've talked to them?" Bernie is tentative and afraid. He needs to establish coordinates. He must assemble reliable data.

"Ion and Gnat. How chic we thought their nicknames were. How millennial. Naturally, I've spoken with them." Chloe stares at him. "Natalie used to tell me what a great mother I was. I had my standard line. I'd say—"

"I'm compensated. I've got my CEO salary, yearly incentive bonuses, stock options and pension plan," Bernie supplies. "Of course, I remember."

"I wasn't kidding," Chloe states.

After a moment, in which he feels dazed and incoherent, and thinks oddly and wildly of hummingbirds and lizards, and how patterns on reptiles resemble certain common skin disorders, he asks, "What did the children say?"

"They're a monolith of narcissism and indifference. They want assurances there's no hostility and the finances are secure. If separation doesn't intrude on their scant psychological resources, it's fine. They require known quantities. If it arrives from two locations, that's irrelevant. Just so we don't necessitate their engagement."

"Is that it?" Bernie senses there is considerably more. His best skill has always been diagnostic.

"Not quite. They both have messages for you." Chloe

pauses. She takes a breath. "And this is the last act of translation I'm going to engage in. After this, you'll have to gather and distill your own information."

"Shoot." Bernie is dizzy. He doesn't want to flinch.

"Ion quit the tennis team." Chloe actually laughs.

"He won the Desert Classic as a sophomore. He's ranked number three in California, for Christ's sake. He has a full scholarship." Bernie realizes he is yelling.

"He knows we can afford it, without his playing. He hates tennis. Thinks it's decadent, imperialistic and retrograde. He quit last year. I've been paying his tuition. Quietly. Part of my job. The choreography, mediation and scheduling aspect."

"What about his major?" Bernie insists.

"He hasn't been pre-med since freshman mid-terms." Chloe avoids his eyes.

"What is his major, precisely?" Bernie is more alert. He understands rage is a form of fuel.

"Urban Design. It's like modern history but with community projects."

"Community projects?" Bernie puts his glass down. "Like Houses for Habitats?" He has a vague recognition of this organization. Perhaps he's seen it listed on intern resumes.

"He's specializing in athletics for the handicapped. Creating playgrounds with wheelchair ramps in barrios. Also, he isn't Ion anymore. He's Grivin," Chloe informs him. " He plays drums in a band. He says it's a good drummer's name."

"Grivin?" Bernie repeats.

"An anagram of his wretched birth name. Irving. I should never have agreed to that." Chloe shakes her head from side to side. "But you were having that affair with the nurse. And I was on the verge of suicide. Guess I just lost that one in the sun."

There is a pause during which Bernie considers the delicacy of the respiratory system and the necessity to gather filaments of air into his body, and keep his lungs oxygenated. "What about Gnat? What about Natalie?"

"No pre med there, either. Sorry. She's in Women's Studies." Chloe examines her hands. Her fingernails are translucent with pearl white slivers at their tips. Or perhaps they are arcs of silver, permanently embossed by some new cosmetic process.

"And? Come on. I feel it, Chloe. I'm down. Kick me hard." The scotch is making him nauseous. He decides to make a pot of coffee and take a Dexedrine.

"She's calling herself Nat and living with a woman," Chloe reveals.

"She's a lesbian?" Bernie tries to concentrate on Gnat, on Natalie. She was an excellent camper. When they rafted the Grand Canyon, it was Gnat who helped erect the tents, identify the correct poles and how to position them. Her natural ability to recognize constellations was exceptional. She rarely tangled a fishing line. Was this unusual? Was her spatial aptitude an indication of abnormality? Had he failed to diagnosis a monumental malfunction?

"Fifty-six percent of her entering class listed their orientation as bisexual." Chloe finishes examining her fingernails. "I suggest we adopt a neutral position."

Events are accelerating in a frantic progression, each revelation is increasingly surreal. Day is assuming hallucinatory proportions. He concludes that his present condition resembles severe jetlag combined with sixth round chemotherapy. And there is, of course, the matter of the luggage. The suitcases packed in the bedroom. She must have arranged for someone to carry them down the stairs and load them into her car.

"Do you care about that?" Bernie manages. "Our daughter is gay."

"Why would I care?" Chloe seems surprised.

"What will happen to the Christmas decorations?" Bernie

asks. He considers their holiday ritual. Chloe and Gnat selected new ornaments for their permanent tree legacy, one for each family member, one each year. The two-hundred-year-old brocade angels with twelve- carat gold threads around their wings from Belgium. The gingham elves with pewter crowns. The silver maple leaves. The glass snowflakes, each with intricate individual facets and panels.

"Nat will take them no matter what. If she goes butch. If she opts for artificial insemination. She'll take the ornaments. And she knew you'd ask that." Chloe is leaning against the wall, her eyes partially closed.

Bernie pours coffee. He removes a bottle of amphetamines from his suit jacket pocket. He takes three tablets and offers the bottle to Chloe. She moves toward it with such unexpected rapidity, he can't determine how many pills she extracts. Bernie watches her hands, following her fingers to where they terminate in glazed nails translucent like the undersides of certain tropical seashells.

"Remember the glass snowflakes?" Bernie asks.

"From Tibet? With triangular amber panels like medieval cathedral windows?" Chloe recalls. "I thought they'd look good as earrings. I imagined them on a young wife on a pyre. Of course, that wouldn't work for me anymore."

"That's what you were thinking? In front of the goddamned pedigreed twenty-two-foot Colorado blue spruce? Ritual incineration?" Bernie places his hands over his eyes. There are numerous anecdotally reported cases of sudden stress induced blindness. He puts on his sunglasses.

Chloe pours herself a cup of black coffee. Her movements are slow, listless, stalled. The room is a series of sea swells. He realizes they are floating like the petals of the flowers that are not lotuses just above the koi.

"And you're putting the fucking suitcases in your car

and driving away?" Bernie is incensed. "Sam Goldberg is your lawyer?"

"He can represent both of us. Or I'll take Leonard and you can have Sam." Chloe offers.

"Leonard is my golf partner," Bernie says.

"We know where all the bodies are buried. It's a cemetery. When in doubt, just keep it, Bernie." She studies the interior of her porcelain cup.

Then Chloe goes upstairs. She returns, slowly and methodically, with suitcases. He's surprised by her muscular arms. She knows instinctively how to balance her torso, shift her weight, and bend her knees. She is barely sweating. She has replaced the kimono with a short beige linen dress with spaghetti straps that accentuate her tanned shoulders. 20 years of yoga and tennis. Then the bags of groceries when the maids disappeared, were picked up by immigration, or beaten up by boyfriends. In between, they had babies and abortions. They visited relatives in their home villages and often didn't return for months. Then the gardeners vanished. Chloe spent days in the garden with a shovel. Yes, she could easily load the baggage into her car. Even the inexplicable cardboard box of shoes. And that is the next step. Bernie considers the heavy carved oak front door that leads to the circular cobblestone driveway.

"What about the jewelry?" Bernie inquires. He always gave her a necklace on her birthday. Rubies in Katmandu. Pearls in Shanghai. Silver and turquoise in Santa Fe. Gold in Greece. He can remember each separate composition of stones and the rooms above plazas and rivers and lagoons where he unwrapped his offerings and fastened the clasps around her throat. Sometimes there were cathedral bells and foghorns, drums from carnivals and parades, waves and sea birds

"I took the diamonds. I left you the rest. They're in my

safe. The key is on my pillow." Chloe pours another cup of black coffee.

"Why leave me any?" Bernie wonders.

"You may need them for bartering purposes later. Sometimes a strand of Colombian emeralds really hits the spot." Chloe lights another cigarette. This is not the behavior of a novice. This is no small stray gesture of recidivism. Does her yoga instructor know? Her aromatherapist? Book Club and the hospital board? And what does she mean by barter? That's a curious concept.

"Wait a minute. Look. This is for your birthday. I got it early." Bernie is excited. It's the amphetamines, cutting through his fatigue, his heavy and unnatural disorientation. Airports are terminals of contagion. A maximum exposure situation. He might be incubating a malevolent viral mutation. Still, he is clarifying his thinking.

"I can't wait." Chloe gazes at her watch.

Bernie walks into his study, the only room Chloe permitted him to decorate, and returns with a small wooden box. "Here," he says. He feels wildly triumphant.

"I'm not interested," Chloe informs him.

Her voice has more energy now. The amphetamines. Perhaps they should take two more. Bernie produces the bottle. Chloe allows her fingers to reach into the pills. She stands near him while he opens the box. A single grayish stone.

"I'm going to have it set," Bernie explains. "It's an agate from the beach in Chile. From Isla Negra where Neruda lived. I went there. I skipped Rio. Didn't you wonder why I went to a river parasite conference in Brazil? I needed an excuse. I changed planes for Chile at the airport. Then I drove. I walked beaches for miles. I found it for you. I pulled it out of the water." Bernie holds the pebble in his palm. His hands are shaking. "Now you can tell me what the stones know."

"Bernie, you're a lovely man." Chloe touches his cheek. "You've made it a wonderful job."

"I want to know what the stones know," Bernie says. "That was your goddamned dissertation. Your personal grail. You were going to decode Neruda's stones and explain them to me."

"That's pre-history, Bernie. You'd need an archeologist to dig back that far. A paleontologist." Chloe turns away from the agate. It looks lonely and ashen. It knows it is an orphan.

"What about the house? The furniture? The paintings? The sculpture? Each sofa a distillation of your personal evolution? That's what you said," Bernie remembers.

"I tried to amuse myself. Forget it. The house is too big for you," Chloe determines. "The kids are never coming back."

"They're never coming back?" Bernie finds himself repeating. The afternoon is a kind of three-dimensional mantra. Phrases are recited, but they are like howls people make on roller coasters, ludicrous vows and confessions. Words came from their mouths, but they are sacraments in reverse, staining the air. They are curses.

"Not for more than a day here and there. Now there won't be the plague of holidays to entice them." Chloe glances around the downstairs rooms, detached and calculating. "Unload it. The market is good now."

"Chloe." Bernie takes a breath. "I love you."

"It's been terrific, really. This is my terminal performance of prophecy on command. My final act of analysis and emergency emotional counsel. OK. I'm gazing into my crystal ball for the last time. It's the goddess of real estate. She says sell."

"Chloe. Let's talk this out. There's more to say. I can say more." Bernie tastes the amphetamines now, an unmistakable metallic sting between his lips. It's spreading through his body; microscopic steel chips, hard-wiring his muscles, his reflexes and agility. She can load the suitcases into her car. But he outweighs her by seventy pounds, and he is wearing leather shoes. One must not discount the element of surprise. Chloe can do head and shoulder stands, she has mastered all the strength and flexibility postures, but she has never been in a street fight.

"OK." Chloe is unexpectedly agreeable. "One final note. That stricture I gave you about only wearing black and gray Armani?"

"Yes?" Bernie closes his eyes.

"I remove it. You should do jeans for a while, T-shirts. Downscale. Lose the Porsche." Chloe takes a silver sandaled step toward the front door.

"You don't love me?" Bernie is confused and chaotic and finds the combination not entirely unpleasant. His trepidation has been replaced by an erratic turbulent energy.

He is blocking the door, with its thick carved oak panels and intricate squares of stained glass implanted in the center and along the edges. Her decorator no doubt looted that from a church, too. And he is not going to let her walk out to the driveway.

"Love you? I'm all dried up in that department. One marriage, 2 children, and the full liturgy of soccer. The 100 unique ornaments I was designated curator for. The secret acts of mediation. Messenger services. Currency exchange. Frankly, specific love isn't even on my radar screen." Chloe seems resigned.

"What do you want? I can give it to you." Bernie is desperate.

"Solitude. Drift. I'll travel. Maybe pen a mediocre verse here or there. It requires a climate you can't provide. You can't survive the altitude I'm looking for, believe me," Chloe says. "And no more question and answer quizzes. No more multiple-choice tests. No more essays."

"Will you take this?" He extends the agate. "You said

swallows and constellations of stars were inside. The mysteries of oceans. Metamorphosis and mythology. Take it."

"No more homework. School's out, Bernie. School's out forever." Chloe sings the phrase, twice.

He thinks it might be an Aerosmith song. Or, perhaps and worse, Alice Cooper. Once he settles the suitcase problem, he's going to play Coltrane on the house speakers at full volume. Dizzy and Monk. Parker and Miles. It's going to be jazz week. Jazz month.

Bernie stands directly in front of his wife. Her suitcases are near the door. She is holding her car keys. Still, Bernie is beginning to get his bearings. There is a machinery in the periphery. He is starting to hear it hum and pump. There are mechanisms. Barter? Deduction is a gift. It becomes a skill experience polishes into a tool. The most fiercely reckless intuitions often prove accurate. And he can see the schematics now. There are blueprints and diagrams and there is nothing subtle about them.

"You don't visit the hospital anymore," Bernie notes. "You used to come for lunch. We had our special noon appointment."

"I couldn't stand all the doors opening to those discreet pastel alcoves. The rooms where women who still have eggs sit. Women with babies in their wombs. I could hear them devising names for infants. They do it alphabetically. Amy. Beatrice. Clarissa. Devra. Erica. Francine. Gabrielle." Chloe glares at him.

"That's a lie," Bernie says, shocked. He wants to slap her across the face.

"Back away," Chloe orders. Her voice is high and thin. It wavers, hangs in the air and loses its sense of direction and purpose. He considers fireworks, how they explode, tattooing the sky with a passionate conviction that quickly dissipates. Then she says, "Do you want the police here?"

Bernie Roth envisions the La Jolla police; two or three freshly painted vehicles parked in the circular cobblestone driveway, each officer tanned and uncertain. He imagines them standing in the marble entranceway below the oasis of stately 60-foot palm trees. The fronds cast unusually vertical shadows like arrows and darts. From certain angles, the house looks like Malta. He once suggested mounting an antique cannon in the turret. And domestic complaints are a gray area. He is, after all, the senior doctor at the hospital. Alternatively, he imagines chasing her car, positioning himself at the end of the driveway, his back against the wrought iron gate, his arms spread wide. She might impale him.

What are his options, precisely? He can shut off the master switch on his computer, of course, locking the garage and gates. Chloe refused to learn how to manipulate the systems. She said she wasn't intelligent enough for such smart appliances. He often worried what she would do in an emergency power failure. Or he could call Ron Klein. Ron is running the psychiatric unit now. A wife with a menopausal psychotic break requiring hospitalization. It happens all the time. Ron owes him a few favors. But favors are a limited resource and he needs to ration them.

"I'm delirious," Bernie realizes. " I need to take something."

The green in his wife's eyes intensifies. It is like observing a river coming out of a mist. Or emeralds just professionally cleaned by sonic wave devices in a jewelry store.

"You're going to open the cookie jar?" Chloe asks. "But you're under suspicion. You swore no more until Christmas."

"That's nine months away. Isn't that unnecessarily punitive and arbitrary?"

Bernie wanders into his study.

This is the only area of the house he has been allotted. He designed it himself in one weekend. He didn't need a decorator.

He ordered over the Internet. The walls are mahogany and the bookshelves contain his medical library, computer files and jazz discs. The lamps are solid brass. The sofa is brown leather like oak leaves in mid-October. The floor is red maple. Chloe disparaged his aesthetics and dismissed his study as aggressively masculine. But she is following him now.

Bernie Roth has always possessed the capacity for strategic action. It might be time to retire now, after all. Empty nest syndrome demands attention. Menopause is problematic. They can build something new, on a beach in Costa Rica or Mexico, perhaps. Grivin can help with the construction. Maybe he can get extra credit course points. And Nat. She can bring her girlfriend. They're probably both good with hammers.

Bernie walks directly to the wall safe and unlocks it. The safe contains one blue canvas duffle all-purpose sports bag wedged against the metal. It fills the entire safe and Bernie has to yank it out. Chloe watches him unzip the bag. Bernie extracts a handful of glass vials. He removes a box of syringes.

The agate from Isla Negra is in his pocket. Later, Chloe will tell him about Neruda, the poet she was enthralled with when they first met. When she recited stanzas about volcanoes and poppies, he didn't hear the words precisely, but rather followed the narrative through her mouth and eyes. It was medical school and he was stupefied with exhaustion. He heard the phrases she offered as a music that was visual. It was a sequence of facial expressions, a tapestry of geometries composed from flesh. Trajectories formed on her lips, which were rivers and bays with bridges, and exited through her eyes, which were green wells and portals that could foretell the future.

Tell me what the stones know, he will command later. I want to be initiated into the language of agates. Show me how they form bodies like infants and feed themselves from stars. And Chloe will comply. She will find the capacity for jazz. It's simple. Saxophones mean spread your legs. Later, she'll laugh at his WMD joke. Her throat will emit sounds that look like strings of rubies and sapphires. She will fall down on her knees and explain everything. She will invent and improvise. He'll help her remember why she has a mouth.

"The usual?" Bernie asks, glass vials in his hand. He prepares a mixture that is two parts morphine, one part cocaine. He prefers the reverse. He taps the air bubbles out of the syringes. "We'll celebrate the birth of god early this year. Take a few weeks off. Reassess our position."

Chloe apparently agrees. She has removed her beige dress with the thin shoulder straps. She isn't wearing underwear. She curls on her side on the leather sofa like a fawn at dusk. Bernie Roth reaches for his wife. She extends her right arm, the one with the good veins. He injects her first. Then he injects himself.

WOMEN OF THE PORTS

They meet at irregular intervals at Fisherman's Wharf. This is the neutral zone, the landscape of perpetual unmolested childhood where the carousel spins in its predictable orbit, and the original primitive neon alphabet does not deviate. Some hieroglyphics are permanent and intelligible in all hemispheres and dialects. No translation is necessary. The carousel doesn't require calculus, rehab or absolution. No complications with immigration or the IRS. Just buy a token.

She phones Clarissa. "I'm here," she announces.

"At the wharf?" Clarissa must clarify the conditions.

"Anemic waves and corndogs that give you cancer. Immigrants catching perch so full of mercury, they explode as they reel them in," she reports.

"What color is the water?" Clarissa asks. "Precisely?"

"Last ditch leukemia IV-drip blue," she decides.

"Half an hour," Clarissa assures her. "I'm coming."

They meet episodically. Conventional friendship, with its narrative of consensual commitments, has proved too intimate and demanding. Between them are houses, husbands dead or divorced, and children known only by anecdote and photograph. Entire strata of their personal history are less than footnotes. Decades passed when they were driftwood to one another, or vessels lost at sea. Or a drowned stranger, perhaps; why bother?

"Our litany of blame is tedious," she once recognized.

"Human perimeters are background razor wire. We're too hip for that shit," Clarissa responded."

"We'll bite it off with our teeth," she offered. "Napalm it. Grenade launchers and M-16s. Tec-9s. We'll have our own Cultural Revolution. We'll go post-modern, but fully armed."

"We'll invent rituals appropriate for our circumstances. We'll whisper endearments while strolling the killing fields." Clarissa was enthusiastic.

"But we'll abide by the Geneva Convention," she prompted. "Despite our emotional residue."

"Directed psychological evolution. It'll be more brutal than weight training," Clarissa agreed. "But we'll become better human beings."

"We'll redefine and transcend ourselves," she said.

It was an earlier autumn on Fisherman's Wharf. It was bluer than Maui, the bay studded with strands of cobalt that looked charged, technologically modified. She had lived two years in a bamboo and chicken wire shack on a nameless river of honey yellow reeds and orchids in the jungle near Hana. She had no electricity. She wasn't in contact with Clarissa then. Clarissa probably doesn't know there are seasons in Maui, too. A faint reddening, a moistening that seems a prelude, and sudden stillness as the mosquitoes enter temporary remission.

"I like it conceptually. But let's go further," Clarissa suggested. "We'll be molecular. Just strands of light from one radiance to another."

"We'll reject linearity entirely," she encouraged. "Sporadic moments of illumination in extreme altitudes requiring oxygen masks?"

"Discreet and unpredictable rendezvous with spectacular voltage. We'll communicate by blowtorch," Clarissa offered. Her eyes emitted an unnatural gleam suggesting rows of votives in deserted rooms and beaches of mica in white sand.

Their psychiatrists were cautiously optimistic. A process of accommodation and evolution was unlikely but not implausible. True, they had failed the traditional strategies of giving and receiving. But the standard methods by which one registers recognition and regret don't apply to them. They had a pact, an armistice with the elements of aggressive radical improvisational surgery. Malignant complications were an acceptable risk. Then they had shaken hands.

Now she sees Clarissa exiting a black town car with darkened windows. She's wearing her usual business outfit — aerobics pants and jacket, oversized Gucci sunglasses and a Giants baseball cap. It's the popular camouflaged movie star look, designed to create the impression you're attempting to be incognito. It's the uniform the narcissistic personality disorder dictates. It's become a global fashion statement. In the malls of all the capitals, passing women might be gangbangers, housewives or soap stars.

Clarissa is carrying not a gym bag, which would be appropriate and predictable, but a Chanel purse with leather quilting and long gold braided handles. It's the second decade of war and alliances are ambiguous and brief. We're polite but alert and suspicious. Vigilant.

They kiss on both cheeks. "You forgot my birthday," Clarissa begins. She dismisses the car and driver with a hand gesture.

"I didn't sign on as a soccer mom. I don't decorate for

holidays. I don't bake or send thank-you cards. I throw away personal mail. You know this," she reminds Clarissa.

"Don't you go to bed at Halloween? And not get up until after Valentine's Day?" Clarissa's voice is light.

"That was my mother," she replies, annoyed. "I just leave the country at certain junctures."

She is fond of Christmas in Southeast Asia — ornately decorated pine trees in air-conditioned hotel lobbies like vestiges from another planet, and bamboo balconies draped in green velvets, antique brocades and holly wreaths. More fetishes. Christmas carols are rendered in versions so mangled by distance and erroneous translation they're almost tolerable. Rivers smell of rotting vegetables, petrol, wood cooking fires and hunger. Air is layers of decaying prayers like a satellite losing orbit, falling down not as metal but as streams of origami. In Bangkok, in December, it's 106 degrees.

"Let's just be here now," Clarissa says. "We know the rules. It's play time." Her mouth glistens with a red lipstick that seems to have small stars encrusted within it. There are implications in the sheen she doesn't want to consider.

The wharf is almost deserted. It's mid-day, mid-week in an undifferentiated season. It's another windswept early November. They walk hand-in-hand down the pier past occasional men fishing and stray teenagers eager for corruption.

"Don't look," Clarissa cautions. "They're contagious. We'll get a contact psychotic flashback."

They, too, grew up in tenements designed for transience, and shabby from inception. The rows of apartments like festering sun sores. They were an integral part of the blueprint for the millennial slums in the sun. They were the penciled-in stick figures on the diagrams.

The Last Edge Saloon perches on the furthest side of the wharf. Their reunions begin there. Clarissa sits in a booth facing the bay on three sides. It's a bold and invitational decision. They'll order expresso and take amphetamines. Or get drunk on something festive, White Russians or champagne. Since she's technically still in AA, she lets Clarissa set the tenor. Clarissa orders a pitcher of Bloody Marys. From a caloric standpoint, it's the obvious selection.

"You still look like a hippy," Clarissa observes, regarding her with an expression that's speciously conciliatory, even condescending. She interprets this as disturbing. Anxiety is inseparable from the air. It's in the oxygen molecules their biochemistry fails to adequately process. There's a perpetual uneasy truce.

"It's my signature classic bohemian statement," she replies quickly. She's defensive and a bit agitated. "I want to formalize our alliance," she begins.

"Want to get married?" Clarissa produces an unconvincing partial smile.

"I want a contract with precise specifications," she replies. "And I want a weapons check."

"Contracts are worthless," Clarissa points out. "They're a wish list for Santa."

She's a lawyer, after all. She knows.

"We could become cousins," Clarissa suggests.

This appeals to her. Survivors of cataclysmic childhoods defined by poverty and isolation compulsively seek validation. They know they lack proper emotional documentation. Cousins evokes a blood connection that would substantiate and obviate certain complexities — the ebbs and flows, droughts and monsoons of their relationship. She wants a device that highlights and justifies their erratic and pathologically intense conjunction. In regions of bamboo and sun-rotted petals, hurricanes are routine and wind propels sand like tiny bullets, and there are too few artifacts. Cousins is an inspiration.

"I could draw up the papers," Clarissa is expansive. "But adoption is superior."

She came to San Francisco when she was 7. Her father, Marvin, had terminal cancer. Her mother was mentally ill. They were bankrupt. She thought heaven was a foster home. If Marvin would just finally die, perhaps she could even get adopted.

"I've missed you like a first love," she says.

"I was your first love," Clarissa reminds her. "And you mine."

They lean across the faux wood table etched with knife gouged gang insignias and logos of metal bands and kiss again. They are both manic this autumn day. They share numerous personality disorders. They're both bi-polar 2 with borderline features. Substance abuse is a persistent irritant. Recently, they've been diagnosed with post-traumatic stress syndrome.

Today's sun turns the San Francisco Bay the purple of noon irises in country gardens in July. To articulate such facets, to know and chart them is a spasm of thunder inside, a tiny birth the size of a violet's mouth. If she extracted this entity from her body, she could present it to Clarissa like an infant.

She examines her almost cousin's eyes. Even through dark sunglasses, they are inordinately bright. Then she senses that she, too, is glowing. Her eyes are brass corridors reflecting fluorescent light. They're both candles today, unusually in sync, radiant with clarity and energy. Clarissa wears a silk scarf, a vivid purple implying motion and vertical waves.

"Like it?" Clarissa asks. "Hermes. Take it. I just stole it on Maiden Lane."

"You still shoplift?" She holds the scarf. It feels moist and sanctified. It reminds her of the Mohave in December, crossing from the east into an inland ocean of relentless purple and mauve waves. The scarf is an embrace around her neck.

"Theft is like guerilla warfare," Clarissa explains. They've finished their second round of drinks. "A thrill kill requires mental discipline. I put it on and keep walking. I know I've had it for years. I bought it on the Champs Elysees. It was raining. I was at the George V. No one could dare question me. And no one does. Let's ride the carousel."

They carry their drinks across the stained wooden planks of the pier. The carousel is closed. Clarissa makes a cell phone call and a man appears. She produces three hundred dollar bills. They wait for the right seats, choosing recently painted twin horses, white and intricately decorated like certain antique porcelain plates, and ride for half an hour. Clarissa vomits twice.

She searches her theoretical arsenal. Is it time for a hand grenade? Should she call for a chopper with medics? Then she remembers her mission. "Are you OK?" she manages.

"I understand how children discover bulimia," Clarissa reports, excited. "It's an accidental miracle."

Despite the gym-suit camouflage, it's obvious Clarissa has gained weight. But even they have taboos. Eating disorders are a forbidden topic. They meet on neutral ground, but there are still no-fly zones, areas of fragmentation and carpet bombs, landmines and IEDs.

Clarissa borrows the purple scarf to wipe her mouth. She's contaminated the silk, but she still wants it back. She thinks, suddenly, of flower bouquets and their inadequacy. The floral arrangements of her life have been too much and not enough. The petals stained, fragile and insubstantial. They were debris.

"If a contract is insufficient, what can we do?" she wonders.

They stand on the wharf where the carousel is no longer spinning. Gone are the circles they inscribed in the too thin aqua air, engraving midnight blue trails like marks made by fins. Somewhere these etchings floated into a river winding to a bay. More invisible origami.

"We could get a tattoo," Clarissa proposes. "Our names together in a heart."

"A tattoo?" she repeats, delighted. "Isn't it painful and dangerous? The possibility of AIDS and infection?"

"But you love needles." Clarissa is annoyed. "You're a professional junky."

"I'm in remission," she replies quickly. There's no doubt anymore. Clarissa is attacking.

In truth, during one particularly virulent carousel rotation, she decided to call a drug dealer in North Beach. It's walking distance, over a steep sequence of stone steps in a cliff. Then the sudden unexpected gate. Within, a creek is dammed and trapped, the water stalls green with slime and duck excrement.

There's a bridge to the Victorian house. She knows the grain in every wooden floorboard and the way sunset displays itself through each glass pane in every room. There's a geometry to how sun impales and dissects the Golden Gate Bridge. If you comprehend this mathematics, you can construct space-ships and time machines with common household appliances. You can turn on the radio and talk to any god.

"You always relapse," Clarissa observes. "And don't you already have AIDS?"

She is shocked. She stares at Clarissa. Even with Gucci sunglasses, there's a distinct softening around her chin, and a loss of definition in her cheeks.

"No. I have hepatitis C." She is angry. "And you need to get your face done."

"What part?" Clarissa is concerned.

They're walking from the wharf toward a tattoo parlor on Columbus Avenue.

Shops offer stacks of cheap plaster statues, saints and

children, dwarves and obese laughing frogs. Someone will purchase and paint these objects, display them, or give them as gifts. They pass display windows offering plastic replicas of Alcatraz, and T-shirts saying PRISONER and PSYCHO WARD.

"What part?" she repeats. "It's not a fucking negotiation. It's a composition. Just give the guy a blank check. And don't use a Marin surgeon. You'll end up looking like a clone. I found an Italian in Pittsburgh."

"I noticed you finally got your father off your face," Clarissa slowly admits.

"Well, the police wouldn't do it," she says with an edge. "And Mommy was in a locked ward."

Slow swells are below the wharf. The bay is a liquid representation of fall. It's in continual transition. All fluid bodies are autumnal and promise betrayal. That's what leaves signify, flaunting unrepentant criminal reds like vengeance and adultery, and yellows like lanterns and amulets. Fall is about packing and disappearing. It's the season for divestiture. Time of the severing. That's the obvious subtext. And it occurs to her that her elation may dissipate. Emotions have their own inexplicable currents and random lightning storms.

She follows Clarissa into the tattoo parlor. "Let's rock," Clarissa says. "Lock and load."

The Eagles are playing. It's "Hotel California," of course. A tanned man with a blond ponytail who looks like a yoga instructor opens a book of designs. *Dragons.*

Butterflies. Demons. Flowers. Guitars. Spiders. She vaguely remembers negotiations involving a fifth of vodka, and a complicated argument regarding the aesthetic implications of scripts. They selected a gothic font. Then she may have passed out.

She realizes they're in an arcade on Pier 39. It's three hours and six Bloody Mary's later. They have gauze and adhesive tape on their shoulders where their names are carved into their left upper arms in navy blue. They're leaving the encircling heart in red ink for their next reunion. Banks of garish video games surround them; hip-hop blasts from speakers in the ceilings and floors. Boys who look part Asian or Mexican are armed with laser levers and plastic machine guns. They keep the real Glocks in their pockets.

"This is not the global village I envisioned," she says.

"That's politically incorrect enough to get me disbarred," Clarissa whispers. She places two fingers against her red lacquered lips in a gesture of mock fright.

The photographic booth is on the far side of the arcade. 4 shots. They've been taking pictures here since they rode buses and walked from Daly City in 7th grade. It cost a quarter then. Now it takes dollars. The photographic session is a ritual element in each of their meetings. It's their sacrament. When they leave the booth, they cut the strip in half. She saves her photographs in the shoebox where she keeps her passport and birth certificate. She assumes Clarissa does the same, but in her Swiss jewelry vault. Or perhaps she just throws them away.

The photographs are a necessary component of their liturgy. They can only see one another by laminated representations. It would be too disturbing and intrusive if they actually perceived one another without artificial mediation. They communicate by email, fax and newspaper clippings.

"Marvin's jowls are definitely gone." Clarissa examines the thin strip of facial shots. "You have cheekbones. Are those implants? Jesus. You're gorgeous. You didn't look this good at sixteen, even. Cosmetic surgery already."

"We're breathing on 40." She is bewildered. Certainly Clarissa comprehends the necessity of proactive facial procedures. This is San Francisco and Clarissa is an entertainment business attorney with a penthouse office above a Chinese bank.

Is Clarissa in denial? Are her medications interfering with her functioning on even this rudimentary a level?

"After you psychologically resolve the slap across the face, and its more damaging verbal resonances—" she begins.

"And that takes decades and costs what? A quarter of a million?" Clarissa is still holding the strip of photographs.

"Then the next step is actual surgical removal. It's a natural progression. It's how to treat emotional cancer. Keep them," she decides. "Get some reference points."

They sit on a bench on the south side of the pier, sun tamed and restrained. The water is agitated, white caps like mouths open, baring teeth. The bay reminds her of a woman in autumn in an imaging office. First the locker, the paper bathrobe, the chatty blond with the clipboard who walks you into the room with the mammogram machines. Then the stasis before the X-rays are read. Yes, the bay is waiting for its results. Poppies encrusted with resins or blood float like prayer offerings in the dangerous toxic waters.

"We used to walk here. What were we? 11, 12?" Clarissa asks. Her mood is also shifting. They're both still drunk.

They hold hands. Her childhood is a sequence of yellows from trailer park kitchen cabinets and the invisible poisons leaking from fathers undergoing chemotherapy. Take a breath of rancid lemon. You've seen the Pacific, reached the end of the trail and don't linger at the edges. They had a final punctuation for that. It was called the iron lung.

"They hadn't invented a vocabulary for us yet," Clarissa says to the waves. "Dysfunctional families. Latchkey children. Remember when I lost my key? What my father did? Jerry tied me up in the carport in pajamas for a week."

"I brought you a canteen with orange juice." She recalls. "And a few joints. You were handcuffed. I fed you like a sick bird."

"How did you get a canteen?" Clarissa asks.

"I took it from the hospital outpatient closet," she says.

Her head is throbbing. She stares at sea swells that are the process by which an autumn forest becomes water. If you understand the bay, it smells of slow burning cedar. Midnight currents are actually leaves brushing the ocean with russet and amber. Waves answer to the moon and immutable laws of spin and fall. They don't get dinner on the table at the appointed hour. They don't carpool or pick up the suits on time, or have the cufflinks and invitations ready.

"Only you know," Clarissa says. She looks like she may vomit again.

She nods. *Yes, only I was at ground zero when it happened. This is why we've tattooed ourselves. We alone comprehend adolescence in the margins of a hardscrabble town in the conceptual latitudes.* The late 50s and their village was subdivided wood frame houses and stucco bungalows nailed in rows like the fruit trees above gashes of alley, oranges and lemons so bitter they burned your mouth.

"We sat next to each other in home room," she offers.

It was 7th grade and they were learning the history of America, but they couldn't find their geography or circumstances in literature. Nature was oaks and maples, not a riot of magenta Bougainvillea, not a blaze of red and yellow Canna bursting through bamboo fences sticky with pink Oleander. Families had two parents and pastel houses behind lawns with white picket fences where characters experienced angst rather than hunger and rage. They didn't sift through trashcans in dusk alleys searching for glass soda bottles redeemable for 2 cents apiece. Gather enough glass and you had bus fare. On a fortunate hunt, you could trap enough coins for lunch.

"Remember digging for bottles for food money?" she wonders.

"I remember what you said." Clarissa smiles. "You said Holden Caulfield would have taken a taxi."

She nods. "Remember our black berets? We were trying to meet Ginsberg and Kerouac. We wore those berets every day. We got lice."

Clarissa shrugs. "We looked for beatniks right here, on this pier. Boys with sketchbooks and guitars. We said we were French. We practiced our accents at recess."

Recess in the region of broken families, of divorces and single mothers, of stigma and words that could not be spoken out loud. Alcoholism. Cancer. Child abuse. Illegitimacy. Domestic violence. The special yellow smell of Sunday evenings when the mothers who worked as secretaries poured peroxide on their hair. The tiny implications of illumination from the one lamp you were allowed to turn on. Electricity was an extravagance. Their San Francisco was a medieval oasis — ocean at your face, mountains at your back. There were warlords at the utility companies with incomprehensible powers. Phones were instruments of terror. It cost money every time you touched them. Long distance calls were rationed, like chocolate during a war. The world as it was, before hotlines that could put your father in prison.

"I still have nightmares about the apartment in Daly City," Clarissa reveals. "At every St. Regis and Ritz, from Beijing to Buenos Aires, I wake up shaking. At the Bora Bora Lagoon Resort Hotel. At the Palazzo Sasso in Ravello, for Christ's sake. The plot complications vary but somehow I'm back there."

"Remember the neighbors?" she asks. They lived next door, with a cement hall between them. She's dizzy and her arm burns.

"The wetbacks and hillbillies? The identical blonds with drawls?" Clarissa is unusually bright. "It was still the Depression. I had a friend once. Another friend, not like you.

A hillbilly. Jerry found us listening to the radio. It was Elvis. Jerry started yelling, 'YΔ1590u're playing colored music? You're putting colored music in my house?' He threw the radio at my face. Took out my front tooth. That's how I discovered caps."

"That was me," she corrects, moderately annoyed. "It was Marvin, not Jerry. And he used the 'n' word."

"We had the same father, metamorphically. A barbarian with bad grammar who thought a yarmulke was a ticket to prison. A guy who could plaster and drywall. They were house painters. When they were employed. House painters." Clarissa stares at the bay.

"Like Hitler," she points out. Then, "Had your mother run away yet?"

"Rachel? She was on the verge. She was morphing into River or Rainbow or something in secret. Preparing for her first commune. After Jerry, a sleeping bag and a candle was a good time."

She remembers Clarissa's mother as a woman sheathed in dark fabrics who sank into shadows, kept her back to the wall, found her own periphery, and rarely spoke. Jerry had pushed her out of a moving car. He kicked in her ribs and put her in a cast. Clarissa's mother, a bruised woman in the process of metamorphosis. Yes, molting like the Hibiscus and Night Blooming Jasmine beside the alleys, sheathed in long skirts, shawls, and kimonos. She was younger than they are now.

Then Clarissa had a family of subtraction and she envied her. All the neighbors had incomplete families — the brothers in juvenile detention, the sisters who disappeared when they started to show. If Marvin stopped lingering, if he would just die, she could have a similar reduction. She could escape the stucco tenements with torn mesh screen doors and vacant lots behind cyclone fences. And the mothers and aunts who rode buses and worked as file clerks between nervous breakdowns.

Even second-hand cars were an aberration. If she was placed in foster care, adoption might follow. She had straight A's and she won the poetry and science competition. Maybe she could be given a new name with syllables that formed church steeples on your lips, like the women in books. She could be assigned a stay at home mother with a ruffled apron who baked cookies and called her Elizabeth, Margaret or Christine.

"Did you realize we were Jewish?" she suddenly wonders.

"I never revealed that. The hillbillies thought we were Christ killers and owned all the banks," Clarissa tells her. "And Jerry said they'd deport us. Send us back to Poland."

"I wanted a bat mitzvah," she remembers. "Marvin said, 'You mean a Jew thing? It costs a fortune to get into that club. They inspect you first. You have to shave your head and show them your penis.'"

"Speaking of Marvin's penis, remember the Polanski scandal? When he sodomized a 13-year-old?" Clarissa asks.

It happened in California. It was front-page news in an era when newspapers were read and discussed. The details were graphic and comprehensive. They were indelible as a personal mutilation.

"Jerry said, 'I knew that guy in Warsaw. He's 5'2. He's got a 3-inch dick.' Jerry mimed the organ dimensions with his fingers." Clarissa repeats the demonstration for her. "Then he said, 'Why is this a headline? What kind of damage can you do with a dick that small?'" Clarissa turns back to the bay.

"Is that when it happened? When you disappeared? The phone was disconnected. I couldn't find you for a year." She tries to form a chronology.

"Brillstein says it wasn't rape. It was an inevitable appropriation. I was chattel. Rachel left and Jerry just moved me into their bedroom. I came home from school and my clothes were in their closet. My pajamas were folded on their bed. Then he found us an apartment in Oakland. He let me pick out curtains," Clarissa explains. "Hey, I was the first trophy wife on the block. It's my mother I hate. She knew what would happen. I was expendable."

"But she came back for you," she says. "She took you to a commune. You went to college. You got out."

"Nobody gets out, for Christ's sake." Clarissa is angry. "You chance to survive."

She examines the bay. There's less agitation, swells are softer and a haze grazes the amethyst surface. The diagnosis has come in. The bay had its biopsy. This stretch of ocean is terminal.

"Didn't Marvin break your wrist?" Clarissa asks. "You had bandages all summer. You had to stay on the pier, reading."

"Mommy did it. She was between mental hospitals. Maybe a weekend pass. Her contemptuous glare. It cut right through the chemo and antipsychotics. She ratted me out. She said, 'Marvin, look, that kid's talking with her fingers again. Don't you know only Jews and Gypsies talk with their hands? You think you're a neurosurgeon? A symphony conductor? You're not even human.' Then she seized my hand. I had three fractured fingers but they took her in the ambulance."

They are quiet. Through haze, sun is lemon yellow on the heavy waters. Accuracy is a necessary component of civilization. Daddy knocked out your tooth. Mommy broke your fingers. There's an elegant mathematics to this, to these coordinates and their relationship to one another. The accumulation of slights. The weight of insults. The random resurrection of coherence. And the way you are no longer blind, cold, and bereft. Then the indelible vulgarity you finally have the vocabulary to name.

Their fingers are entwined. She notices Clarissa is wearing a platinum set VHS-1 Tiffany diamond of at least 4 carats. And a gold Rolex with the perpetual oyster setting. She withdraws her hand.

"You know how it is," Clarissa dismisses the implication. "When other women evaluate their black velvets, I consider a cool set of razor blades."

"So you transcend the genre?" She is enraged.

"What genre would that be? Survivors of squalid adolescences? Best aberration in the most abhorred class?" Clarissa looks at her, hard. Her red lipstick with the embedded stars are like tiny metallic studs or hooks. They help you shred flesh.

She considers their shared childhood; their parents had been disenfranchised for generations. They were pre-urban and unprepared for a remote town perched at the edge of the implausible Pacific. Appliances overwhelmed them. The garbage disposal must never be touched. What if it broke? The refrigerator must be strategically opened and immediately shut. What if it burned out? And their offspring became mute with shock, there in the dirty secret city, deep within a colossus of yellow Hibiscus and magenta Bougainvillea, behind banks of startled red Geraniums and brittle Canna.

"We are what coalesced at the end of the trail. After the bandits, cactus and coyotes. We are the indigenous spawn of this saint. His bastards," she realizes.

"We were spillage," Clarissa replies. "Don't romanticize."

Everything is suspended. The bay is barely breathing. Perhaps it's just been wheeled back from a fifth round of chemo. Maybe it's hung-over. Or slipping into a coma. It needs a respirator. Come on. Code blue. It needs CPR.

"The immigrant experience, my ass," Clarissa adds.

"But we have instincts." She is exhausted. Her arm with its gauze-bandaged shoulder extends. She can talk with her limbs now. Marvin and her mother are dead. She gestures with her fingers, a motion that includes the bay, an outcropping that is Marin and Sonoma, and a suggestion of something beyond.

"We understand ambushes and unconventional warfare. We're expert with camouflage," Clarissa agrees, offering encouragement.

"They'll never take us by surprise," she responds. She feels a complete lack of conviction and a sudden intense longing to get a manicure.

Silence. Palms sway, windswept and brazen. Vertical shadows from fronds appear without warning, random spears. One must relentlessly improvise. Holden Caulfield would get knifed in the gut.

"I have to go now," Clarissa abruptly announces. "But you look stunning. I'm impressed. Have you considered a wardrobe update? Do shmattes prove you're an artist? Listen, I brought some Prada that were sized wrong. I'd sue if I had time. They're in my car."

"That's OK," she manages. *This is emotional aerobics for the crippled*, she thinks. Then, "I appreciate the gesture."

"I don't have a generous impulse in my repertoire." Clarissa is tired. "This is a search and destroy in the triple-tier. But we must keep trying. Let's end our reunion with a celebratory benediction."

This is their ritual of conclusion. They exchange tokens of mutual acceptance. It's how they prove their capacity to transcend themselves. It's the equivalent of boot camp 5-mile runs in mud and climbing obstacle course ropes in rainstorms.

"I brought a postcard you sent me from Fiji 16 years ago." She produces it from her backpack. She reads it out loud. "On the beach under green cliffs, I feel God's breath. I make my daughter smile. She laughs like an orchestra of bells and sea birds fed on fresh fruits. Her hair is moss against my lips. How pink the infant fingernails are. I wish you such sea pearls." She offers the postcard to Clarissa.

"I forgot that completely." Clarissa doesn't take the postcard. "That was Anna. A guy with the name of a reptile, Snake or Scorpion, took her away on a Harley to Arizona. I sent you newspaper clippings."

"She testified against you," she tries to remember. "In that divorce."

"I was accused of witness tampering. I almost lost my license," Clarissa says, and stands up.

She returns the postcard to her backpack. Their reunions are conceptually well intentioned. But leaches and bloodletting were once considered purifying and curative.

There is a long pause during which she considers radium poisoning, Madam Curie and the extent of her fatigue. Then she asks, "You still doing the venture capital thing? Private jets? Yachts to beaches too chic to be on a map? Everybody loses but you?"

"When the Israeli money dried up, I thought I was through. Then the Persians. No sensibility and billions, all liquid. An entire race with an innate passion for schlock. Payday." Clarissa is more alert. "Then détente. Russian mafia money poured in. Cossacks with unlimited cash. Who would have thought?" Clarissa places the strip of photographs in her Chanel purse. And, as an afterthought asks, "What about you?"

"I'm getting married," she says. "I'm moving to Wood's End, Pennsylvania."

"Jesus. The grand finale. OD in a barn with a woodstove? Twenty below without the wind chill? Your halfway house skirts in a broom closet? What now? Another alcoholic painter fighting his way back to the Whitney? Or a seething genius with a great novel and a small narcotics problem?" Clarissa extracts her cell phone.

"Fuck you." She is outraged.

"I apologize. That was completely inappropriate," Clarissa says immediately. "Forgive me, please. It's separation anxiety. We have difficulty individuating. Partings are turbulent. The overlay and resonances are unspeakable. But Brillstein says we're improving."

"You're still with Brillstein? Jerry's psychiatrist? The Freudian with the high colonics and weekend mud baths?" She stares at Clarissa. She's so startled, she's almost sober.

"He's eclectic, I know. But it's like a family plan. I'm grandfathered in at the original price," Clarissa says.

The stylish phone opens; the keyboard glows like the panels on an airplane. It's the millennium and we have cockpits on our wrists. Clarissa's phone is voice activated. She says, "Driver." Then, "Pier 39. Now."

"Does your arm hurt?" she wonders.

"No pain, no gain. My dear cousin," Clarissa smiles. "Keep your finger on the trigger. We must soldier on. Our cause is just."

She realizes Clarissa has already moved on. The conference is over. The documents will be studied. Further discussions to be scheduled. My people will calendar with yours. We'll synchronize by palm pilot.

Suddenly she feels she's on a borderless layover. It's last Christmas in India again. She began in a broken taxi 5 hours from Goa. Then a 6-hour delay in the airport and the run across the tarmac for the last and totally unscheduled miraculous flight to Bombay. A day room for 7 hours. The flight to Frankfurt and another day room and delay. Finally, the 14-hour flight to New York. 70 hours of continual travel and she was just finding her rhythm. She could continue for weeks or months, in a perpetual montage of stalled entrances and exits, corridors and steps, tunnels and lobbies all in vertigo, in free fall, where no time zones apply.

They are no longer holding hands. A distance of texture and intention forms between them. The geometry is calculated. Not even their shadows collide.

"Another bittersweet reunion barely survived," Clarissa says. "My beloved almost cousin."

"And you, my first and greatest love," she replies. "Another high risk foray we deserve purple hearts for."

"We'll get red hearts next time. Our next tattoo." Clarissa produces a small false smile. Her lips are stiff beneath the lurid lacquer coating.

They kiss on both cheeks. The glitter has departed from their eyes. They've slid into an interminable foreign film they have neither interest nor affection for. But she knows the name of Clarissa's lipstick now. It's called Khmer Rouge.

There's a certain pause just before sunset when the bay is veiled in azure. It's the moment for redemption or drowning. Inland, cyclone fenced freeways carve cement scars beside bungalows with miniature balconies where parched Geraniums decay in air soiled from the fumes of manufacturing and human wounds. The bay is a muted defeated blue, subjugated and contained. At night, they pump the antidepressants in. Or maybe there's enough Prozac and beer already in the sewage. Pollution turns the setting sun into strata of brandy and lurid claret, smears of curry and iodine. It looks like a massacre.

"Listen. My car can take you where you're going," Clarissa offers.

Clarissa's driver has short hair, a thick neck, aviator sunglasses and an ear attachment like a Secret Service agent. Clarissa indicates the car door. It is open like a dark mouth with the teeth knocked out. And she's waving the purple scarf like a banner. She refuses to admit that she doesn't know where she's going. She turns away and starts walking.

"Look. The Prada coat that doesn't fit right," Clarissa calls, waving a patch of blue silk with both her hands.

She turns away and starts walking. If those are words issuing from Clarissa's mouth, which needs immediate surgical attention, she can't hear them. There are shadows along the boardwalk and alleys bordering residential streets with ridiculous insipid seaside names. Bay Street. Marine Drive. North Peninsula View. Who do they think they're kidding?

Keep walking and shadows find you. They're the distilled essence of all harbors and bays. They taste like a wounded sherry you can drink or pour on your cuts. Shadows are graceful and do not require explanations. They know you're more dangerous than they dare imagine. They cannot fill in your blanks. Simply surrender and they do everything.

There are no neutral zones. They're an illusion, a delusionary construct, like movie and real estate contracts. Satellites map each zip code and tap every telephone. Cities are enclaves between combat arenas. We are born with weapons of mass destruction. They're within us from inception and we pass them down the generations like poisonous heirlooms. It's ground zero now and forever. She senses the car moving behind and away from her, and she's grateful. She hopes Clarissa loses her license and becomes destitute. She should have her hands amputated like any other thief. Then she should get a slow growing undetectable ovarian cancer that metastesizes in her stomach and brain. The Russian Mafia should gang rape her while the Iranians eat caviar and watch. In any event, she never wants to see Clarissa again.

THE PROFESSOR'S WIFE

It's a brisk, wind-thrashed morning in early April and Professor Malcolm McCarty is riding his bicycle along Maple Ridge Road toward campus. His bike is winter gray and weathered, with a wire basket attached in the back and front. It's ideal for transporting books. He purchased it from a Sorbonne classicist during his first graduate school sojourn in Europe, and despite the shipping expense, he knew he would cherish it.

Malcolm has an intuitive sense of his emotional parameters, his range and repertoire. It's an unwavering internal mechanism of measurement that gives the impression of confidence. Some perceive it as arrogance. It's not. Rather, it's a trick of the genes he was born with, a small gift, like absolute pitch and eidetic memory.

Not that he knows himself, of course. Who can purport to possess that gift? Still, Malcolm McCarty exercises a consistent ability to articulate and prioritize the morphology of his sensibility. In a millennium of inchoate folly, even rudimentary self-awareness is considered impressive.

There's ice on the road from a recent snowstorm, and with characteristic lethargy, the town of Allegheny Hills has not sent out plows. If he was the sort of man who shrugged, and he isn't, he might be tempted to do so now, to convey his indifference to the condition of Maple Ridge Road. As a man of implacable aplomb, insignificant external details do not affect his fundamental purpose.

Professor McCarty is completely disinterested in the exchange of verbal banalities and displays of conventional gestures. That's the sort of behavior junior faculty refer to as body language. *Body language*, he thinks derisively during faculty meetings, wondering if any of the new boys have read a Shakespearean sonnet. Or more accurately, any sonnet.

He remains calm. He conceals his contempt for the assistant professors from California and eastern seaboard cities. It's the principles of the institution he's devoted to, not the transitory personalities. Let them come and go. Milton and Chaucer are permanent like the universal law of gravity, the force fields and the speed of light.

Malcolm McCarty believes universities are akin to the monasteries of Europe's Dark Age, the last repository of illumination in a barbarous era that lasted a thousand years. During particularly offensive curriculum discussions, where the canon is autopsied and body parts assigned to what is indisputably the province of women's studies, ethnic sociology, film appreciation and abnormal psychology, Professor McCarty maintains his restraint. He has an appreciation for grace and the discipline of modulation.

In the third decade of his academic service, Malcolm recognizes that bureaucracy eventually reduces and degrades. He's become strategic. Junior faculty present passionate justifications for *Hip Hop: The Poetry of the Present*. They're not arguments, but clearly rehearsed theater pieces. It's a charade with syllables intended for another format entirely. Twitter? YouTube?

Given these rules of engagement, a monosyllable is appropriate. A simple no. He has a reputation as the man of the no. He's their anchor, their barricade, their unrelenting referee. He instinctively recognizes where the borders of civilization are and when there's an incursion. His sense of violation is absolute. He's been department chair for two decades.

Invariably these boys and, increasingly girls, move away. On, they call it, as if Boston and Los Angeles automatically conferred clarity and vision. He can define them with the elegance of a simple equation. Movie theaters with ornate facades + plazas selling the paraphernalia of diversity + concoctions with curry from Cambodian villages = an unassailably better destiny.

During their last faculty meeting, he glanced across the Formica table in the conference room. Their oak table disappeared one weekend and the replacement appears to have come from the student cafeteria. It's leached beige plastic, no doubt assembled by teenagers in Malaysia or the Philippines who have no concept of what a conference table looks like or what its purpose might be. They don't know much about the Imperial Examinations, either.

Malcolm McCarty was looking for Bob Lieberman, his staunchest ally. They came to the College of Northern Pennsylvania at precisely the same time. It was spring and nearly thirty years ago in the placid era before the vulgarization of culture. There was a before, when the knowledge of literature was a necessary attribute of the intelligentsia. Books were discussed at dinner parties where wit and controversy engendered a verbal choreography similar to performance art.

Malcolm McCarty wasn't alone. Bob Lieberman can bear witness. They saw the delegitimizing of the experimentalists and the subsequent round-up of the stylists, the stilt dancers who parachuted for locomotion. When asked for proof of authenticity, the stylist held out his palms and smiled. There it was, stigmata on demand. Then the critical apparatus, the intellectual's compass, collapsed.

This was before the college was called CON PA. Or as the students say now, without irony, the Con.

An excessively thin, completely bald man is occupying Bob Lieberman's regular chair, the one with wheels and torn leather upholstery decorated with masking tape like bandages. The stranger is picking his nails with a Swiss army knife. Malcolm will have him removed by security. He reaches for the department phone and simultaneously realizes that it is, in fact, Bob Lieberman. It's a maliciously vandalized rendition. The sixty-six-year-old version of his former colleague and confidante is unrecognizable. He's progressing through his collection of miniature instruments with intense concentration. He's a slow moving chameleon extracting a filing tool.

Their recent conversation was disappointing. Bob Lieberman had taken to staking out his office and ambushing him. He'd suddenly spring from a nook in the corridor as Malcolm walked toward his office.

"You can have the 49ers on Sunday. Give me eight points," Bob proposed.

Was this an attempt at appeasement? The official line was ten. Malcolm was suspicious.

"Why this generous offer?" Malcolm asked. "What do you want?"

"The spring grad seminar," Bob admitted.

"Have a topic?" Malcolm didn't want to know.

"The genius of Bob Dylan." Bob Lieberman offered a partial smile so small, it seemed purely conceptual. He looked feral and wizened and his skin was dull gray.

"Take it to the curriculum committee," Malcolm said. He reached his office and pulled the key from his pocket.

"You are the curriculum committee," Bob pointed out, following him.

"What did I say last time?" Malcolm was annoyed.

"I believe you said not in this life time or any other," Bob recalled.

"Correct," Malcolm replied, his key in the slot; he opened his office door. Bob Lieberman was still there. Then Malcolm shut and locked the door.

Bob Lieberman succumbed to a student, an older student, a returnee as they currently phrase it. He was exculpated by technicality. Malcolm considers Bob's behavior an ethical violation. His fall from grace occurred in broad daylight and slow motion. Bob Lieberman defiled his principles and vows. He ignored logic and loyalty and, in his defining moment, he didn't go down with his ship.

Bob divorced his wife, the daughter of a celebrated Israeli cellist for Christ's sake, and married a woman with a spawn of grandchildren from various sons and daughters, half-children, stepchildren and assorted offspring from implausible liaisons with adoption complications. Some children kept returning to the screened porch at sundown like hungry dogs, and after a year they were considered found.

Bob Lieberman stopped writing. He said he didn't feel the urge anymore. He was making furniture with his soon to be bride. He'd bought a pick-up to transport his pine benches and square squat tables to craft shows.

"I have no regrets. Make a novel. Make a bench." Bob shrugged.

His new wife draped herself in floral housedresses

resembling tents. Her grandsons in the army had phrases from Corinthians tattooed to their arms. The granddaughters were in jail or missing. She had given them the names of gems and intoxicants, as if intentionally scarring them from birth. Amethyst, Jade and Crystal. DUIs, possession with intent, and burglary were considered routine events. Then the multiplicity of in-laws with tawdry soap opera lives, passing around photographs of a half-child's grandson from three liaisons past. Hadn't Patricia in one of her Women's Club scholarship activities sponsored that returnee?

Naturally, there were repercussions. Bob Lieberman began teaching *Literature of Cinema*. His students viewed movies based on marginal novels and were encouraged to write one book critique a semester — down from the original six. Encouraged was the operative word. Not required. They weren't even middle school book reports. The latest crop of barely literate students was evidence of the College of Northern Pennsylvania's extreme bottom-feeding strategies.

Patricia assumed they would continue including Bob in their social activities — their dinner parties with the deans, barbecues for visiting scholars, the President's Tea, and their annual excursion to the theater in Philadelphia. It was surreal to envision Bob and his new bride at a flute recital, sitting on one of the white linen sofas in the President's living room, drinking beer directly from the bottle. The new President from Yale, no less. Not to mention his Wellesley wife.

"Things happen," Patty said. It was an assertion, and she didn't cushion it.

"Things don't happen to a disciplined man. That's the point. Discipline." Malcolm stared at her.

Was that complaint on her face, he wondered, that puffing around her mouth? His wife was losing her moral resolve as she was her skin tone. There were no gradations, only a universal softening. No one was responsible. That's the collective mantra. Everyone was damaged and inevitably must stall, collide, derail. Relapse was the consensual norm.

"People change. He wanted a family," Patricia offered, carefully. She was controlling herself.

"He has a family," Malcolm reminded her.

"Rachel lives in Tel Aviv. The boys are in yeshiva. Then they go in the army," Patricia replied.

In the monolithic void of political correctness, communication is labored and deliberately vague. Spontaneity and improvisation are no longer acceptable conversational implements. Awkward silence is preferred. Between predictable statements, there's a pause for the constant evaluation of potential areas of offense. Fear is the variable of state. We are losing our vocabulary, and our ability to differentiate, Malcolm thinks. We're losing our sense of obvious distinctions the way we're losing our collagen and flexibility.

"What should he do? Stitch a scarlet letter to his chest?" Patricia asked, her face a mask, her voice shrill.

"He should return his pension and resign," Malcolm replied. "He should carry bedpans in a UN refugee camp."

Malcolm McCarty vividly remembers Bob Lieberman in his previous incarnation. In that version, indelible as a recurring nightmare, Bob Lieberman was an impassioned artist in the midst of what would be a seven-year ordeal culminating with his second unpublished 689-page novel.

Bob's wife, Rachel, telephoned Patricia. She was hysterical, Patricia reported. Yes, again. Apparently Bob had moved into the barn, and no longer ate or slept. He was emaciated, naked and incoherent. Rachel was threatening to leave him. Patricia insisted he intervene.

Malcolm rode his bicycle slowly to the Lieberman house and considered the metastasizing situation. This wasn't his first rescue mission. Last year, he'd accompanied Bob to open mic readings in Scranton and Penn State. There was a winter blizzard on each occasion. Malcolm drove and Bob practiced reading his material out loud.

"I only get five minutes," Bob explained. "But all the bigshots will be there."

The venue proved to be a shabby basement room under a biker bar. Schedules for AA and NA support groups were tacked to the walls. **LIVE AND LET LIVE** and **ONE DAY AT A TIME** were nailed into the plaster and formed a continuous horizontal line at eye level, like a bar. The script was rendered in black block letters with curious curves suggesting South Pacific tattoos and something vaguely gothic. It was an insistent male hand and misguided, Malcolm thought, a shabby attempt to use repetition as a method to disguise a renegade nature. It was unconvincing.

The eight or nine attendees were talkative college students dressed entirely in black who looked like professional mourners. Their long fingernails were lacquered and resembled the backs of certain beetles. They chatted into gadgets and rarely glanced at the podium. Bob trembled as he read. He was inaudible.

An egg timer was set at the five-minute mark. Bob was startled and confused when it rang. He'd only read two pages, badly and much too fast. He glared at the bell like it was a guillotine.

There was punch in plastic cups and a paper plate of stale crackers. The bigshot, an undergrad in a black hoody who'd published an underground journal called *Scranton Scribes*, said, "Terrific words, man."

Bob executed an abstract bow and hunched further into

himself. He leaned close to Malcolm and whispered, "I need my eyeglasses next time."

On the way back, the highway was almost impassable. There was only the black of the ice covering the road and the deeper black of the dark.

"Writing is a criminal act. Artists employ the methods of professional criminals. We have the same repertoire." Bob began. He was earnest and attempting to be reasonable. "We trespass, break and enter, burglarize and rob. We assume aliases and engage in fraud. We lie, omit and impersonate. We collect family history for the purpose of unmasking them. The only reason we talk to anyone is to practice dialogue. Tell me that's not true," he looked at Malcolm.

"Autobiography is traditional," Malcolm observed.

"We call these entities composite characters. Bull shit. We're arsonists and assassins. We lure and trap. We're mercenaries. We violate and desecrate. We autopsy the living, and exhume the dead for interrogation. Then we deny everything," Bob concluded.

"Original and well-stated," Malcolm managed. This was not the first time Bob Lieberman had articulated his theory of the artist as outlaw. Malcolm was gripping the steering wheel and he couldn't see the painted lanes on the highway.

"Artists invented home invasions," Bob posited. "We've been doing it for millennia. Some confections demand intrigue and a clarity possible only by obsession. To master the page is to know origami. We are the shifting tectonic plates. We are the calamitous disruption that causes seismic ruptures."

Bob Lieberman tended to speak sporadically. When he broke the surface, like a diseased whale about to beach himself, his words came in a rush, energetic, wind-charged and inflamed. He favored improvisational epiphanies and driving loosened him up. It was unfortunate. Bob's literary theories were painful. But his rhapsodic descriptions of the creative process were tortuous.

"A poem is like a one-night stand, unexpected and exotic. It happens in Katmandu or Vienna, or on a train or ship. Objects and gestures are heightened and indelible as they happen. Exaggerations demand and receive permanence. Are you following me?" Bob asked.

"Absolutely." Malcolm was enthusiastic.

"A poem is neurosurgery. It's a blood sacrifice. You amputate your limbs with a dull penknife and no anesthetic. That may bring you a single stanza. Maybe." Bob paused, presumably to allow Malcolm to fully comprehend his concept.

Malcolm couldn't distinguish a separation between the ground and sky. The pavement was glistening, glazed and scaly like crocodile hide.

"Anyone can write a poem," Bob unexpectedly said, contradicting and negating himself. "I prefer the short story. It's like a love affair that distills and sanctifies."

Malcolm steeled himself as Bob described the russet fluttering of October dusk. Maples were citadels of light and nothing was peripheral.

"On the other hand, a novel is a marriage." Bob hesitated. "It can consume and gut a lifetime."

Malcolm McCarty agreed.

"No one is born a novelist. The deformations of the personality necessary to achieve the artist's altitudes are not intuitive. The sacrifice and solitude. You must make yourself a fertile wilderness before you can be a breeding ground," Bob clarified. His tone suggested confession.

"I see," Malcolm tried.

Bob Lieberman laughed. He was on the edge of hysteria. "You can't possibly understand," he immediately replied. "You're just an academic."

"Right you are," Malcolm agreed. Then he skidded off the road into a long shallow ditch, barely missing a frozen maple tree. Snow was up to his thighs as he examined the damage. The fender was bent nearly in half. It would have to be replaced.

Malcolm took two shovels from the trunk. He handed one to Bob and began digging.

Bob Lieberman leaned against his shovel and directed his words to the dark. "I know the moth kiss of the page that both denounces and saves. I've had a spiritual intercession. It's remarkable, incalculable. I know what resides in the vast aubergine corridors of fall. That's where our bridges and mirrors are, our biographies, diaries and footnotes. That's where our real selves are, in the aubergine corridors where streetlights suffocate the night."

Bob described his transformation while Malcolm dug the car out of the ditch. Artists cast shadows that have nothing to do with their bodies. Bob admitted he was merely an apprentice. When he's an adept, levitation and spontaneous combustion will be unremarkable frequent occurrences. Artists are clairvoyant and instinctively know procedures for invisibility and seduction. One must avoid the debris of the ordinary to be purified by solitude. Bob's neurons twisted as lines and paragraphs deposited themselves on the page like shells seaswells swept onto sand. Channels beneath his flesh ignited. He was beginning to cast spells and translate languages he didn't know. He was aware of the risks, the toxins and ancient fevers and plagues he exposed himself to. Artists accommodate lethal agents and come to crave them.

"We are the absolution we see," Bob concluded. He handed Malcolm the shovel, sat back in the car, and let Malcolm drive him home.

Later, Malcolm drove Bob to an open mic night at Penn State. Bob claimed he was having an anxiety attack. He took two tranquilizers and changed his outfit several times in front of a mirror. He finally selected his stylish Barney's black gabardine funeral suit, a black shirt and black tie.

It took five hours and the highway was closed, roads barricaded and wind brutal. They climbed stairs and walked the corridors of two buildings before finally locating the basement room. **SNOWED OUT** was taped to the door and the door was locked. Bob turned the handle anyway and threw his shoulder against it. Then he cursed for an hour.

Malcolm was forced to stop in Maple Corner's. Two trucks had collided, several cars were involved, and the vehicles were surrounded by police cars, fire trucks, and ambulances with flashing red lights. It was an updated version of the protective circle wagon trains used. Paramedics passed with stretchers and gurneys.

Malcolm managed to maneuver to the shoulder and navigate into the parking lot of a closed coffee shop. They'd probably be there all night.

Bob was sullen and agitated. Malcolm wanted to turn on the radio but feared Bob would call it polluting noise and cause an argument. Then he noticed Bob was leaning against the car door, sleeping, his inaudible pages between his fingers.

The landscape reminded him of a black-on-black Rothko painting from the mid-60s. But it lacked the nuances and sense of luminous immanent tragedy. It didn't even have the promise of suicide. Malcolm fell asleep, rehearsing his speech for in court when he sued Bob Lieberman for the twisted fender.

Malcolm slowly pedaled to the Lieberman house, leaned his bicycle against a side gate, and walked directly to the barn. He was resolved. He pounded his fist against the raw wood. Then he knocked again.

Bob Lieberman opened the door half an inch. A khaki wool blanket was draped across his shoulders, but he was, in fact, naked.

"Did I wake you?" Malcolm inquired, casually.

Bob Lieberman squinted in the sunlight, glanced behind Malcolm as if he expected more and worse, and edged back into the barn. He was furtive and already retreating. He resembled a small mammal — a harp seal or otter — sensing capture.

"I don't sleep." Bob was offended. Clearly, sleep was too trivial a state for an artist.

He motioned Malcolm into the barn with two stiff fingers. It was a reluctant invitation. Malcolm glanced at his living quarters. Bob had painted the barn wood black. The room was Spartan. Malcolm noticed a desk with a small lamp, his Smith Corona typewriter, and a metal folding chair. A sleeping bag was on the ground. Papers in the shape of fists and plates of decayed food were scattered randomly across the ground.

"I can't talk now," Bob said. "I'm working. Obviously, this novel should be written in Africa."

"Making progress on the void?" he ventured, cheerfully. Bob's novel was set in the void of a century that could be the past or future.

"There is no void. That's the point of my novel. The void is festooned with orphans, runaways, and skeletons of drowned babies." Bob was angry.

There was no obvious place to sit. Malcolm leaned against the barn wall and realized the barn wasn't entirely empty. Photographs of goats, elephants and zebras were tacked to the wood walls. Bob had constructed a sort of altar with crates and burlap, and random objects were placed on the top — two oranges, glossy opera programs and a red hawk feather. Perhaps they were offerings.

His desk was cluttered with assorted items — a bud vase

with a bouquet of calligraphy pens and sharpened pencils, a magnifying glass, sequins in a glass bottle and a crystal candy dish with fragments of debris that might be gravel or seashells. A cocktail glass was filled with erasers and paper clips and surrounded by dozens of thumb-sized bottles of white correction fluid and extra typewriter ribbons.

Reams of blank paper and a box of black and white magazine photographs were under the desk — children alongside railroads who looked abandoned, high-rise apartment buildings with balconies where sheets and T-shirts hung drying on ropes strung across an alley in a favela, and city plazas with cathedrals and pigeons on smooth gray stones seemed familiar.

The wall beside his sleeping bag was decorated with photographs of elephants and savannah sunsets. Bob had apparently attached squat candles to a pine branch and hammered it into the wall. A rusty iron cowbell, two marimbas, gourds and a tambourine were near his sleeping bag. Bob was still inhabiting his poet as shaman persona.

"Are you engaged in voodoo?" Malcolm decided to ask. "What are these objects?"

"Talismans. I'm a method writer. I told you, this book should be written in Tanzania. I'm compromising and it's dangerous," Bob said.

"Sure," Malcolm replied. "It's a slippery slope."

Maybe the barn was an attempt to represent the pre-verbal Paleolithic cul-de-sac of Bob's void. His faux escapement was designed to evoke a primitive era. Fire was a recent invention, and cave painting, glyphs, prayer and barter didn't yet exist. There were no permanent myths, but only transitory seasonal entities with inconsistent affections and powers.

Bob's protagonist was two-foot-high and clawed. Zubo, Master of Meteors, invented flight and wildfires. He carried an acetylene blowtorch, and rode on four-humped camels and the backs of disabled satellites and deserted space stations. His hobby was scorching cities. His consort, Zima, ruled rivers and inland seas, and derived pleasure from drowning children. She lured them and wrapped them in strands of red kelp. Strangled children washed up on shore, drained and weightless. At nightfall, the tribe gathered their dead daughters and sons and praised their generous gods.

"They're hundreds of mutations and thousands of generations from triangular arrowheads. They don't even have fishing nets and drums," Bob had clarified.

His novel's scientific premises were fallacious. Bob was a technical illiterate and absolutely ignorant of the principles of basic physics and anthropology. His fundamental concepts were irredeemably offensive, ridiculous and unpublishable.

"Do you believe words clarify and redeem? Treaties and vows? Alliances? The Geneva Convention? Covenants and promises," Bob abruptly asked.

"Yes, Bob. I certainly do," Malcolm replied.

"Words are tadpoles and microscopic worms. They're eons from vocal chords, grammar and vocabularies. The growls of hyenas are superior. Hyenas come in after the jackals and before the kites. Autumn brings wolves in packs of forty. They're hungry." Bob shuddered. His eyes were unfocussed and mottled with a filmy residue like storm clouds. He should definitely be checked for glaucoma.

Bob Lieberman took off his eyeglasses. When he was intensely passionate, he often removed his glasses. When he assumed the guise of an artist, and fueled from within, the external world was a foul and unnecessary distraction. On several occasions, Malcolm had seen Bob pull off his glasses with a wild, awkward flourish, toss them to the floor and step on them.

"I'm not sure anymore. Syllables are ashy pebbles escaping from some hole in your face. They're transient and insubstantial, peripheral and irrelevant." Bob paused and evaluated the elephant pictures. "They're how to fill rooms with ghosts."

Bob was his closest colleague and, as department chair, he was responsible. Malcolm leaned against the barn wood and sorted through his options.

"Do you know what's at the end of the universe?" Bob asked.

"No," Malcolm said. "I do not."

Bob Lieberman told him the universe was immensely vast but ultimately finite. There's a river at the end, sliding slow and dense with chunks of gray agate behind the obscure insult of smoke. The last bend of the river unexpectedly ends and there's a final colossal but graceful trestle, above ridges of sweet William, Geraniums and ferns. Spring is bold and unrepentant and scented with terror.

"We're always crossing bridges, losing our wallets and waiting for planes. We pretend we know where we're going. We attend to our watches, springing forward and falling back. We're aching for lamplight, a pier, an alley or mooring we recognize. We all need a cot for the night." Bob's voice was soft.

They considered the end of the universe in silence.

"Your wife stole Rachel's gold compact and tennis bracelet," Bob told him. "She takes things whenever she visits."

"I'll look into that," Malcolm offered.

"Rachel said she's a kleptomaniac," Bob Lieberman revealed.

Malcolm nodded his head.

"Something's stirring in the electronic soup. An emerging patois that isn't codified. We don't know its morphology or sensibility," Bob observed. "Or what it wants. Don't assume progress is benign. I'll tell you this. It's birthing itself and it's savage."

"I'm following you," Malcolm said.

Bob Lieberman suddenly leapt from one foot to the other.

"When I merge with my persona, I'll birth royal lepers," he announced.

Malcolm looked at his watch. "Time to get dressed," he decided. "There's a new open mic on campus. Got your car keys? OK, let's take a short drive."

Bob Lieberman immediately acquiesced. He clapped his hands and spun around several times in a circle. Professor Malcolm McCarty found a towel on the floor and wrapped it around his waist. Then he drove Bob Lieberman, barefoot and hallucinating, to the Briar State Hospital. They held him in a locked ward for 30 days.

It was never right between them again.

After tea and before dinner, Malcolm McCarty typically spends forty-five minutes on his stair stepper. He listens to the NPR feed from Pittsburgh when the wind is right. He used to find *All Things Considered* entertaining. Then he realized all things were not considered. Or perhaps all things were considered in all the same ways. He suspects topics are selected alphabetically. Farming in Finland and France. Faulkner. Fire fighters. Freud. Futurism.

"Isn't there personal evolution?" Patty demanded. She had followed him to his study. She's still talking about Bob Lieberman. "Do you accept that possibility?"

"I accept entropy and the effort to battle it," Malcolm answered, no longer engaged.

"Let's not even go there," Patricia said to his back. She slammed the door shut.

This is a slogan she repeats with regularity. *Let's not even go there.* His students also say this. It's a global idiom. Verbal contagions suddenly appear. A TV celebrity utters a colloquialism and it becomes the coin of the realm.

Certain moments loiter in the dusk and do not dissipate. That awkward conjunction when he failed to recognize Bob Lieberman is one of a series of misidentifications. He had a similar experience at a conference in China three or four years ago.

Malcolm McCarty was in the hotel restaurant, weighing the nuances of the menu, the possibilities of twice-rinsed bird nest soup, sea moss and eel with river fish, snake and infant pigeon. A woman sat next to him. Her tangy metallic perfume was an unexpected intrusion and he recoiled. The scent permeated her skin. He thought of rancid cooking oil rising from woks in hundreds of millions of muddy alleys. Her overly painted mouth was the red of a degraded calligraphy rendered in that so-called Shanghai coast prosperity. The encrusted lips parted and he was startled to hear Patty's voice.

Patricia's hair had been darkened in the hotel salon and festooned with pearls. They protruded from her skull on shiny black sticks. She wore an inordinately red silk dragon scarf around her neck. An odd whitish powder was lacquered into the crow's feet around her eyes. It reminded him of lime in gullies and trenches and uncountable pots of spoiled broccoli and spinach. He considered the pollution of the Yangtze and Yellow River under a moon the Han have charted for six thousand years. He managed to say, "Good evening, dear. Come to me, my dragon lady." He bowed and kissed her hand.

They had just returned from a two-day journey on the Perfume River. A fiercely painted red and yellow barge in the shape of a dragon had taken them to a village in the mountains. It was puerile and redundant but they remained moderately festive. In the town square, vendors with crutches offered counterfeit cashmere shawls and enormous pear-shaped melons with dagger-like spikes were sold from a 70-year-old flatbed army truck. The neon was graceful; pinks lingered on the water like lotus blossoms. Translation was possible, he decided, but it's drained, anemic and ghosted. The difficult was discarded and the ambiguous omitted. Simplification was the global standard. We can cross the great fluid expanses but there's a price.

After wars and cholera, plagues and harvests and string quartets, we arrive at our penultimate destination. In between, we manage to recognize our wives. We smile, take their hands, noting that their fingernails are painted like a butcher's. We tell them they look like a warlord's concubine. We remember we are returned from the sea. We have cheated death again.

In mid-morning few vehicles are on the approach to campus and there are no pedestrians or bicycles. Professor McCarty has the reputation of being both the first and last man on the road. It's said you can use him as a calendar. His daily bike rides begin in March and continue until Thanksgiving regardless of storms and wind chill. Weather is an insignificant external phenomenon like fashion, like the long hair, strident turquoise jewelry and buckskin-fringed jackets of his graduate years.

Now the exaggerated baggy pants and body piercings of his current students. They dye blue and magenta streaks in their hair that accentuates their absurdly white skin. Apparently the take-home message of the millennium is to avoid the sun. This they can do, hoops sprouting through their noses and eyebrows. They take buses to Erie to have bolts driven into their tongues. Their faces often swell and require antibiotics. They crucify their mouths as if intuiting they have nothing to say. They veer toward silence and shade and concentrate on the gadgets in their palms. They're albino zeroes.

Recognizing the universe mathematically is an ability Malcolm was born with. It's precisely these instincts one must nourish and protect. It's a curious paradox. In the service of authenticity one is labeled recalcitrant and eccentric.

Professor McCarty earned his undergraduate degree in physics. Then he realized the divisions of most unusual derivation came not from numbers but syllables. They were orders of magnitude more unpredictable and dangerous. The ferocious recklessness of a pen and mouth deserved the astonishment awarded delinquent asteroids. No celestial body compared to the delirious, high-wire, no-net orbits of a poet. By then, he'd discovered Keats, Byron and Shelly.

In the Allegheny Mountains of northwest Pennsylvania, April is still winter and ice smells of a permanent absence without the impulse of invention or revision. The air is odorless and bleached. It's what a terminal man dreams when all sensation is removed. There are no lavender Crocuses pushing up from snow, no Tulip necks or frail Hyacinths. No daughter arranges snow flowers in a basket. There are no flowers or daughters or baskets. There's only the cut of cold. In the end as in the beginning, the knife. And the curriculum committee thought the Elizabethan Period was irrelevant.

Patricia McCarty watches Malcolm ride confidentially down Maple Ridge Road. The day is Attica gray with a texture suggesting metal, bad food, child abuse and felonies.

In the Allegheny foothills where Pennsylvania becomes New York State, they call the border Penntucky. Here the erasure of possibility has the sheen of aluminum shedding, losing its edges and purpose, elegance and nerve. Surfaces are like ditch-water in night rain where you can't see your face. Corroded swingsets tilt above punctured tires, cars rust in backyards and the daughters don't return. The boys come back between tours in Iraq and prison. They're bums with palms outstretched for money.

There's an ashy arithmetic to explain this geography and

how it creates its own self-perpetuating stain. Thirty-five-year-old women have emphysema, can't comprehend email, and spend $500 a month on satellite TV. They leave their babies in the same diapers for weeks.

"Why do they do that?" Malcolm wondered.

"They like to hear them cry," Patricia replied.

"And the TV bills?" he asked.

"What should they be doing?" Patricia demanded, angry and defensive. "Prepping for their MCATS? Their bar exam?"

Malcolm thinks character is constructed from consistent decisions. And the women of the hollows and trailer parks deliberately make malevolent choices. He is completely wrong. Volition is not a component. Their circumstances are an inevitability within the system itself. Is there a hierarchy of ignorance? Is the inability to evolve aesthetics criminal? Is it a sin or a felony? What is their punishment? Imprisonment? The stake?

Malcolm is accustomed to pronouncing judgment from his elevated perch. Of course everything he touched responded. He planted their garden, along with the garden each successive college president's wife held the Spring Tea in, along with the Trustee Luncheon, and the barbecue for the rare stray Pulitzer novelist. Malcolm tracked the sunlight effortlessly, laying out the first plots, digging holes for Lilac trees and Ornamental Plums. Malcolm made vegetables appear. With a roll of twine and two consecutive Sundays, he planted seeds for tomatoes, peppers, corn, carrots, and pumpkins. He supplied some offhand, barely conceived weekend formula and solved the problem. Abracadabra.

The following spring, he built the gazebo and granite fountain. He filled the car with stones from the Genesee River. He cut and pruned. Later, he added on the sunroom and restored the fireplaces.

"How do you know all this?" she wondered.

"I was an Eagle Scout," he replied. He spread his lips into a sort of smile. When he laughed, it was curiously without sound. He produced a sort of translation from where he really lived. It was distorted by distance and impossibilities and his face stalled in a ghastly mime, as if he had palsy.

Patricia had three brothers but she was the one they called professor. Adjunct as it turned out, despite Malcolm's efforts. Adjunct. Without the office or letterhead, prestige or pension.

They could have retired to Florida. Malcolm had almost agreed. There was a moment, a window they call it now, and then the window closed. The door shut. The entire room was erased.

It was after the unfortunate business with Bob Lieberman and his sordid divorce. Then his lurid remarriage in the disco lounge of Flint & Bow Indian casino.

"How did he meet her?" Malcolm was driving home.

"She was a server in the cafeteria," Patricia said.

"They bonded over Jell-O?" he asked.

Patricia looked at him. "What do you really think?"

Malcolm didn't hesitate. "He should commit seppuku."

Malcolm doesn't realize that personal catastrophes strike the distinguished and the negligible. Honor is not a factor. Some devastations aren't reported on the evening news. That's why she avoids headlines. What's important are the back pages, the obituaries in small print and the corrections in pale gray.

Celestial aberrations can assault you as you bend to adjust a lamp. Uncharted comets leave trails of dust like shed feathers. Some phenomena can't be described on a chalkboard. Conventional symbols are inadequate. They're not like the fundamental significance of triangles or how to manufacture machine guns. Everyone comprehends the principles of the obvious.

In Allegheny Hills, it's said things come easily to Professor

McCarty. His first interview provided an immediate position. Provost Kruger, with his chapped lips and shredding in pieces like tiny fish scales, was making what would be his final appointment.

"I want you to stay," the Provost revealed. "It's personal."

"Well, of course I'll stay," Malcolm replied. It was an unusually warm May. Maples budded on hills in patterns of red nubs like fallen constellations. It was a forest of kissed mouths north and south for three hundred miles.

"Winter is difficult. Locals are a fifth generation underclass and profoundly mean. No employment since the oil wells. We don't have a movie theater. There's no restaurant." Provost Kruger paused. "But, for the self-contained man."

"Yes, of course," Malcolm said immediately, though it went without saying.

Patricia was in her back-to-the-land phase. They brought the retiring engineering dean's house on Maple Ridge Road. That summer, Mac constructed a gazebo in the meadow. Patricia was twenty-four and wore long gingham print skirts that weeds and grasses stained. Not stained, but rather embossed with a pale green filigree.

Malcolm painted the gazebo white. He built two benches by the stream and scattered wildflower seeds. But it was Patty's garden. Patty, barefoot, carried baskets of tomatoes individually wrapped in newspaper like swathed infants.

The house was encircled by a hundred-year-old apple orchard, most of them twisted and feral. Late spring was honey yellow. The afternoon air contained something ancient, with complicated properties like grainy amber and the barely detectable imprint of wings.

In mid-summer, the ring of apple trees was a gold circle promising everything. The sweetness of inflamed, seductive yellows gave him a sort of vertigo. He looked at Patricia and thought, *This is a yellow I'd go to hell for, sin for, lie for and marry*. It's what he imagined late summer afternoons could be, subtle and refined like rarities in antique shops. The air was a vagrant intoxicating dust.

There was a particular moment Malcolm uses as a reference point. It was an August afternoon in a sudden warm rain. He was watching Patty kneeling on the ground. Afternoon was glazed and fragrant, intricate as a gold locket in which you engrave the names of your daughters. Patty was moistened like a European movie star shot through a Vaseline lens. He realized it could be Thursday in England or Italy. In rain all landscapes are vulnerable and slow. Rain renders history manageable. Events are compressed to the size of a canvas or a door.

And Patty became all women who walk chestnut lined boulevards and city parks. She was a synthesis of all women eating oranges imported from Portugal who sit in meadows beside statues of composers, princes and poets.

Hummingbirds came — so many the air churned with propellers and tiny buzz saws. Cardinals and enormous iridescent blue jays resembling dwarf peacocks appeared. He was professor of the air and he conducted the elements.

He meant to say birds churned the air, but instead he wrote *churched* in his journal. And hadn't they been, if not happy, some version so close as to be nearly identical?

Patricia McCarty remembers that particular summer as a relentless fragrant ache. Its extravagance, its garlands of gold-hued embellishments flaunted themselves and made her dizzy. Possibilities for both absolution and ravishment rose on their own accord. Her body was awkward and shuttered. She was a fever of mutually exclusive impulses. She had found her own inland sea. She knew herself as a solitary, but she was afraid to be alone. The mewling of red fox woke her and the autumn moon was an unadulterated silver that burned.

That summer she was pregnant. She didn't tell her husband. In early autumn, she took a bus to Pittsburgh alone and aborted it.

Patricia recognized her urge to escape and disappear. There must be schematics with details of the necessary phrases and gestures, and anecdotal accounts and stories in small print at the end of newspapers. She suspected it was a process. Each year, at CON PA or a neighboring college, St. Joseph's, Allegheny Tech or even Penn State, a young woman inexplicably vanished during spring or Christmas break.

Lydia Kepler, 21, an attractive brunette from Baltimore, went to the campus library and inexplicably vanished. She was a nursing student with a graduate school fiancée and an affection for cats. She was on the tennis team and twice weekly volunteered at the animal shelter. She had no record of delinquent or promiscuous behaviors.

Denise Kaplan, 19, went to the Pittsburgh Macy's to purchase winter boots and didn't exit the building. Her boyfriend, Ricky, was waiting for her in his car. He waited until the store closed and then called the police. Her sorority sisters were shocked and her desperate parents posted a reward for information. Denise, a popular sophomore, was a member of the chorus and the Sierra Club. She was an avid skier. The Pittsburgh police were "mystified."

Ruby Marie Johnson, 22, a senior pre-med student from Philadelphia, was last seen walking to her part-time job at Brenda's Bakery. She was the oldest of six siblings and an honor student with a full scholarship. She planned to work with disabled children in the inner city. She tutored biology students, and had the role of Miss Hannigan in the campus Theater Arts Society's production of *Annie*. The production was cancelled and detectives described her disappearance as "disturbing and inexplicable."

Patricia wondered where the lost women were. Perhaps they were under the ground, speaking in a language with fluid syllables of rain and creeks and damp chimes. It was a local dialect of tinny trinkets and rumors. It was said there was an ocean to the east, vast, implausible gray, pre-human and incontrovertible. The vanished women don't believe this. They can select their beliefs and devise their own hierarchies of necessity. They're a-historical and immune.

Patricia kept a scrapbook of stories about missing women. She also collected obituaries of the murdered ones. When her scrapbook was full, she threw it into the Genesee near Hamilton Bridge.

Patricia wasn't convinced that all the unaccounted for women were kidnapped or trafficked runaways. They weren't abducted by extraterrestrials. They didn't have amnesia. Some women chose absence, and Patricia suspected shedding an identity was liberating.

That fall she makes an appointment with the psychologist in Wood's End. Dr. Hernandez has a suspicious reputation including allegations of statutory rape and numerous suspensions. But he's the only psychologist in the county. Dr. Greg Hernandez is a handsome man, forty, with an auburn beard and striking sea-blue eyes that don't quite focus. He wears dark tinted glasses and chainsmokes.

"I want a divorce," Patricia begins. It's the first sentence she speaks.

"Do you have sole and separate assets?" he asks, reaching for his lighter. "Bank accounts and credit cards in your name only?"

She shakes her head no.

"How will you buy a plane ticket? Or hire a lawyer in

Philadelphia? What are your skills? How will you earn a living? Can you type and use computers?" Dr. Hernandez inquires. "And where will you go?"

Patricia stares at him. Then she looks down and examines her shoes.

"Has your husband physically abused you?" he asks. "Broke a bone? Sent you to ER?"

Patricia shakes her head no.

"Does Professor McCarty hurt you?" the psychologist tries.

It's a simplified version of his previous question. He thinks she is stupid. Patricia is tempted to explain that the mere existence of her husband is intolerable. She doesn't.

Then Dr. Hernandez asks insipid questions from a notebook. Where and when was she born? She names the month of her birth; he smiles, encouragingly.

"I'm winter born, too," he tells her.

Does she have siblings? What are their names and occupations? Is she a conservative or progressive? What's her opinion of politicians and capital punishment? Does she go to church and vote? Does she have a pet? A hobby? A child? Insomnia, nightmares, and eating disorders? Does she believe in damnation and redemption?

Is he proselyting? Is he taking a poll? Is he a census taker? Will he recommend her for jury duty? His questions are designed to induce sleep. She realizes he's trying to hypnotize her. Patricia considers leaving the office, going home and getting in bed. He's just another passing snake oil salesman and she has all the right answers. Still, one must veer on the side of caution. Diminutives and mediocrities can stumble on a rare inspired intuition. It can happen by accident.

Dr. Hernandez holds a pen, makes a brief notation in a notebook, and offers her another smile. Patricia notices his teeth are white and even. He enjoys showing them off.

"When were you last arrested?" he asks, looking at his pen.

"Arrested?" Patricia repeats. She laughs. She has good teeth, too. "Why ask me such a question?"

"You look guilty," Dr. Hernandez replies. "Tell me about your lover."

Patricia is startled. "You think I'm unfaithful?"

"It's possible," he says.

"I've been married nineteen years," Patricia informs him.

"But not successfully. You want a divorce," Dr. Hernandez reminds her.

"Yes," Patricia replies. "I do."

"Why are you angry?" the psychologist wonders.

"I'm not angry," Patricia replies. She feels completely composed.

"I think you're hostile," the psychologist decides.

They sit in silence. The leather on her last pair of black high heels is worn and shabby. She needs to go to Pittsburgh and buy a new pair. If she lived in Florida, she wouldn't have to bother with boots and the cedar winter closet with its stacks of gray cashmere sweaters, down jackets, scarves and gloves and all the tedious rest. She'd just wear sandals.

"I suspect you have a secret," Dr. Hernandez says. "Tell me. You'll feel better."

Patricia assesses the condition of her shoes. She'll replace this pair and buy another and then red stiletto heels.

He stands up abruptly and walks from his desk toward her. He takes long aggressive strides and positions himself above her. "What's your other name?" he suddenly demands, his voice raised, forceful and direct.

"Other name?" Patricia repeats. She's completely alert.

"Who else lives inside you?" he persists.

"I beg your pardon," Patricia says.

She watches Dr. Hernandez retreat. He reaches for his

gold lighter and lights another cigarette. He needs to conceal himself with smoke. He's an amateur.

"Why does your husband laugh without sound?" Dr. Hernandez wonders.

Patricia shrugs. She finds it impossible to form a sentence.

"Don't you find it curious?" Dr. Hernandez persists.

Patricia says no. Out the window, roadside cemeteries of corn stalks and piled husks are littered. *In the Allegeny mountains we navigate by tombs*, she thinks.

"Maybe somebody punched him in the mouth," the psychologist suggests. "You might think about that. We'll explore that next week."

She agrees and thanks him. On the highway, she considers the legions of untraceable women, solitary in towers of light, in stucco and in brick tenements, in trailers and farmhouses. Soon autumn will turn tawdry. Then the freefall vertigo of winter dusk. Perhaps the discarded were hiding in shoulder high grasses and Russian Thistle. They're taking the pulse of thunder and memorizing varieties of grey — antique pewter, tin, pebbles beneath a rot of fog, and the sly silver of a bread knife. The women recite the incarnations of erasure in six languages. No one knows what the men do and no one cares.

When Patricia approaches Maple Ridge Road she stops the car. *Other name*, she thinks. She allows herself to laugh out loud. What a fuckhead. She rips Dr. Greg Hernandez's appointment card into pieces and throws them out the car window.

One winter, when blizzards were virulent, car crashes epidemic, and the college suspended classes, Malcolm taught himself Mandarin. On journeys to conferences in China, he engaged in constant conversations with colleagues, waitresses and taxi drivers. Malcolm asks bartenders where they were born and if their fathers farm with water buffalo. Mac's at his best with strangers he won't encounter again. Professor McCarty, the part-time landscaper and ethnographer.

Patricia finds herself drawn to calligraphy. She has a desire, small as a shiver, to write in an Oriental script composed of symbols telling stories of ruined fortresses and crossing bodies of water. They're creation myths that explain how the universe began and why it continues. If she had special pens, ink sticks and an apprenticeship in brush strokes, she might know the answer. She could have scrolls made from rare woven fibers and moth wings, and the core would be comprehensible.

Patricia thinks everything in Chinese sounds brutal and enraged. It's all harsh threats and hoarse insults. Malcolm asks a janitor to describe his childhood and if he'll be able to find a wife. She wanders museums alone, devising her own idiosyncratic translations. They're not literal but rather inspirations. It's nothing she would soil a paper with or dare spoil the air with her mouth, not even if she whispered.

She runs her hands across the archetypal hieroglyphics etched into three-thousand-year-old stones. They're the original Braille, she decides, and closes her eyes. Some knowledge can only be transmitted tactically. Patricia only memorized a few characters — *woman and man, big, market, heaven, sea, fish and baby.* It was enough.

She prefers hieroglyphics to calligraphy. Characters resemble fishhooks and litters for concubines. Bent trees struck by monsoon lightning recur in a rash like seasons. She recognizes elephants and canoes, and a woman in a typhoon.

Hieroglyphics are more primitive and comprehensible. Their narratives are urgent. They're the headlines of history. They're like fossils in amber.

"You have theaters between your fingers," Malcolm

observes. It's the tone he employs for undergraduates. He must be preparing for his office hours. And he means he's given her this, defined the perimeter and secured the borders. Constellations rise from the ground and vast star systems replicate themselves on the sides of rocks. Self-contained men and women recognize and appreciate this.

"Yes, of course," Patricia replies, prepared to kneel in dirt. In truth, she thinks gardening is boring and back-breaking. Today is bolts of steel or a river of washed rags. Malcolm says she should prepare beds for Tulips and Daffodils.

She could put on her jacket now and walk through mud and patches of ice into the forest of striped trees, curiously nude and obscene. The self-contained know miniature cities float where you stand and villages lit by votive and prayers grow under your watering can. Patricia stands at her front door. Then she realizes she doesn't want to go there.

Malcolm McCarty is in his office, examining a hundred-year-old book he chanced to find at a rummage sale. The book is leather-bound and surprisingly heavy. The pages are composed of a paper not currently in use. The cover is engraved with the names of the author's family in gold letters. His children and siblings and their occupations and locations are also listed. In this aspect, the book of another century possessed the qualities of a family bible. There was nothing disposable about it.

Malcolm McCarty planned to bring it to his senior seminar, to pass the book around the room and encourage his students to respond. Yes, touch it, feel the ebb and flow of the hand-set typeface. Books have oceans inside them, yes.

The content is unremarkable. But he wanted to show his students that books were once designed to endure like artifacts

— an ivory inlaid table, a grandfather clock or gold charm meant to be worn at the throat. In the previous century, a book was an heirloom.

Now he realizes his students would be indifferent. They prefer books bound with glue that dissolves and composite paper of inferior substances that yellow and shred. A writer can anticipate outliving his books; he had planned to note this and pause, allowing his senior seminar to consider the implications, the irony and tragedy.

His students don't expect books to alter the orbit of worlds or be memorized. They don't believe a book can change a single molecule of their lives or give them one second thought. The shoddy construction of modern books asserts they're of the moment and don't need glass cases for protection. They aren't distillations of personality or character in the monumental chaos of unforeseen events and complex ambiguous circumstances. They won't be reread or gifted to children. In fact, his students donate or discard them. They leave them on beaches and in airport terminals. They toss them in trash cans. His students share an aversion for trash and they're careful not to litter.

It's the first tentative knocking on the door of his official office hour's morning. Professor Malcolm McCarty glances at the door. He relishes the ritual of this, the sound of a hand against wood, uncertain but determined. It's a gesture ancient as fertility dances, bare feet on mud under a full moon, and men drumming. He knows his assigned part, walks to the door and stops. It's the arrested moment of expectation before the grotesque tedium of student indifference and obfuscation. This pause is like a signature in pencil on a lithograph or a single voice reciting on stage. It's an intimacy that demands obedience and complicity. As he opens the door, he senses spring in the ice under Hadley Hall, differentiating and assembling itself.

"It's Cindy Carlson. Candy's sister," the stranger says. She calls herself *it*. "You know. C.C.," it says.

"Yes?" Malcolm feels an imminent irritation.

He knows C.C. She's one of the middle-aged locals they've rounded-up to enroll. She's what they term a returnee. C.C is fifty-one and working on an undergraduate English degree. She's been a sophomore for three years. They choose English because they suffer from the delusion that they speak the language. They believe it's easier than that compendium of border wars called history. Or the math you need a protractor for. That's called geometry. But they can read headlines in scandal sheets, recipes and satellite TV schedules. They assume Conrad and Melville will be similar. Words. More words. Many pages of words.

Obviously, C.C. sent her sister to deliver the inevitable excuse. She's been in a car crash. A limb was unexpectedly amputated. Thieves stole her purse at gunpoint. As fate would have it, her final exam was in it. Or one of her wayward spawn is in an institution and the police, social workers and doctors have mandated her presence.

"She can't come no more." The woman takes a breath. "She got the pneumonia. Got put in the hospital."

Malcolm McCarty must adjust his vision to clarify this current generation. He sorts through piercings and tattoos, noting how white they all are, the boys tall and the girls soft and heavy. They have pale skin like porcelain that accentuates their vicious out-breakings of acne. They wear the universal uniform of blue jeans and bulky navy sweatshirts with attached hoods concealing much of their faces.

"I'm sorry," Malcolm McCarty says. He leaves the office door wide open.

His secretary glances up from the computer she doesn't know how to use. He spent six hundred dollars of his dwindling

Visiting Lecturer funds to enroll this perpetual sophomore English major in computer classes and she can't put headers on documents. Cut and paste is a dangerous wilderness she won't enter. It's her version of Hawthorne's dark forest.

"Sit down." Malcolm indicates the one chair in front of his desk. "Please."

He remembers Candy Carlson. C.C. lives in Harmony Hollow. It's six miles from campus as the crow flies. And that's the one thing that does fly in Allegheny Hills.

He'd been there once before at the request of the enrollment committee and Women's Club. Patricia had repeatedly requested he visit. Then finally and officially, in her capacity as secretary of Women's Club, she had insisted. Patricia, liaison to the perpetually unfortunate.

His wife collects what crawls out of the hills and hollows — the disabled, amputees, women born with legs of different lengths, and schizophrenics. Her last project was an Iraq vet tractor repairman with a limp and stutter. Patty was stirred by the man's momentary desire to acquire sufficient grammar to procure a contractor's license.

"Is that a dream?" Malcolm inquired. "Do we differentiate inspiration from banal aspiration?" Not even an aspiration, he decided, but an impulse such as the severed arm feels. A few random neurons flicker and spasm, and his wife was sharpening pencils and baking pies, her face alert and prepared for her latest squalid enormity.

"Chris has PTSD," Patty informed him.

The vet, in dirty jeans and a wildly stained Sex Pistols T-shirt, reveals a shabby impulse to improve the self he doesn't have. He borrows money and doesn't return it. He offers to do Patty's grocery shopping in Wood's End and skids into a ditch. One side of the car collapses like smashed tin and oak branches crack the windshield. He doesn't call but hitchhikes home instead. He schedules lessons and doesn't come. He has to bail out his ex-brother-in-law. His girlfriend's in a diabetic coma. His grandfather has Parkinson's. A horse stepped on his stepson's foot.

Patricia waits with her posture adjusted, her hair just washed and brushed, and pencils ready. Malcolm assumes her tutoring missions will continue indefinitely. One summer night when rosehips have infiltrated the air with the unmistakable scent of cinnamon, Chris honks from a pick-up. He's drunk and high on meth, and drives up and down Maple Ridge Road, shooting out their windows with a deer rifle.

Malcolm McCarty telephones Sherriff Murphy in Wood's End. Patricia protests, pulls at his arms, moans and falls to the floor screaming, "Hang up. O god. Hang up."

"She's improving the world one hillbilly felon at a time," Malcolm says.

The sheriff laughs. He's amiable, a sturdy man, tan, with an athlete's build. He moves with graceful assurance, comfortable within his body. Probably ex-military. Women are no doubt drawn to him. He has the quiet certainty of a man who has been tested and recognizes his capacities and limitations. A straight shooter, Malcolm decides, unhurried and attentive.

"Your wife's a nice lady. But she can't treat country folk same as faculty. They're accustomed to abuse. If they don't get it, they're suspicious and resentful," the sheriff explains.

Malcolm is surprised when the sheriff accepts tea in a floral porcelain cup. Patricia has gone to bed.

Sheriff Murphy, casually taking inventory of their living room — the piano with a silver candelabra Patricia found in the flea market at Clignancourt is beside a bluish art nouveau vase with yesterday's roses. The walls are decorated with scrolls of muted Yangtze River landscapes — fishing boats, huts at the sides of rice paddies and bridges in fog.

The sheriff glances at the carpets. Malcolm carried the rugs back from Kashmir in rolls like twin boa constrictors around his neck. He went to the Philadelphia airport to retrieve the cobalt blue chandelier Patricia bought in Prague. It was rush hour and custom agents interrogated him for three hours and threatened a full body search. He brought the box home and the directions were in Russian. He remembers. It took him an entire weekend to hang it.

"This all insured?" Jim Murphy asks.

"Yes, of course," Malcolm says.

Sheriff Murphy stands up. He's wearing black polished boots. He takes a small notebook from his pocket. "Want to make a formal complaint?"

Malcolm says no.

"I'll arrest him anyway," the sheriff decides. Then he extends his card. "You may want to call me."

"Why?" Malcolm is puzzled.

"Can't insure the future," Sheriff Murphy observes. "You might need a hand some time. I'm a good person to know."

Malcolm McCarty entertains the notion that Jim Murphy is threatening him. Maybe it's the prologue of a shakedown. There's something wrong but he can't quite determine what it is. He dismisses the idea and lets it drift into the night.

Patricia's new project is a farmer's wife who can't read. She's dyslexic and somewhat deaf. Her father considered her too retarded for school. Her stupidity enraged him and he took out her two front teeth. She's been at River's Nest Motel in Belleview since she was 11. She has attention deficit disorder and they make her do all the laundry. Patty lists a litany — misogamy, physical and verbal abuse, and predatory lawyers. Malcolm nods and excuses himself.

Her current pupil cancels lessons, naturally, claiming car problems. Her boyfriend demonstrates his rage at her uppity disrespect by breaking her arm in three places. But she's persisted and become Patricia's triumph. The woman can now awkwardly sound out rumors about movie stars with morning sickness and divorces.

Malcolm McCarty objected to the forced visit to her residence. C.C. in her natural state, so to speak. In situ. Then he relents. He drives a staff car, listening to the wind and remembering Patricia in graduate school. She's crossing Strawberry Creek at Sather Gate carrying sequined bags of strawberries and miniature sunflowers. At this precise moment, thousands of women are crossing bridges carrying parasols and net bags of fruits and breads, orchids and pastries called moon-lit doe and spring angel. Women walk on riverbanks beneath redwoods, frangipani and palm trees. He was studying Chinese poetry, and realized all constellations are in alliances, haunting and elusive — *Afternoon of the Woman Lost at Sea, Night of the Burned Boy, Squall Morning after Falling Stones, Feast of Old Man Feeding Demons.*

Candy Carlson waits outside. She's a washed-out blond with a manipulative whine and a hallucinatory sense of her poetry and its place in human consciousness.

"I'm better than Plath," C.C. informs him, hand on her hip. "I got more experience. I'm wiser."

Sometimes a monosyllable is unnecessary. In fact, it would be excessive. Malcolm nods his head.

Her trailer rests uncertainly on a low muddy rise surrounded by rusting bicycle and appliance parts. Gutted mattresses and plastic bags of rags decorate the yard. It's returned to its original condition, reedy weeds and shoulder high thorny thistle cover the scarred metal remains of what might have been a playground. She wears a mini skirt, red stiletto heels, lipstick and perfume. Chickens pass blindly near her right foot.

"Free range," C.C. says, laughing heartily.

Chickens poke through the corroded swingset tilting above punctured car tires, rusting wires and pieces of children's toys. Afternoon is like dusk. It's an unusual demarcation of the day and it contains an austere gravity. C.C. leans against a slat of barn, smoking, and beckoning him into the trailer with her fingers.

"Beer?" She studies him. It's abstract, but not entirely impersonal. "No. You're a coffee man. And you're on duty."

She produces an inappropriate smile. Her lips are distorted from Botox injections and emphasize her sullen pout. Despite decades of cynicism and disappointment, real and imagined, her mouth is prepared for the kiss that isn't coming.

She puts a spoon of instant coffee in a *Star Wars* mug and fills it with warm tap water. He places her application form on the table. The Women's Club secretary has filled out the difficult areas, like social security number, date of birth and address. All C.C. needs to do is sign. Yellow post-its are attached to the signature lines.

"My ship's come in," C.C. says, immediately turning to the financial aid package page.

Yes, it's your ship, dear, Malcolm thinks. But it hasn't anchored. It's on the horizon. Contagion stalled it at sea. It's abandoned but for caskets in rows like April Hyacinths.

C.C. applies her signature and recites her list of difficulties. She must be transported to and from campus by car. There's no bus service in the hollows. She doesn't have a phone and her electricity is shut off. Naturally, it was someone else's mistake. She uses her hands for emphasis as she speaks. Malcolm notices her fingernails. They're broken and discolored.

Some women are like old lamps, stained, discarded in thrift stores and attics. Two bucks. Professor Malcolm McCarty knows these women. They have insomnia, run red lights drunk and collect divorces and abuse. They're bad swimmers with a diabetic's thirst. They swallow bilge, oily kelp, and a colossus of salt. Bloat shuts them up. He wants to stitch her lips closed.

"I got books of poems already done," C.C. informs him. She points to a stack of three-hole binders. Eight, Malcolm guesses, maybe more.

"Patricia told me. Women's Club is sponsoring you." He takes a symbolic sip of tepid coffee. "Proudly. Everyone is delighted to have you on board." Malcolm replaces his mug on the table and stands up.

"You don't look all that pleased," C.C. notes, stabbing out her cigarette and lighting another.

She drinks beer from the bottle. Typical aggressive confrontational tilt of the hip. Too much noise in the eyes. She falls asleep with the TV on. She never turns it off. It's her sole companion, the one pal who doesn't let her down.

Some women scar everyone like radiation. Husbands. Neighbors. Infants. Failure makes them narrow and raw. Some women smell like cancer. Their skin is the texture of disaster. Rashes. Lice. That's what Patricia brought home from her volunteer year at Wood's End Hospital. But there was something intangible that couldn't be scrubbed off — a sense of ruined linoleum, of trailer park faux wood plastic paneling, and food from a can like a dog.

"See, you don't know me like Women's Club," C.C. begins, voice simultaneously a rebuff and a plea. "I was married up to a soldier twelve years. I lived in Okinawa. Texas. Germany. I've seen things."

"Yes, of course you have." Malcolm is almost at the car. He keeps walking.

"Hey, mister professor," C.C. calls. "I was global from the jump. Think the bang's in Bangkok? Wrong. They got porn in Berlin you wouldn't believe. Think Plath knew that?"

It's a rhetorical question, he decides. He drives recklessly fast and Harmony Hollow is behind him.

Professor McCarty is holding office hours. C.C.'s sister extends four more notebooks. "She wanted me to give you this," the sister says. "It's her final paper." The sister pauses. "Women's Club's coming to visit. They sent a real big flower arrangement. You know, real flowers, not plastic. She'd sure appreciate you visiting."

"I'm sorry, I'll be out of town." Malcolm picks up his calendar and manufactures an obstacle. "A conference in Chicago."

He rides his bike home to Maple Ridge Road. Afternoon settles on him like a soiled blanket. He isn't prepared for Patricia. How could he be? Patricia is suddenly agitated and abrasive. He's twice repeated the story of Candy Carlson's epic journey to campus. She was walking in snowdrifts with her *Norton's Anthology* in a plastic bag and her grade school rhymes printed in pencil. She doesn't know cursive or how to type. He feels cold. His hands. Perhaps he should start wearing gloves.

"C.C.'s in the hospital?" Patricia is stricken.

"Yes, C.C.," Malcolm McCarty clarifies, wondering how well his wife knows her and the extent of her misguided emotional involvement. Good old C.C. She expected him to drive her to campus, as if he were a bus service or butler. Her condition was so exceptional it necessitated private squiring. This after the Lieberman affair, when no male faculty would even have a brief conference with a female unless a secretary was stationed on watch.

"These women feel themselves coming apart like the landscape," Patricia informs him. "They have a capacity for lyricism"

Malcolm nods his head. The table is set for tea. He sits down.

"C.C. was transcending her circumstances," his wife says.

"Transcending her circumstances? I think not. In point of fact, she was walking an icy road in high heels. Smoking, no doubt." He replaces his teacup carefully in the saucer's floral center. Another domestic bull's eye.

"She was hiking to your class. She was carrying your books," Patricia raises her voice and glares at him.

"Transcending her circumstances," Malcolm repeats, annoyed. "That's a soundbite. Her situation required decades. It's a process, for Christ's sake." All at once he's unexpectedly frightened.

Malcolm walks into his study. C.C. needs more than decades. She needs divine intervention and electric shock. He's unsteady and angry. This is the new order. One wishes to be a singer, a TV show hostess, an architect or engineer, and the whole mechanism of struggle and revelation is extinguished. The planet is succumbing to magical thinking. He's seen the global village. It's a millennial cargo cult under an atrocity of lurid neon.

"You were born with a stick for a spine," Patricia says, pushing his study door open without knocking. "That stick is up your ass. Don't mistake it for a backbone."

Malcolm is stunned. He hasn't heard Patty say 'ass' before. He thought her genetic code precluded forming a certain strata of words. The inexplicable vulgarity was shouted with intensity.

"Is it focus, Malcolm? Or are you blind?" Patricia positions herself next to his desk and leans into the wall. She's obviously prepared to stay.

Malcolm McCarty remembers graduate school, the books, the eyestrain in libraries with inadequate light, and the relentless deprivation. How hungry he was, filling his pockets with crackers and packets of ketchup from cafeterias. He ate this later, reading, underlining and memorizing. What did he fail to notice?

His mother was in the hospital that last semester. Each weekend he drove a borrowed car to San Diego. He underlined passages while she slept. He was revising his dissertation. His mother was hideous. Choking and sobbing sounds released themselves from her body, as if she were already buried and now lived underground. His mother, with her feline mews and growls. Then the weeks of strangling, as if the individual events of her life had coalesced and formed a rope. In the act of breathing, she was hanging herself.

All Things Considered is coming from Pittsburgh, battered by static. It sounds feeble and distant, partial and disabled. It might be posthumous. What are they saying? Tractors in Thailand and Tunisian Theater? The tumultuous tale of Tin. Tsunamis in Taiwan?

Malcolm McCarty is losing his linearity. He's thinking about blueberries and Patricia in the anointed yellow summer of creeks and bridges and sly moons. He doesn't know why he's lying on his study floor in what is now inexorably night. Something is cleanly and queerly pounding in his head. Not an aneurysm, he decides, but a newly formed, uncharacterized disease.

It's a retrovirus, a hybrid mutation hatched from the millennium itself. It's come from the juxtapositions of travel that should never have been taken conjoined with alien objects, texts and sacramental vases stolen from tombs. Some artifacts have glyphs that explain everything. Why the Buddha came and went and what he thought when he pretended to smile. You can trace the first characters with your fingers, but you're holding this stone under the eerie distorted neon of Shanghai dusk. The air is humid and soiled and his hands are violently shaking. Hands so cold they're turning his arm numb.

"You don't know women," Patricia screams. "You fucking asshole."

Can his wife be saying this? He studies her mouth. He tries to read her lips. A huge o is forming. Is it another vastly inappropriate anatomical reference? There's a buzzing in his ears, not insects, but birds in cages. It's the Hong Kong market, warehouses the size of airplane hangars, boxes and crates and bamboo cages of canaries and parakeets stacked to the ceiling, all a glistening sordid yellow as if they had swallowed torches.

A disciplined man does not drop to the floor like a wind-ripped maple leaf. First they decay, infected and jaundiced. They're contagious, spread to the pines, and it becomes a forest of hepatitis.

"Call 911," Mac instructs. "Now." Each word is a stone, carried on his back across snowdrifts, and mortared with his blood. He isn't talking but building pyramids, one enormously heavy boulder at a time.

Why isn't this woman placing his head on her lap? Why isn't she dialing the telephone and taking his pulse? Can't she see he needs a blanket? Why is she turning away, walking past him and staring out the window?

"Mac, all those spelling tests and optional extra credit essays. All those book reports and book reviews and book revisions that always come at Thanksgiving. What did it get you, really?" She turns and stares at his face.

His wife is a stranger who purports to understand calligraphy and claims an affection for gardening. She's entirely false. He's observed her in the orchard and she rarely prunes a branch. She feels revulsion for the ground and her headaches are a too convenient camouflage. Patricia is a fraud with a collection of cripples and illiterates she captures and enslaves. She's a pathological liar with a secret agenda, scrapbooks he's forbidden to touch and dresser drawers that are locked. That's where Rachel's bracelets are. How has he come to this juncture with such a person?

Patricia is doing something with flames. Perhaps it's a ritual of propitiation. She's removing a paper from her pocket. It's a document. She's setting it on fire.

"The results of your echocardiogram," she reveals. "Seems you have a bit of a valve problem."

Patricia lights a cigarette with the flame that's charring the paper. A vault problem? Her cigarette is infecting the air, making the individual molecules harder to gather and trap.

He realizes the sheriff wasn't threatening him. It was a warning. "Sheriff Murphy." Malcolm tries to sit up. He's resting on his elbows. "Call. Now."

"Sheriff Murphy? The Romeo of Wood's End? You're so Elizabethan," Patricia muses, inhaling and exhaling streams of silvery smoke. "Let's not even go there."

She expels flames because she's a dragon. She's Zima, the river goddess who drowns children. She rides a camel with four humps and wields an acetylene torch.

"You're MacBeth's wife," Malcolm McCarty realizes.

"You're a pompous little prick," Patricia laughs. "I'm Medea."

Professor Malcolm McCarty is having auditory and visual hallucinations. It's from the sickness pitching him to the floor that's rocking like a vessel at sea. Of course, such diseases are inevitable. He's simply the first to encounter this particular virus or spasm or whatever it is taking his breath absolutely.

Bob Lieberman knew something was coalescing in the electronic stew. A global patois rose from the verbal graffiti and smiley yellow faces. It's savage. Flames come out of its mouth.

His arm is numb. He can't he feel his hands. An enormous aviary is puncturing his jaw and exiting through his forehead. All the stone steps, temples and bronze bells, carved wooden bridges, rivers and orchids, blueberries and gazebos are losing their clarity and dissolving.

Professor Malcolm McCarty knows he has the right to define and name this phenomenon. But it's virulent and accelerating. In the sky, an armada of zeppelins pass trailing banners announcing *Feast of Old Men Feeding Demons*, *Night of the Burned Boy* and *Woman Lost at Sea*. He watches them glide by. How will he assemble the data, derivation and trajectory? Jesus Christ. He will die first.

A GOOD DAY FOR SEPPUKU

Tommy Sutter rides his bike along Maple Ridge Road from Wood's End to the college. It's precisely twelve miles from his house on Lincoln Street to the campus and he's ridden this road thousands of times

Sometimes he passes Professor McCarty and waves. Professor McCarty teaches at the College of Northern Pennsylvania and only wants to talk about bicycle construction, the intractable stupidity of his students and books. Has he read *Catcher in the Rye* yet? What about *Zen and the Art of Motorcycle Maintenance? One Flew Over the Cuckoo's Nest?* His wife, Patricia, comes out on the porch to announce that they're retiring to Florida. Tommy nods and pedals on.

He has an affection for the campus. It's an outpost where the forest is tamed and paved paths lead to known and predictable destinations. The four-story brick buildings rise at measured distances from one another, asserting order, the unquestionable triumph of the scientific method, and the value of geometry.

He enters through the main gate, where a twelve-foot-high

marble statue of Galileo stands on a granite pedestal. An inscription detailing his life is engraved on a bronze plaque. Tommy's memorized it, but he feels the act of reading it justifies his presence.

He watches football games — he's seen Penn State, the Nittany Lions from Altoona, and the Pittsburgh Panthers. The college has an ice-skating rink, and a chess and science club. He's a member of both. He enjoys the sense of other people, their accidental jostling and sudden random clusters, how strangers brush arms or legs, then suddenly splinter into distinct smaller tributaries. It's like a chemical reaction.

Tommy Sutter's boyhood is solitary. His father, Joshua Sutter, is the Wood's End veterinarian. Everyone calls him Captain. There are constant emergencies. His father's suitcase is packed and he can disappear in minutes. Cows cough with respiratory disease and yellow mucus leaks from their eyes. They have stillbirths, lesions on their teats, infections and parasites. Horses come down with influenza and tetanus, pulmonary hemorrhages, and colic. They get leg fractures, skin cancer and encephalitis. Sheep have bloat, meningitis, fungus and fevers.

The country folk bring Dr. Sutter deer and lamb meat, chickens, and bags of corn, tomatoes and carrots. They bake breads and blueberry pies. When they come to town, they stop by the clinic with baskets of eggs, jars of applesauce and milk in gallon jugs. It isn't payment for services rendered, they're all in debt, but token offerings acknowledging his father as intrinsic to Wood's End. The clinic is part of the spine of the town — necessary as JJ's General Store, the sheriff's office, United Methodist, St. Stephens, and the post office.

His father gives the meat to Sheriff Murphy. His mother doesn't want flowers and she refuses to make stews. She's a vegetarian. The storeroom is littered with Mason jars of decaying Irises, and Lavender and Mint are buried beneath the acrid smell of alcohol, Betadine, astringents and pipe and cigarette tobacco. Ivermectin for the horses is a subtle and insistent musty scent like apples in mud. Pink antibiotic leaks from gallon bottles and looks like bubblegum.

The clinic storeroom is off limits. His father smokes cigarettes in secret there and paces in circles. He keeps his files on the floor and can immediately locate what he needs. He's memorized precisely where each case is — baskets of roses gone stiff, foul eggs and collapsed tomatoes form a perimeter along the back wall. There's one oak cabinet and it is locked.

Then there's an outbreak of bluetongue that could kill off half the sheep in the county and his father leaves for a week. Goats stop eating, get infested with worms and turn mean from arthritis. The fields are actually composed of wounds, abscesses, dysentery and viruses, foot rot, liver flukes and lesions.

His father picks up his doctor's bag and dozens of keys sway between his fingers. They're held by a large bronze disc. It's the Governor General's Gold Crescent Award. His father drilled a hole in it to accommodate all his keys. He has keys for the clinic and storeroom, the locked oak cabinet, the house and Buick, and numerous small silver and gold keys in odd shapes he doesn't recognize. Tommy assumes they're for camouflaged doors his father keeps hidden. The tiny keys are delicate and look designed to fit jewelry boxes and dollhouses. Or mailboxes in other counties.

Sometimes his father has to go to the horse farm outside Harrisburg. He's signed a contract, after all. They have seventy thoroughbred racehorses and need him to examine a new arrival. Two horses are shivering. One is limping and off his feed. There is blood in the barn.

Sam Markowitz often telephones from Erie. He's scheduled twelve surgeries in three days, and he's desperate. He begs his father for help. Sam is seventy-nine. He has glaucoma and his hands tremble. Latex gloves give him hives, he wheezes and can't breathe. Poor Sam can't retire. His wife has cancer and Sam has to keep up their insurance. His father can't refuse. Then he might drop by Cornell for an emergency conference on rabid red fox and rabid raccoons. A frat kid got bitten and the trustees funded a research grant six hours later.

"All frats are naturally rabid," his father observes. "This kid's a business major with a room temperature IQ. I wouldn't give him a tetanus shot. Truth is, I wouldn't give him a tourniquet."

Joshua Sutter has a reputation as a man of fierce convictions. When he makes up his mind, it doesn't change. Some consider him arrogant and stubborn. But it's generally agreed that he's smart in an uppity way, and he has steady hands.

His father is 6'5" but seems larger. He uses his whole body unapologetically when he speaks. He bends his knees, and his hips move side to side as if performing a two-step. He spreads his arms wide for emphasis and his limbs punctuate the air.

Joshua Sutter has a melodious voice and a deliberately slow delivery. His movements are calculated and languid. He wants to be certain you see him coming. His father rarely raises his voice. He's committed to the discipline of modulation. He claims it's part of being professional.

His father's red hair is long, past his neck, and falls around his face in ropey tendrils like kelp. Tommy thinks his father's hair is a distraction — like the red cape of a matador and the misdirection of magicians.

Joshua Sutter is given to overly nonchalant entrances and exits that conceal quiet flourishes. His father actually has a repertoire of sly moves. He's sleek and subtle and travels inside shadows. His Buick is the color of winter. It has 300,000 miles on it, and a bumper sticker that says **Make Love Not War**.

His father is always getting in or out of the Buick, humming

"Tambourine Man" and "The Times Are A-Changing" with a corncob pipe jammed between his teeth. His riverboat gambler's hat seems to float on top of his red hair, perched like a large nesting bird. His hat is ivory and made from shantung straw. Its wide brim conceals his forehead and bends at an angle, permanently shading his brow and left eye. He has black, red and white hatbands. Sometimes he wears his red and or black, triple-rose brocade vest, and has an entire drawer just for his sleeve garters.

His curls tangle and swirl like ocean waves he doesn't bother to brush. He carries his doctor's bag and suitcase in one hand, and presses a bottle of scotch to his chest with the other. Keys dangle from his middle fingers and a hundred dollar bill is folded into a little square in his palm. When they shake hands, the money transfers to Tommy's palm and adheres to his skin.

"Keep yourself in feed," his father says. "Have a problem, call 911."

Just before he drives away, with the engine already running, his father motions him closer. This is the conclusion of their ritual. His father reaches in his pocket and presents him with a silver dollar. "Buy a lottery ticket," he advises. Then the car is gone.

Tommy believes his father can will himself into invisibility. He's magical and his doctor's bag and big brown leather suitcase are somehow suspicious. His father is a circus with rings of acrobats, clowns, strong men and limping horses smelling like rained-on apples. He's the grand master. His suitcase must be filled with confetti, ready to burst in a storm of gold flecks, and silver sparkle fireworks that could escape and resound like ricocheting bullets. Then plumes of purple smoke would pour through the house and into Lincoln Street. He has miniature missiles in his suitcase, and milk snakes coil in his folded brocade vests and sleeve garters. His father invented the universe. Time didn't exist until he devised watches and clocks.

Tommy thinks his father can pull rabbits and lambs from his special riverboat gambler's hat. He can extract water buffalo, mammoths, and make golden eagles fly from his hands.

Tommy frequently examines the Buick. He's disappointed when nothing is added or subtracted. He knows precisely what's in the trunk — remnants of a tool kit, a parka, card decks, playing chips from the Flaming Arrow Indian Casino south of Altoona, a Frisbee, and two bottles of scotch. In the glove-box his father keeps chocolate bars, two cartons of Marlboro 100 cigarettes, and his expired driver's license.

Tommy watched his father install a cassette player. But he didn't buy anymore cassettes. He only plays three tapes — *The Best of Bob Dylan*, *The Best of Frank Sinatra* and *The Best of Cream*. On a recent reconnaissance, Tommy realized his father doesn't have a single map in the car.

"Maps are for people who care where they're going," his father said, corncob pipe in his mouth, hat covering his forehead. Then he's walking out to the gray Buick that's so identical to the gray air, it's camouflaged.

Tommy Sutter spends his boyhood in the vast green chambers of the forest that begins at the backyard gate. The forest is an inland sea with wind currents the texture of waves. He's disguised and protected here. Trees are mysterious and practice their own forms of sorcery. They communicate with gestures revealing their intentions. They are agile mutes and natural mimes. Their language evolves seasonally. Branches sway suggestively to one side, offering a deer path he follows, zigzagging to the creek beneath stands of sepia and glazed young oaks.

He jumps the creek to ridges of brazen scarlet and vermillion maples. They're a battalion of renegades. He calls that Revolution Hill. Low slopes are intricate displays of leaves turning cinnamon, cordovan and oxblood. They remind him of the leather and high- ceilinged rooms at the college. He names this path Library Road.

Some maples look dipped in wine, burgundy and sherry. A good chemist could take the separate elements of autumn and distill them. The first chemists were alchemists. A superior chemist could put them in a bottle and drink it. That's the hazard of maples and the lure of clarets and grenadine.

Oaks are sturdier. Their strewn leaves resemble buckskin, pelts, leather patches and gourds. He could gather them, and devise clothing and weapons. Or he could graft them on for hands. Tommy is certain he could survive winter.

The forest is an engine, a wind-fueled orchestra. Oaks are anchors and provide a steady rhythm. On the banks of 5 Eagle Creek, the maples are younger and subdued. When dry, their leaves rustle like tinny castanets. That's Gypsy Ridge. The west-facing slopes go brown and brittle early. He can step on them for percussion. He calls this section Death Row.

He knows where he is and rarely encounters anyone. It's his forest and he can orchestrate it.

Tommy was angry. The week began with a rare family discussion about his request to join Boy Scouts. He needed twelve dollars for dues and a uniform. His father said no.

Tommy offers to clean cages in the vet clinic. He'll wash the storeroom floor.

Betadine and iodine leak from ten-gallon jars and fall in streaks like stalled creeks polluted with rust. Pink antibiotic drips thick like spit-out bubblegum. The floor is encrusted with what fell and lodged between the layers — pens and keys and business cards, cotton balls, swabs, gauze and coins are permanently laminated. Each year the county health department cites the clinic for multiple violations.

"That's my Sargasso Sea," his father said. "I like it as it is."

Tommy rarely has a specific desire that he can articulate. He doesn't want a Walkman, a *Star Wars* video or a guitar. But Boy Scouts is an urgent necessity. He must make fire from sticks and the movement of his wrists. He wants to learn Morse code and how to send smoke signals. For an astronomy badge, he'll identify constellations and the Pleiades meteor shower in August when the troop camps out for a week at Hamilton Mountain.

Tommy doesn't know how to say he longs for companionship. He can't recognize his loneliness, how remote and distant he is, how stranded. He's sympathetic to the moon, barren, pock-marked and futile. Rogue asteroids excite him. They're fearless delinquents without rules. When satellites lose orbit, and are condemned to fall back to earth as incinerated pieces, he mourns their fiery extinction. He has no idea why.

During their formal family discussions, he talks in a rush about knots, lassos and securing boats at docks. The principles of aerodynamics are demonstrated by archery. He mentions badges for cooking and house repair. He's nervous and passionate and senses defeat. He wants to dig for arrowheads and fossils in amber, and recognize archeological sites from Indians and wagon trains.

Tommy is trying to create a dialect in which he will be fluent. Perhaps it's a language of ropes, flints, canvas tents and sticks that transform into flames. He's small like his mother, with thin wrists and ankles, and doesn't play sports with his father. He isn't chosen for teams or after-school football. He is trying to survive.

"Your thoughts are so primitive and generic, I can't process them," his mother says, taking off her apron.

After dinner his mother goes to clay class or a lecture at the college. Woman's Circle meets once a week and she's taking another sewing class. Democratic Club is mandatory. The county has never voted democratic, not even for Roosevelt. Of course the cause is futile. That's why it's so important, his mother tells them. She's president and has to open the door and start the coffee pot. She has the only set of keys.

"Uniforms and saluting lead to Idi Amin, the shithead Shah of Iran, and that bastard in Iraq," his father says. He stands up. "I can't support that."

Tommy feels betrayed. He rides his bike to the college, barely noticing the rain. No one is outside, not on Lincoln Street or Maple Ridge Road. Campus is deserted. As usual, he reads the plaque on the marble statue of Galileo. Then he rides home in the dark.

It's the cusp between fall and winter and he's uneasy. The zone of transition is like a frontier where there are no rules and the unpredictable is constant. Wind rips random paths through the forest and maples' leaves fall in the shape of broken hearts, mouths, and twisted upended shells. The sun thins as if strained through a colander. Tommy knows the architecture of November. It's an anatomy of edges and pebbles, gravel-mouthed thunderstorms, and abandoned nests finches left. In the planet's shift, he has the sensation he may fall off the world.

He's surprised to find Captain waiting for him. "What have you got in that backpack?" he asks.

Tommy takes out his compass, flashlight, buck knife, matchbooks, and paperback copy of *On the Road* that Professor McCarty gave him. He doesn't like it and isn't reading it.

He places the items on the table near his father. He doesn't have a canteen. He drinks from 5 Hawk Creek below a colossal maple. It's one of the oldest in the forest and invariably turns a bold magenta. Its leaves stay on as if somehow attached past the first freeze. The bark is thick and complex, a sort of Braille he tries to read with his hands. There are epics beneath his fingers, formulas and footnotes. Puncture such a tree and the history of the world pours out. Cut it down and time stops. He calls the place where he drinks Cistern of the Sage.

Under the lamplight his tools are a paltry assembly. They're squalid and starkly inadequate.

Captain examines the contents of his backpack. He picks them up one at a time and evaluates them.

"A substandard Cro-Magnon could rule the planet with this gear," his father decides. Then he opens a statistics book.

Tommy can't translate his emotions into intelligible sentences. He recognizes his father is wrong, but he can't go further, can't say *You're an unreasonable, selfish man.* He believes he'll someday navigate back through time, return to precisely this moment, and say, *You're a bully and narcissist. Give me the money.* He doesn't yet know that what is lost cannot be retrieved.

His mother is gone the next day. After school he finds a recipe card taped to the refrigerator. Under the list of necessary ingredients for banana bread, she's written *Going to New Mexico.*

"Dad, we have to call the sheriff," Tommy says. It's past dusk when he rides to the clinic, holding the recipe card in his hand. "File a missing person report."

"Jimbo's an asshole. Give it a few days," his father replies. "She'll come back when she wants."

His father hasn't spoken to Sheriff Jim Murphy since the problem with the PETA brigade from Pittsburgh. Tommy chanced to be at the clinic when the delegation arrived. He watched six women get out of a van and enter the clinic.

They have a list of requests. They want his father to board stray dogs and cats in his storeroom until they're adopted. 'Rescued' is the word they use.

His father is flabbergasted. They're inundated with strays as it is. At spring break, students from the Con drop off kittens and puppies on the clinic grounds. They throw cats out of car windows, and kick puppies from cars. Sometimes they drag dogs to their front lawn in Wood's End.

"I'm an innkeeper for strays?" His father is infuriated. "Not in this life."

His father calls Sheriff Murphy. Jimbo drives his patrol car to the clinic. His father demands Jimbo arrest the delegation from Pittsburgh. The sheriff glances at the women in pastel suits and high-heeled shoes. They aren't whores or white trash passing bad checks and selling dope. They aren't hippies bad-mouthing America and whining about Salvador. They look like high school principals and doctors' wives and smell like Reagan and golf.

'What for?" the sheriff wonders.

"Trespass, conspiracy to intimidate, harassment, and monumental stupidity," his father informs him.

"Hold on, Red," the sheriff cautions.

"Call me Red again, I'll knock your lights out," Dr. Joshua Sutter threatens. He makes a fist.

His father has extraordinary hands, long and wide, and his fingers are monumental, graceful, sculpted and purposeful. The bones are clearly articulated like mountain ridges on old globes.

"Kids in the hollows eat paint chips and bark. Vets sleep in bushes beside highways." He waves his big-as-branches arms up and down, and in a diagonal implying lightning. Then he spreads his arms apart suggesting the wingspan of an eagle or a flying dinosaur.

"Can't do much about that," Jimbo decides.

"We're mass killing peasants in Central America. And they have bleeding hearts for kittens? You kidding me, Jimbo? These folks," his father pauses and glances at the Pittsburgh delegation, "have the St. Vitus of the 80s. It's highly contagious."

"Can't help you there, either," Jimbo says.

Tommy waits a week. They eat frozen dinners, canned soup with crackers, and have Papa Paulo's pizza delivered. His mother used a battered Betty Crocker cookbook. Wednesday's meatless lasagna passes, Thursday's fried chicken with wild rice, and Friday's tuna casserole. His father reads a book about differential equations and makes notations in the margins. Periodically, he briefly glances up and says something about the sheriff.

"Jimbo's a coward and fool. He got his purple heart for shooting himself," his father reveals. "Dropped his .45 on his foot and it discharged. What a dick."

Tommy stays in his room. He doesn't have a single arrowhead or fossil trapped in amber. Amber is how history punctuates itself, assuring that some specimens don't disappear. It's like an exclamation point.

"Dad," he begins.

"Don't call me Dad." His father closes a text book and looks directly at him. "Dad is for whiners. It diminishes and offends me. I'm not just your dad. I have other aspects. Other facets."

"What should I call you?" he wonders.

"Call me Captain like everyone else," his father instructs him.

"Where do you think Mom is?" Tommy asks.

"No idea," Captain says. "At least a million women disappear every year. Could be more. Police find their cars on back roads. The FBI discovers their suitcases at airports and bus depots. Women vanish like smoke. Poof."

His father draws out the word, *pooooofff,* and waves his magician's arms toward the ceiling. It's a gesture meant to imply the infinite universe with its inexplicable laws and paradoxes — its force fields, dark matter, black holes, sudden blindness, spontaneous combustion and vanished mothers.

On Sundays when his father is gone tending to sheep and cows, Tommy walks to Madison Street where three churches in a row occupy the whole block. Covenant Baptist, then Central United Methodist and All Saints Lutheran. He makes himself inconspicuous and watches women pass in their special church clothing. They wear big floppy hats, their good shoes are polished, and they have their dead grandmothers' rhinestone pins on their coat.

When they are close, almost brushing him, he breathes in their skin. This is what fascinates him, not the singing or sun beating itself against stained glass, but the powdery floral dust rising from the necks and hair of discreetly perfumed women. It's this muted citrus and tea rose he wants to breathe, internalize and own. This is what he must analyze and possess. It has nothing to do with religion.

On his 14th birthday, Captain presents him with a color TV. Sheriff Murphy carries the over-sized 40-gallon aquarium from the display window of Peter's Prize Pets. He has a bucket of water with guppies, neons, red barbs, butterfly rams and angel fish. There's a bag of coral and gray pebbles and a small wooden box with a ship to sit on top of the gravel bottom. The ship runs on batteries and sends out distress signals in what might be Morse Code. Jimbo produces two birthday hats, candles and a cake from Brenda's Bakery. Jimbo impales candles in the icing and Captain and the sheriff sing Happy Birthday. They're out of tune. Tommy blows out the candles and doesn't make a wish.

Later, Captain helps him set up the aquarium. They rarely have a project together and Tommy is disoriented by the thrill.

"What's your major?" Captain asks. "Austerity and solitude?"

"Biochemistry," Tommy answers.

"Sit alone in a lab with tubes in racks and shakers? Count

how many molecules can disco on a pin?" Captain returns with a glass of scotch. "Don't make the mistake I did. I hate my job."

His father loathes being a veterinarian. Animals bore him. They're too predictable and the stakes are too low. Sheep or cats, horses or dogs, mice or mammoths. Captain often threatens to quit. After all, he has other facets.

"Go to medical school, Thomas. Nothing serious like surgery. Dermatology is the best bet. It's an overlay."

Tommy doesn't go into the forest in winter. Trees thin to sticks embedded in deep snowdrifts. Hills resemble the aftermath of an atomic blast. Their nudity is obscene. It's a sacrilege. His birthday gift TV only receives two channels. The news from Scranton or Philadelphia, and preacher shows. The fish die one by one. His sunken ship no longer sends out distress calls in a smart sequence of three quick red beams every fifteen minutes. The batteries are dead.

Tommy suspects distress calls fail to lead to search and rescue. There's the matter of encryption and current conditions. His ship is in the Mariana Trench and nobody is listening.

When he was in second grade, he realized his parents didn't actually speak to one another. They only appeared to inhabit the same house on Lincoln Street. But they broadcast on separate frequencies in encrypted codes that changed every day. That's when he recognized the futility of distress calls. There're actually posthumous messages. By the time you say *May Day May Day* it's too late.

Six months later, his grandfather, Horace Bowen, telephones. The Captain and Horace aren't on speaking terms.

"Well, son," Horace begins. There's a pause, as if his grandfather is taking a deep breath. "Seems your mother got a touch of malaria in Africa. She called me for money. They flew her to Germany. She's OK now."

So she didn't go to New Mexico after all, Tommy is startled to realize. She joined the Peace Corps instead and they sent her to Arusha in Tanzania. She was teaching girls to use sewing machines in a village called Mosquito Creek. They were making aprons with Mt. Kilimanjaro stenciled on the front. They'd sold 231 at the airport when she became infected.

His grandfather, Horace Bowen, has a northern accent with rolling a's that are languid but defined, like smooth sandstone boulders slowly sliding down a hill. He lives in an Amish village in Manitoba, Canada. That's where his parents are from. They grew up on adjoining farms. His mother won the Governor General's Gold Crescent and was going to Berkeley, California. But she had somehow detoured and married Captain instead. She was sixteen.

"Is she coming back?" Tommy asks.

He hasn't spoken to a relative before. He doesn't know what the boundaries are. Should he tell his grandfather that his heart is broken and his father ignores him? And they just eat pizza and canned soup? Should he say he needs his mother with her Democratic Club, clay classes, and stained Betty Crocker cooking book with the pages falling out?

Everything is unfathomable and abstract. Manitoba. Tanzania. Germany. And suddenly a man who is his mother's father has appeared.

"Is she coming back?" Tommy asks.

"She didn't say," his grandfather tells him.

"Why did she run away?" he wonders.

"That's not for me to know," Horace Bowen replies.

"Did she have a message for me?" Tommy is urgent.

There is a pause in which his grandfather seems to make a

decision. "It was a short call and went by fast," his grandfather says. "Bad weather here. I have to go."

It's the second Christmas since his mother departed. Tommy no longer believes she was kidnapped by a band of marauding killers, or struck with a rare amnesia. Nothing fell on her head from the sky. She wasn't stolen or abducted by extraterrestrials. He recognizes that she deserted him.

Over a million women disappear every year. It's a phenomenon. Sometimes cars with wallets and passports and antique bracelets are found on abandoned country roads. Suitcases with nightgowns, photographs, wedding rings and ski jackets are discovered in airports and bus stations.

It's possible to triangulate location from accidental remnants. A red taffeta dress with ruffles, hoop earrings and castanets wrapped in tissue paper next to a book titled *Spanish Basics* suggests a certain trajectory. A wedding gown, flannel baby blankets and a two-hundred-year-old lace communion dress made in Belgium indicate other possibilities. But his mother didn't leave a trace.

Tommy is stunned. He realizes history isn't absolute. It's flexible and offers competing narratives subject to editing and deletion. He has trouble falling asleep. He hypnotizes himself by deriving rudimentary mathematical theorems that can be solved and replicated. This is the prayer that works. This is grace.

Tommy finds the Christmas decorations in the attic and brings the boxes to his father. Captain has appropriated his mother's bedroom for a study. He's moved in a desk and bookshelves, a new sofa, his stereo and TV. He's put a lock on the door. Tommy has to knock.

Captain doesn't look at the box he's holding. Strands of green and red bulbs and his mother's childhood ornaments are inside — the miniature gingham dolls with yellow yarn braids and brass button eyes, the cotton snowflakes, each distinct in size and embroidery and the fifteen angels with her name rendered in pink thread. One for each Christmas. Someone who loved her sewed her name in twig-like stitches. Tommy senses they intended to impart a further message in a deliberate script like hieroglyphics.

"Let's give it a rest," Captain says.

They don't put up the Christmas lights or drive to Mike Moretti's lot with its hundreds of freshly cut trees that are fragrant with some dusty, distilled essence of pine. They don't buy a Christmas tree for his mother's ornaments or put a wreath on the front door.

Captain closes the clinic just after Thanksgiving and doesn't plan to reopen until mid-January. He pauses on his way to the Buick and counts out five crisp hundred dollar bills. He indicates the table where ten silver dollars are arranged to form a squat pyramid. His suitcase and doctor's bag are already in the car.

His father hasn't cut his hair since his mother left. It's so long he ties it in a ponytail with a rawhide string. Wind knocked off his ivory shantung straw hat that hides his forehead and part of his left eye. His father doesn't want anyone to see what he's thinking.

Tommy has retrieved the hat and his father puts it in the cardboard box he's carrying toward the Buick. The hat rests on top of packages wrapped with rows of inordinately festive reindeer tied with pink and blue bows.

"I've got bloat and colic from Pittsburgh to Harrisburg," his father says. "I've got Grass Fever and Nile Fever and widows and orphans in 12 counties. Ho ho ho." He doesn't smile.

"What about me?" Tommy asks. He expects his father to tell him to dial 911. That's what he said last Christmas.

"Something happens, I expect you to take care of it," Captain said. "Time you man up."

Caroler's from St. Mary's and St. Stephens United Methodist offer an unenthusiastic truncated version of "Santa Clause is Coming to Town." As if sensing the desolation within, they quickly move on through thickly falling snow. The porch light is burned out and the only illumination in the house is the lamp in his bedroom. When the carolers arrive, he turns off the lamp.

The house is a black hole on the street. It's a mouth with the front teeth knocked out and it's snowing hard.

Mrs. Riggs, the mailman's wife who lives two houses down Lincoln Street, brings him plates with leftover dinner — sometimes it's turkey and mashed potatoes with gravy, ham and cornbread, or beef stew and biscuits. When the pharmacist's wife, Mrs. Sissick, bakes, she sends one of her sons to deliver pieces of pie and bags of ginger snaps.

Sheriff Murphy passes in his pick-up and issues a blizzard warning through a bullhorn. Then he parks and walks in through the front door. Tommy hadn't realized the sheriff had a key.

"Got a bulb?" Jimbo asks. "It's creepy dark. Probably scared away the preachers. You hiding?"

The sheriff puts in a new bulb on the porch. Then he opens kitchen cabinets and counts soup cans.

"No tree?" the sheriff observes.

"Mom's got the best ornaments, too." Tommy says. "The snowflakes and dolls."

"And the angels with her name in pink thread? I loved them," Jimbo says. "Hey, I'm looking for power lines going down. Maybe people trapped in cars. Want to help out?"

Tommy shakes his head no.

"It's your civic duty. I'll deputize you," Sheriff Murphy offers. "Come on. Let's go."

Tommy follows Jimbo over snowdrifts with a flashlight. Just outside town proper, a power line is dragging in snow, partially buried and emitting sparks. Jimbo hands him a fire extinguisher and tells him what to do. They find Mrs. Rossington in her car in a snow bank and dig her out with shovels. The sheriff wraps a blanket around her shoulders and calls paramedics.

Tommy hasn't seen the Christmas decorations in town yet. They stop and walk to the square. The Christmas tree is thirty feet high and encrusted with sparkling lights, large red balls and extravagant layers of tinsel. An angel sits on top.

"Want a beer?" the sheriff asks.

He shakes his head no.

"Hot chocolate?" Jimbo offers.

Tommy accepts hot chocolate and stares at the tree. He's forgotten what Christmas decorations are. Their elegant, fierce sparkle is fearless and assured. Holidays are a punctuation, too. They're a pause or semi-colon in the winter, a flare promising the possibility of spring.

When the phone rings, he assumes it's an ambulance or hospital. The governor declared a state of emergency and Sherriff Murphy closed the highway in both directions.

"Now, son, your mother's had some trouble in Chicago," his grandfather Horace begins. "Seems she burned her underwear. Got arrested for indecent exposure. I bailed her out. Don't know where she went."

The snow outside is four feet deep, almost halfway up the lampposts. He likes the way Grandfather Horace calls him 'son.'

"Why did she do that?" he asks.

"Some women's liberation protest," Horace Bowen says.

"Why do I have to call dad Captain?" Tommy wonders.

"Well, son, he believes he's gambling on a riverboat in a past century," Horace reveals. "Truth is, he was born bad.

Forty-six hours in labor and eleven pounds, ten ounces. Nearly killed his mother. She ended up dying at thirty-one."

"Did she have red hair?" he wants to know.

"Nobody in six generations of this colony had that hair," his grandfather assures him. "Born like that, he was. Full head of crimson curls. Whole scalp covered. Some thought it disturbed his thinking."

Tommy is blond like his mother, small-boned and blue-eyed. His father has a mutation that interferes with his judgment. It's a form of plaque barricading his syntactical flow like a dam in a creek. It's a genetic heresy animals sense. In fact, Captain's antipathy to the limited animal repertoire may have a more complex source. Maybe he's receiving encrypted signals from another galaxy. When he's a biochemist, he'll analyze this abnormality.

"He didn't file a missing person report," Tommy tells the man who is his mother's father.

"She's not exactly missing, son," Horace replies. "She was in Cook County Jail last week."

School will be closed tomorrow and the roads impassable. Tommy knows he'll be inside all day, scooping up dead angelfish with a ladle and eating canned tomato soup. His mother used the a Betty Crocker cookbook and he knew what dinner would be when he woke up. Meatloaf on Monday with beans and mashed potatoes. Wednesday was lasagna and raison and carrot salad.

"Maybe I could visit sometime," he offers, cautiously.

Tommy is shy and frightened and trying to man up. He's in a cross current and has the sensation that he may fall down. He has frequent episodes of vertigo that he doesn't mention to anyone. He's grown five inches this year and feels his bones straining. His voice has changed, and he barely recognizes it. He may look entirely different when school resumes. Maybe he can assume an alias and start his life over. Or maybe he'll be invisible.

Tommy knows he's a compendium of accurate observations, but when he tries to assemble them, they collapse as disassociated images. Maybe he has a touch of his father's contagion. That's why Captain didn't want him to join Boy Scouts and get an astronomy badge. In Boy Scouts he might have stumbled on Captain's mystery with a telescope.

He wonders what his grandfather Horace Bowen thinks about the Heisenberg Principal of Uncertainty and reincarnation. What exactly is human nature? Do the Amish believe in Jesus and eternal damnation? Are they pacifists like his parents?

Tommy's perceptions are vivid but contradictory. He believes in the scientific method and also the surreal and fantastic — charms and spells, demons and the afterlife, voodoo and the curses of shaman. In this plateau of overlapping riptides, he's afflicted by alternative selves diverging and reappearing with clarity.

He's convinced some can foretell and move objects with their thoughts. It's a sensitivity some are born with like perfect pitch and eidetic memory. He wonders if the Amish believe in ghosts, vampires, evolution and a flaming hell. Who qualifies for punishment? Do they support capital punishment and hang the guilty? Do they cut off the hands of thieves? Is there a hierarchy of transgression? What about mothers who run away from their sons?

Tommy exists in spasms of sharp insight and overwhelming grief. He's so many ages at once, he entertains the notion that he's living his incarnations simultaneously. Galileo recants but gets house arrest anyway. Leo Szilard crosses a London street in 1922 and invents critical mass. He patents it and doesn't get a dime. Copernicus's books are banned and burned. Marie Curie is enraged and demands the return of her hands.

At White Sands, Oppenheimer chants, "Now I am become Death, the destroyer of worlds," in Sanskrit. Teller calls the FBI and rats him out.

"I know a lot about bluetongue and colic, abscesses and bacterial infections," he finally offers.

"Sure you do, son," Horace says. "I'll think on it."

His grandfather telephones the following summer. Tommy is observing pink finches with binoculars. They've constructed nests in the eaves of the porch between twisted branches of Wisteria his mother planted. There are blue finches, too, and huge raucous blue jays. A pack of grackles stayed a noisy week and flew away. Robins with burnt orange breasts search for worms on the lawn. A pair of small cardinals keep crashing into the front windows.

"Kamikazes," his father says, walking out to the Buick. Captain has a particular distaste for birds. "Somebody dares bring me a parrot or canary, I'll eat it."

Tommy has read the biographies of physicists, chemists, biologists and astronomers. Many began as naturalists. Science is about observation. He has a book titled *Birds of Pennsylvania* with photographs and descriptions he finds confusing. He can't establish an absolute border between black and charcoal gray. It depends on the sunlight, passing clouds and sight angles. The question of how they are flying is ambiguous. He's watches nuthatches, Carolina wrens, and chickadees. If he'd joined Boy Scouts, he'd instantly recognize raptors. Their wings flutter and ripple as they fly. Are they hawks or turkey vultures? Captain is in a poker tournament at Flaming Arrow. Last month, he finished third.

"Your mother got in some trouble in Tucson, Arizona, son," Horace Bowen tells him. "Seems she was sleeping on a golf course. They charged her with trespassing and vagrancy. Dragged her away in cuffs."

"Is Mom crazy?" he finally dares to ask.

"More like scratching an itch with a blowtorch," Horace says. "She used to chase lightning. Didn't play with dolls. Wouldn't touch them. She treated them like poison. She was barn building at 10. Then she wins the Gold Crescent. First time a girl won. Just turned 16. She had a perfect score. They couldn't deny her. She had scholarship offers from Harvard and McGill. She was packing her suitcase."

"Where was she going?" he wants to know.

"Berkeley, California." Horace says.

"What happened?" Tommy asks.

"He came back on a motorcycle. Claimed he bought it for twenty dollars. He's wearing a black silk cape and top hat. Looks like he's going to a party with the royal family. He's moving like a feral cat, fast and balanced and graceful-like. So tall, you have to look up to see his face. It sets an attitude. Everybody's craning their neck and he's acting like nature exalted him. Big as a hill, he is, and a certified veterinarian. Talking all lofty about Woodstock and stopping the Vietnam War. He's waving his arms around like an orchestra conductor. Few years before, he won the Governor General's Gold Crescent, too."

"I know," Tommy says.

"Her score was better," Horace informs him.

"Why did you let them stay?" he wonders.

"They were purified by sincerity," Horace answers. "Two wildfires, they were. We thought they'd put each other out naturally."

"What happened?" Tommy asks.

"Wind changed direction," his grandfather replies.

There is a pause. It expands like accordion suitcases with concealed compartments with zippers and flaps that snap shut.

You could put the forest past 5 Eagle Creek inside, all of Revolution Hill, Gypsy Ridge and Cistern of the Sage. But if the wind abruptly stopped, the suitcase with the forest would drop through the ground. A tunnel would open and you might fall to the core of the Earth.

"Can you make her come back?" his voice has wavered, then cracked.

"I surely cannot," Horace immediately replies. He's surprised.

"We can get a private detective. He'll find Mom and bring her home." He's absolutely certain Sheriff Murphy will go with him. They'll track her down, leap out and grab her. Jimbo can put her in handcuffs and carry her back.

"You can't pluck somebody from their destiny," Horace tells him. It's a chide. "You can't walk on water or raise the dead. He can call himself Captain. He can say abracadabra. He can dance with a bear. But we each have our own destiny. Understood?"

"Yes, sir," Tommy replies.

Captain is preoccupied and rarely speaks. It's as if words have failed him. He doesn't eat for days, then devours all the soup in the kitchen in one night. Tommy picks up twenty-three cans from the floor and the wrappers from two boxes of crackers. His father has taken to going to Brenda's Bakery and buying a dozen donuts. Pink boxes of glazed, jelly and old fashioneds with white icing are stacked next to the soups and scattered on the floor of his study.

His father parks the Buick near the clinic, plays his Best of Dylan cassette, but can't force himself to get out of the car. He explains that his legs feel like wood and won't respond to his commands. He goes to a physician in Philadelphia and returns with a bag of medicines. Later he claims he's allergic to them.

"It's like dipping my head in a bucket of cement," Captain says.

His father says he wants to take a shower, but there's an abnormality with the water. Days aren't washing off like they should. There's a thickness to the water, a sense of stained inks, the skin of the drowned, and what's leaked from gutters. It's the run-off from ruined lives in apartments with storm clouds in them. Lovers shout insults in a patois implying punishment and exposure. Outside, trees shudder, seized with vertigo, and Cancan in the nervous breeze. Constellations vanish as they scream. Captain says he needs to investigate the pipes for corrosion and rust, or something worse.

His father goes to another doctor in Boston. Captain walks in circles in his study for hours, often all night. Tommy hears his pacing even when Captain is barefoot.

Captain has an entire shelf of medicine bottles. One morning he throws them against the wall, gathers the scattered pills and tosses them in the trash. He can't fall asleep and he can't wake up. Then he cuts clinic hours to afternoons only. Blue circles form under his eyes and he's pale as a toad's belly.

They don't celebrate holidays. No one visits and they aren't invited anywhere. It's as if they've also vanished. Occasionally, they watch football on his father's TV. They go trout fishing twice.

"I hate all God's fucking critters," Captain often says as he passes, humming "Tangled Up In Blue."

Tommy is torpid and becalmed in his bedroom. Captain claims he won't extricate himself from Lincoln Street. His father thinks he'll just carry his bag of dead guppies and the stain of no merit badges into a future he's already despoiled.

Captain makes it clear that medical school is mandatory. Or else he'll end up an assistant professor in a make-shift lab with teenage assistants. They'll break the minimal equipment and he'll have no budget to replace it. Tommy's going to put himself in prison with a 25-to-life sentence.

"Studying for the priesthood?" Captain asks, staring down at him. Tommy sits at his desk and feels miniaturized and incompetent.

He checks the mailbox every day. Tommy is convinced a communication from his mother is coming. Logic dictates an exchange of addresses and photographs, and Christmas and birthday cards. She will provide a detailed explanation. At the least his mother will send a postcard.

Tommy wonders if she considered what would happen to him on Lincoln Street in the barricaded late evenings when Captain anchors the Buick and returns from a twelve-day prowl. Captain makes the house shake when he walks in, stamping ice from his boots. His hat, sprinkled with snow, is barely attached to his kelp-red tangle of hair, and his father's head almost brushes the ceiling. Captain doesn't say hello. He may fast for days or devour all the soup in an hour. He claims his head is encased in bricks. Then he goes into his study. He closes and locks the door.

Tommy is certain his mother will come to his high school graduation. That's why he cut his hair short and bought a three-piece suit he can't afford. That's why he's valedictorian.

Tommy stands at the podium on stage and surveys the auditorium row by row, memorizing family groupings and searching for solitary women. His mother is thirty-three. It's spring and she'll wear a pastel suit with high heels dyed to match and pearls around her neck. She'll have a short stylish haircut and a square hat like Jackie Kennedy. She'll smell like Hyacinths and blueberries.

"Joining the Marines?" Captain comes up behind him. "You all dressed up for Mommy?"

Captain slaps the back of his new pin-striped suit as if he wants to leave his handprint on the fabric. His father wants to soil and brand him. There's nothing friendly about it.

"She's not coming, Thomas. She's not sending birthday gifts or Christmas cards. No postcards, either. Just like I told you." Captain smiles.

It's ambivalent and unconvincing, Tommy decides. His father is afraid she might actually appear. Then he'd be accountable. His father's face is the wrong postcard.

Captain is wearing his riverboat gambler's hat, and his one sports jacket. He hasn't taken it to the cleaners for years. It's covered with cat and dog fur, and stained with sheep urine, cow pus and blood. Streaks of Betadine resemble skid marks from a collision that permanently scarred a highway. Yellow paint-like smears encrust his sleeves. It's mucus that leaked from the eyes of sick cows. Hay protrudes from his pocket and sticks in the brim of his hat. Captain doesn't own a tie. His father calls it a statement.

"I'm going to Cal," he informs his father.

"You're never getting off Lincoln Street," Captain replies.

"I wouldn't say that," Jimbo offers. He's wearing his dress uniform. It's obsidian black and trimmed with gold. The buttons and braid on his cap are like lanterns. He's polished his shoes and he's wearing white gloves. They're stark against his black uniform and seem pasted on and detached from his body.

"Where's Cal at?" he asks.

"Across the bay from San Francisco," Tom tells Jimbo.

"Sounds like he's leaving town." Jimbo glances at Captain. "Getting the 49ers, too."

"We'll see," his father says.

During Tom's senior year, his grandfather telephones on a warm late afternoon in spring. Redwoods in an accidental row form an uninterrupted dark green fence in front of his bungalow. Their bark smells like wharves and cinnamon. There's no wind and the bay is a pale blue devoid of whitecaps. It's asleep. The only motion is seagulls passing.

"She's done it this time, son," his grandfather begins. His tone is weary and distant. "Seems she's been sleeping on Venice Beach in Los Angeles. Been there a while, too. Living in derelict hotels and camping under a pier. They charged her with vagrancy, illegal use of public lands, and selling without a vendor's license."

"Selling what?" he wonders.

"Seems she had a stall on the boardwalk. She'd find shells and driftwood. Make necklaces and such." Horace tells him, "I had to get a lawyer."

Tom envisions his mother wearing an apron with Mt. Kilimanjaro stenciled on the front. She's sewn on dozens of extra pockets. She's in the tide line, collecting what's fallen from cargo ships. She's found paper umbrellas printed with pink peonies and cranes, and a piece of fuselage from a plane thought lost off Zanzibar. Once she found a swallow's nest with six undamaged scarlet eggs. She won't talk to cops. She's taken a vow of silence and they wouldn't believe her anyway.

During his graduate school summers, Tom drives to Los Angeles, finds a hotel on the beach, and walks for days searching. He picks up tiny top shells and small-ridged clamshells and carefully places them in his pocket.

In late afternoon, Tom sits on the pier. He recognizes that all ports are mythical and primal. It's the beginning of time and oceans don't have permanent names. It's before the Silk Road. Women are routinely abandoned near wharves. They're collateral damage from an intrigue gone astray.

His mother wasn't born in Manitoba. She came from a village on a delta where fields are fertile with sunflowers. Barges brought spices, statues of new gods, perfumes, mirrors, and capes made from the feathers of jungle birds. His mother became a woman of the wharves. When they're hungry, the women rip barnacles off pilings with their hands and eat them raw. They knock their teeth out and their fingers bleed.

Tom saves the seashells in his box of mementoes where he keeps the card his mother tapped to the refrigerator, the banana bread recipe with *Going to New Mexico* written in her hand. He also keeps the postcards of where he's been.

Tom thinks his mother is also walking on boulevards and beaches, examining postcards, studying angles of light and shadow. There are questions of dusk versus sunset, and how to distill the details. She's not satisfied with a sunset lacerating the sky and the waves below bluffs stitched with palms.

Tom knows there's a treacherous complexity in sorting stylized images, condensed and tamed. His mother recognizes the conventional but it's without thrill. It's overly familiar, simplified and false. When his mother finds the right postcard, the one that explains everything, she'll send it to him.

He visits laboratories the size of walk-in closets where post-docs sleep on the floor under saddle blankets. Experiments are monitored every three hours. They hire six assistants for each position. They wait to see who survives.

He interviews for a job at a Swiss pharmaceutical. He can tell immediately that he's not who they want. It's like a chemical reaction. When he mentions cloning and mapping the genome of a virulent cotton fungus, the men wince.

Captain plays poker with R&D guys from Monsanto and arranges an interview for him. His appointment is at 2. They don't call him until 4:45. Three men sit at a long mahogany table. The older man gestures to a low metal folding chair. Tom sits there. When he mentions growing protein crystals for X-ray and computer modeling, the two younger men immediately leave the room.

The older man says, "I've got to get the phone."

There is no phone. Nothing is ringing. Tom is paralyzed, waiting for clarification or an explosion. Two minutes pass. His organs are leaking out, and he presses his hand to his gut. Another minute pass. Tom picks up his briefcase and makes his way out of the building.

Captain calls from JFK on his route to Seattle. He has a cell phone but doesn't use it. He prefers the random and increasingly rare phone booths he finds on highways and on the edges at airport terminals. He's made the final table at the World Championship of Poker in Las Vegas. Girls in high heels and bikinis carry out trays of cash. He finally won a championship bracelet. Captain has a blog and he's interviewed on ESPN. Now he's invited to private games and picked up by limousines.

"I just played some guys from Du Pont," his father begins.

"Did you win?" Tom is alert. He's interested. He's at full attention.

"I got hot cards," Captain says.

Their conversation is how they embrace. They talk sporadically, and at Captain's discretion. His father demands thousands of miles of suffocating mist, gutted nests finches left and mountain ranges to form a barricade between them.

"Listen. I talked to their R&D boys. Biochemistry is strictly 20th century. You missed virtual reality and A.I. Better transfer to med school," Captain advises.

He doesn't congratulate him on his doctorate. He didn't come to graduation either. Tom's accomplishments are too trivial for a comment or handshake.

"I appreciate your concern," Tom manages.

"You'll wind up an assistant professor at a bankrupt shithole. Broken equipment and no budget," his father actually raises his voice. "Get off Lincoln Street, kid."

His father telephones when he has time on his hands. It might be a break in a tournament, a plane delay, or a bout of insomnia.

Between them hay is spooled on the edges of fields of pumpkins. There are roadside cemeteries of corn stalks and piled husks. A bloated post-harvest moon rises and consumes the sky.

His mother goes underground, underwater. There's a language for this, fluid syllables of rain and thunder and damp chimes. It's a local dialect of tinny trinkets and obscene bells in corridors of mirrors with lightbulbs that sting and all of it is repeated in glass, in glass, in glass until she is lost.

His father calls back. His plane must be delayed. "I can get you into Cornell. It's not too late," Captain tells him, his tone urgent. Then he abruptly hangs up. They must have announced his Seattle flight. Tom feels slapped.

Horace Bowen telephones a week later. "I have bad news, son," his grandfather says. There is an overly long pause. It's a silence with lead in it. It's a metal vestibule. "Captain's dead. Funeral's on Friday."

Thomas doesn't ask what happened. Maybe Captain was ambushed by rabid raccoons. Or PETA sent assassins. He is still angry.

The cemetery is surprisingly crowded. He instinctively searches for his mother. She isn't there. He's found 60 Bowens in Manitoba. None of them have come. But the sheep and goat farmers from the pasturelands are here in their church clothes. And all the dairy farmers, the mayor, and president of the Democratic Club. The head of the county health office and her assistant have brought a wreath. The new young doctor from Colorado, probably working off med school debt with two years of rural service, offers his condolences. Mrs. Rakov, the librarian, asks if he's seen his mother. She remembers her; of course, no one could forget her.

Thomas recognizes two CON PA lawyers in black suits and red ties taking notes. They're no doubt on assignment, making sure no student pet abusers are posthumously charged. Men in jeans, baseball caps and sunglasses lean against the fence at the back of the cemetery. Town cars are parked on the street. Thomas assumes they're poker colleagues.

His neighbors from Lincoln Street stand near his father's grave. Mr. Brody, the retired math teacher who lived next door, pushes his walker across grass. He pats him on his shoulder. Phil Cossink, the pharmacist, with his added-on sunroom and attic turned into a playroom for his three children has come with his sons. They're college students now and wear suits. His wife reminds him that she brought him Christmas dinner in a blizzard when he was alone.

A developer places an arm on his shoulder. The stranger has a ruddy face and he's breathless. His father's property up to 5 Hawk Creek was sold at auction. The developer plans to build 40 Cape Cod houses with swimming pools on 30-acre parcels.

"I respect natural environments." He is hearty, almost festive. "I'm not considering blading."

That means he's going to chop the forest down. Thomas turns his back and walks away.

Sheriff Jim Murphy, in his black dress uniform and white gloves, stands at his side, their shoulders brushing. Thomas notices Jimbo is wearing his purple heart. He hasn't seen it before. The velvet is vibrant and George Washington is depicted in the center in gold. No clergy preside. There are no eulogies.

The sky is the brilliant untarnished blue of intelligence, prophecy and magic. It's the sky of an earlier time when brutality was confined and sporadic. The cobalt sky is naked, not a blue humans know, but the blue of tapestries, epics, and cities still bearing their ancient names. Syracuse, Ithaca, Corinth and Thebes.

Then he chances to look directly at a woman wearing a black hat with a long veil and a black dress past her ankles. She looks like Central Casting sent her for the role of a Greek widow. She slowly approaches and introduces herself.

Samantha Markowitz is from Erie. She has fair skin with freckles that blend in together, turning her cheeks a moist peach. She embraces him and trembles in spasms. Her 12-year-old red-haired twins sob. Then Lillian Johnson is weeping in his arms. She doesn't have a horse farm. She lives in a brick house half an hour north of Harrisburg. She's a nurse. Her sons, Joshua and Justin, are red-haired dermatologists in Philadelphia. They're at least 6'3. They shake hands. His father's other sons have excellent eye contact and their business cards are linen and embossed.

Samantha and Lillian are sturdy, handsome women, 40ish he guesses, and fleshy. Their voices are soft and their words sparse. Of course, Captain wouldn't want women who dazzle. The spotlight must remain fixed on him, the narcissist.

"You all squared away?" the sheriff asks.

"Nobody's all squared away," Thomas remarks in his father's tone.

"I hear you," the sheriff replies.

"See much of him?" Thomas asks.

"Captain got more social when you went to college," the sheriff says. "That euthanasia crisis dragged on. He knew the clinic was doomed. He expected malpractice suits and he wasn't ready for the tournament circuit. Made his depression worse."

Thomas remembers. His father had flown to California to discuss it in person. He shared a house with two other students and his father had ignored them.

"This euthanasia craze gives me pause," Captain said. "It's a plank of the PETA doctrine. They're symbiotic. Point is, the fundamental principles are unsound."

Tom asked how and why. He enjoyed his father that spring California day. Outside, layers of magenta Bougainvillea embossed the bamboo backyard fence. Four hummingbirds drank sugar water. He poured Captain coffee. His father's hair hung in a braid halfway down his back. It resembled copperheads and milk snakes he found near 5 Hawk Creek at Cistern of the Sage.

His father wore a new hat, a black Stetson, blue jeans, his size 16 Doc Martin work boots, and a Grateful Dead T-shirt. He'd bought one of their cd's.

"Which one?" Tom was curious.

"The one with Dylan covers," Captain replied.

Then Captain explained that euthanasia was a terrible death. His father was restless and distracted and his eyes seemed cluttered. He paced, chainsmoked, and stared at the floor as he talked.

"You can't fool some critter you've had for fifteen years. They recognize the carrier and the sight of it induces pure terror. In the clinic, they're assaulted by the stench of critters in pain. They smell death."

Captain said it could take him three days to give them a lethal shot. By then, the critters are sick with shock. Their owners don't realize they're consigning their pets to three days of abject suffering. In winter, maybe longer.

"What do you suggest?" Tom asked. He realized that if the clinic closed, his father would have an awkward transition.

"It's a town of 3,400 with 8,870 registered weapons. They love that critter for fifteen years, sleep with it in winter, feed it from their plate. It's their responsibility to end it," Captain said. "Take the critter out back and put a bullet in his brain. Wait for a pretty day, sun shining. Let him see some robins. In a microsecond, it's lights out."

"You don't have an ethical problem," Tom ventured. "And who knows? Maybe you're right. You're senior faculty, Captain."

Later his roommate asked, "What's your father do? Is he a roadie?"

"He's a vet," Tom answered, a bit off-balance.

"Gulf War?" his roommate inquired.

"No. He's a veterinarian," Tom replied, his tone crisp. "And a professional poker player."

"So he's a professional liar," his other roommate offered.

Tom smiled, uneasy, and rode his bike to the library. He hadn't thought of his father that way before. A professional liar.

The Con weekly, *Galileo,* devoted a three-page article to his father. They included Captain's allegations of conspiracy, and undue and misguided influence from PETA in Pittsburgh. His account of the plague of kittens and puppies criminally deserted by students was vivid. What did they imagine happened to critters dumped out of cars? Some magical intervention? Maybe Jesus would feed them? It was animal abuse and punishable by imprisonment and fines.

"I'm not an innkeeper," Captain stated. "And I'm not an executioner." The *Galileo* quoted him and put his statement in bold.

"That was his finest moment," Sheriff Murphy says. "It had a kind of grandeur."

Thomas agrees.

"Captain had a restless nature. He was cursed. Born bipolar," the sheriff says. "He was lonely. He'd stay here for days."

Thomas is surprised. "What did you guys do?"

"Smoke pot, watch TV, drink some and talk. He tried to teach me Texas Hold 'Em. I didn't have the math for it. Plus, Captain was plain out lucky. You have to go the river, he'd tell me. It's a game of blood. Every hand is seppuku. Captain had the statistics cold, and cards just came to him. Only two outs and he gets one. Flushes, full houses, trips. It was uncanny. But he was obsessed with law suits."

Thomas remembered the quiet sustained furor in Wood's Hole. His father closed the clinic a year later. By then he was playing professionally. He was on the circuit with men barely twenty-one, and constantly moving across the county, often by himself. Captain called him from airports. He'd come in second at the Commerce Club in L.A. and was going to Palo Alto next. Then Vegas, Atlanta, Houston and Miami. He'd take off a few days before going up the coast to Atlantic City and Foxwood Casino in Connecticut.

"I talked to Lily and Sam," Sheriff Murphy says. "Good stock and hardworking. Agreeable. And he sure put his mark on those kids."

"Accommodating," Thomas decides. "Easy come, easy go."

They are driving to the wake at the sheriff's house. He notices Jimbo has the Governor General's Gold Crescent on his key ring.

"I wanted a token," Jimbo says, uncertainly. "You mind?"

Tom shakes his head no.

"Want something? Lawyer in Vegas has documents and keys for you."

"He ever file a missing person report?" Thomas asks.

"No," Jimbo says, after a pause. "He did not."

"Captain didn't have a single friend," Thomas realizes.

"I wouldn't say that," the sheriff replies.

"I looked around. All I saw were people who paid him," Thomas concludes. "And the ones with his chemistry. The ones he contaminated. Blood captives and customers."

"He was a big man," Jimbo notes. "What was he? 6'5"? 6'6"? Lot of terrain inside. Low lands and peaks and marshes."

"Ever read Conrad?" Thomas suddenly asks.

"Dennis Conrad?" the sheriff replies.

"Tell me, Jimbo. What did he die from?" Thomas wants to know.

"One 9-millimeter to the back of the head. Instantaneous. Robbery. Kid killed him for the poker bracelet," Jimbo tells him.

Mourners mill around the living room and sit at a picnic table outside. He stands with the sheriff in the kitchen.

"Did you know about them?" Thomas glances in the direction of the living room. Lillian and Samantha sit on the sofa, one child on either side, like human bookends.

"No clue," Jimbo says.

"Think they knew about each other?" He studies the sheriff's face. He's grown a gray moustache that suits him. Sunlight turns it silver. He's handsome, not distinguished, but a man who's seen his share. A man with stories, rugged and confident. And worldly.

Jimbo says no.

"Figure there are others?" Thomas wonders.

"I'd bet on it," Jimbo says.

"Clinic's a worthless outdated shambles. It's a tear-down," Thomas tells the sheriff, and shrugs. His father didn't have an appetite for money. He ran on some other and more exotic alien fuel.

"I remember when they built it. Just Captain and your mother. I lent them the tools. Your mother enjoyed painting. And she was terrific with a hammer. She did the whole roof," the sheriff said. "What was she? 17? She carried you in a big blue wicker Easter basket. She sewed the curtains. Went to Philadelphia for the fabric."

"What were they like then?" Thomas is interested.

"Different. They stood out. Looked like they'd stepped out of a painting. Clothes all velvet and embroidered. Regal.

Called themselves beatniks. They were intense. Truth is, they had crazy eyes. Both of them," Jimbo told him.

Thomas considers their crazy eyes. "What happened?" he asks.

"People were scared. Crossed the street to avoid them. Captain so tall, your mom tiny, but feisty and mule-stubborn. First few years, Captain seemed to take hold. Then he hit the wall. Your mother twisted in the wind. Did a year of nursing school at the Con and quit. Carried notebooks of poems and threw them away. Started the theater group," the sheriff remembers.

"You were in that?" Thomas is surprised.

"Thought I could meet women," Jimbo admits. "Can't meet them in church or a bar."

The dermatologists from Philadelphia sit on the floor with the twins. They're playing Monopoly. Lily and Sam have managed to brush their hair and rub rouge on their cheeks. Samantha has removed her veil. They're going to meet halfway in Briarwood for Sunday brunch. They're sisters now. Lily passes a plate of cheese and grapes around the room. Sam pours lemonade into paper cups.

Thomas squats beside his half-brothers and half-sisters. He notices the twins have all the hotels on the board.

"See much of him?" Thomas directs his question to the older boy, Joshua, the dermatologist with his father's name.

"Hardly saw him after he turned pro," Joshua said.

"We'd watch him on TV," Justin, the younger brother, offers.

"So what you'd do together?" Thomas wants to know.

"Went to Red Lobster in Oakdale mostly," Joshua says.

"We went to a movie once," Justin says. "And we played Frisbee."

"Maybe twice," his older brother says. It's a correction.

Thomas nods and walks back into the kitchen. The sheriff hands him a beer.

"We did *Cat on a Hot Tin Roof*. That's a play by Tennessee Williams," Jimbo says.

"Right," Thomas nods.

"After a week, your mother hung it up. Said she didn't want to live inside someone else's architecture," Jimbo remembers.

"What did she mean?" Thomas asks.

"She could see all the pieces. And it lost its meaning. She saw the whole and the ending," Jimbo explains. "Captain the same way."

"Was she depressed? Maybe angry?" Thomas wonders. "Just seventeen with a baby? She resent it?"

"Captain was a roller coaster. Your mother started novels and burned them. Then astronomy. Captain went to New York. Got her a real telescope. But she'd see the schematics and get paralyzed. Said her mind was full of corridors with thousands of doors. Open a door, there'd be another corridor of doors. She got tangled in complexities. Said her head was a house of mirrors."

"Don't imagine the Captain was much help," Thomas offers.

"Captain was a complicated man, no doubt," Jimbo confirms. "But she loved you, Tom. She stayed as long as she could bear. Maybe longer."

"I thought he was a magician," Thomas reveals.

"Captain was tricky, no question. Listen. My old man passed two, three years back. Cirrhosis. Never saw him take a drink." Jimbo glances at him. "You can't know a father. They're all magicians. Got two million years of strings and mirrors in their pockets."

Thomas thought his father had invisible instruments, tiny silver crescent scalpels for scraping off celestial tumors and shined metal tools like amulets for a royal child. He was an alchemist. He invented airports and machine guns, banks and cops, fossils and dinosaurs. He had the patent on arrowheads and missiles. He owned the triangle, scotch and pot and two accommodating women. His father had the license for fire and canons, telephones, vaccines and museums. He could hypnotize and infect you. He carried the contagion under his riverboat gambler's hat and tucked inside his Doc Martin size 16 boots. Then he slipped into his gray Buick and vanished. He didn't need a map. He was clairvoyant. That's how he knew which cards were coming.

"I used to think I could move through time. Go in and out, adjust circumstances and decisions," Thomas says.

"Maybe you can," Jimbo replies.

"Captain didn't even show me how to shave," Thomas is angry. "He wouldn't let me join Boy Scouts."

"He was unreasonable." Jimbo agrees. "I told him so."

"Know why they came here?" he asks.

"They hitchhiked. Trying to get to D.C. for the big protest. Somebody let them off at the Con. They walked in," the sheriff says.

"How he'd choose being a vet?" Tom wonders.

"Tougher to get accepted than med school back then. Captain had exclusive proclivities," Jimbo points out.

"My grandpa Horace told me Captain died," Thomas says. "How'd he know?"

"I'm still wired in. I call a constable in Hughes, one town over. We have an arrangement. Amish don't have phones. Maybe he delivers a note." Jimbo smiles.

"Were you in love with her?" Thomas suddenly asks.

"I sure was," Jimbo said. "Still am. Second summer, she organized a Bloomsday Festival. June 16th. That's my holy day. Whole town and half the country folk came with costumes.

She made a dress with white lace and carried a silk umbrella she'd painted Peonies on."

"She was Molly," Thomas guesses.

"You bet. She read the last pages and I had to leave. Sat in my pick-up crying.

"She was five foot two and spoke with the voice of an oracle. You don't expect a woman that size to talk like that, like a senator. She got a certificate of recognition from the Irish ambassador. It's all framed up in the library. But she didn't care. It was just another door into another corridor of doors."

Millions of women vanish every year. They buy wigs and dye their hair. They don't want to be found. Jimbo hands him a beer.

Thomas walks Lily and her sons to their car. Then Samantha and the twins. They're going to have Thanksgiving together. He'll join them, of course. And bring Sheriff Murphy. Thomas nods enthusiastically and watches them drive away.

"Captain said I'd never leave Lincoln Street," he tells Jimbo

The sheriff nods. Jimbo is a big man, too. Maybe 6'2". He looks like he played college football. It occurs to Thomas that it's awkward, just the two of them standing close in the kitchen of an empty house. They've unexpectedly exposed themselves as criminals and cowards.

It might be the first epoch of the Quaternary Period, Thomas thinks. It's the Pleistocene, two million years before the codification of laws and hierarchies, county health regulations and merit badges. Everyone wears mammoth pelts and complains about the cold. There's no PETA and men have as many women as they can feed.

Thomas is suddenly and inexplicably stiff with shame. He glances at his watch.

"Ever strike you odd? Two Governor General's Gold

Crescent winners in an off-the-grid Amish village? Nothing but prairies, cattle and sunflower fields?" he asks.

"I'd call it statistically impossible," the sheriff says, unequivocally.

"Mind if I ask you something?" Thomas looks directly at the sheriff.

"Shoot." Jimbo smiles.

"How'd you get your purple heart?" Thomas asks.

"Toenail fungus in Da Nang," Sheriff Murphy replies. "My whole outfit had it. Gave us all purple hearts and sent us home."

"You didn't shoot your foot?" Thomas is surprised.

"No," Jimbo admits. "But the truth was embarrassing. I made up a cover story."

That's how we live, Thomas realizes. We step on IEDs and our skin peels off. We stumble on, certain an intervention is coming, a reprieve. We invent small fictions like patches sewn over torn cloth. The headlines of our lives are mere approximations of a complexity we could not characterize in the chaos of constantly flowing emotions and circumstances. We are all stars with our events compressed and encrypted. We are what loiters in erratic orbits in the vast ocean of night.

"What was Captain thinking at the end?" Thomas asks.

"He got a kick telling me about who he played with. What their houses were like. Press a button and the living room turns into a tennis court. He'd play with Mark Zuckerman and Bill Gates and the smart boys from Google and such. Lots of hedge fund guys and dudes named Phil," Jimbo says. "The Captain didn't give a rat's ass about gadgets and the future. He was moving to Cannes. Last thing we discussed."

"Cannes?" Thomas repeats.

It's the end of an Indian summer afternoon. They walk

outside and sit on the backyard grass. The forest is an extravagance of maples in transition. Leaves are yellow as candles purified by prayer, and an unrepentant criminal red like vengeance and adultery. There's a linear continuity to this, a cause and effect he can almost articulate and arrange like an equation.

Thomas notices a swingset, monkey bars and a sand box with red and blue plastic buckets and small shovels. Vestiges from Jimbo's last marriage. Was that the third or fourth?

"See them much?" Thomas indicates the swings.

"She up and moved to Oregon. Two hundred miles from an airport," Jimbo says. "Claims she doesn't have a phone."

"Maybe you can get the Hughes constable to ride over," Thomas offers.

Jimbo laughs. "People tell you everything. They're social by nature," the sheriff reveals. "They confess. They put their sins and ambitions on bumper stickers. They show you where the bodies are. But they tilt their words and disguise them. It's in plain sight if you know how to listen."

"Do you know how to listen?" Thomas thinks to ask.

"I got a good ear," Jimbo says. "Good eyes, too."

"Think she'll come back?" Thomas asks.

Jimbo looks at his polished back shoes. Then he shakes his head no.

"You believe in destiny?" Thomas suddenly wonders.

"Didn't use to. But I'm coming around," the sheriff says. "Here's an anecdote. Few autumns back, a little girl fell in the Genesee near Hamilton Bridge. Pretty girl, four years old with pink bows shaped like cats in her hair. Name of Amanda Leaf. A pick-up crosses the bridge. Lady happens to look out the window. Lucinda Hopper, forty-six, a homemaker with three sons, spots the girl in the current. George Hopper, fifty-one, hits the brakes. They're trying to get to Butler but they took a wrong turn. They both jump in the river. Everyone drowns. I recovered the bodies. Point is, they didn't belong on the bridge to begin with."

After a while, Thomas says, "Thanks for all this." He points at the room where the mourners have been and gone. He opens his arms wide, trying to encompass the day the Captain and his mother walked into town, how she painted walls and built the clinic roof, and carried him in an Easter basket. He pauses at the door.

"Hey, Jimbo. Captain did have a friend," Thomas realizes. "You were his only friend."

"I appreciate that," Jimbo says.

Thomas thinks there should be more. He fights an impulse to fall to his knees and beg the sheriff to adopt him. He can rent a room in Jimbo's house. Or maybe he needs to find a sharp rock or bat. The sheriff's hunting rifle, an old Remington 30-30, leans against the kitchen wall. Jimbo's probably wearing his pistol. He's stronger but Thomas has the element of surprise. Thomas wants to embrace the sheriff but doesn't. He suddenly wants to put a bullet in Jimbo's gut and watch him bleed out. They shake hands.

"I'll call you," Thomas says.

"You do that now," Jimbo replies.

It's not all gone if someone with a good ear is left, Thomas decides. The forests of his boyhood, rinsed with henna and dyes from antiquity, the houses on Maple Ridge Road and Lincoln Street, and the people who inhabited them linger, anchored in a part of the memory no one has deciphered. They're embroidered into our biochemistry and their words come out of our mouth.

In his room on Lincoln Street, blue guppies with yellow fins and cherry barbs with intricate braded sides float to the surface. His butterfly ram was supposed to live four years but didn't. Tommy pulls them out with his fingers. His sunken ship gives up on distress calls.

Captain holds his car keys between his long, sturdy middle fingers. The key ring is attached to his Gold Crescent bronze prize. It's the size of a silver dollar but seems like an artifact from an ancient civilization. He invented the universe, currency and barter. He may devise navigation and counting next. Then geometry, philosophy, and the schematics of how to beat the house.

"I've got bluetongue and red tongue and tongues with rows of high-heeled Cancan dancers," the Captain said, whistling "Tambourine Man." "I've got Nile Fever, Grass Fever and some vile viral nightmare from Cambodia. I got widows and orphans from here to Honolulu. Ho Ho Ho."

Captain revealed himself, but Thomas couldn't interpret his code. His father's choreographed entrances and exits were confessions repeatedly reenacted. He committed seppuku every time he walked out to the Buick. How had he failed to notice?

His red-haired, pre-med, twin half-sisters shake pompoms as they pass. Amanda Leaf climbs out of the Genesee. Her voice is a sequence of miniature azure bells. Her hair is still wet and clouds of sapphire moths circle her face.

The dead and the missing exert a field that doesn't dissipate. Gestures and phrases have half-lives. Silences are deserted plazas, dusty, throttled by wind where the last goat starves. Omissions are a dereliction.

His mother stands on a sandbank. Kelp stretches out like a henna crocodile. She reaches inside the seaweed and pulls out amber dragon fangs. *For you, Tommy. Now I can come home.*

The most spectacular and irredeemable crimes have no

official designation, no official code number or prison sentence. They're boulders in the Genesee where little girls drown. They'll be here when you and your loves and the concept of love itself is gone and there's no statute of limitation.

Hailed as one of America's foremost writers of short fiction, KATE BRAVERMAN has been included in nearly every preeminent story collection, including Ben Marcus' *New American Short Stories*, Tobias Wolff's *The Vintage Book of Contemporary American Short Stories*, McSweeney's, *Best American, Carver, The Paris Review,* and *The Norton Anthology of Short Fiction.* She is the author of many books including the groundbreaking novel *Lithium for Medea,* which caught the attention of Joan Didion, Janet Fitch, Rick Moody, Greil Marcus, and others, identifying Braverman as a remarkable literary voice in American letters.